PRAISE FOR
Manda Collins

"When I pick up a Manda Collins book, I know I'm in for a treat."

—Tessa Dare, *New York Times* bestselling author

"[Manda] Collins is a delight!"

—Elizabeth Hoyt, *New York Times* bestselling author

"Manda Collins reminds me why I love historical romance so much."

—Rachel Van Dyken, #1 *New York Times* bestselling author

"Manda Collins writes sexy and smart historical romance, with a big dash of fun."

—Vanessa Kelly, *USA Today* bestselling author

"A go-to for historical romance."

—*Heroes and Heartbreakers*

A Spinster's Guide to Dukes and Danger

"The mystery unfolds effortlessly, delivering a slew of suspects, tantalizing clues, and danger around every corner without ever overshadowing the love story. This sensual romance will have pages flying."

—*Publishers Weekly*

"Compelling, evenly paced, and delightfully fun."

—*Kirkus*

"Collins keeps the heat smoldering between the well-drawn main characters in this installment, and the mystery keeps the pace moving nicely... [for] fans of Julia Quinn and Evie Dunmore."

—*Library Journal*

An Heiress's Guide to Deception and Desire

"After delighting readers with *A Lady's Guide to Mischief and Mayhem*, Collins is back in fine fettle with another fetching mix of sprightly wit, nimble plotting, and engaging characters that is certain to endear her to fans of historical romances and cozier historical mysteries."

—*Booklist*

"The mystery drives the action while the romance provides the heartbeat of the story, and the two weave together to create a well-plotted, entertaining tale for fans of both genres. Expectations and prejudice based on class and gender are scrutinized throughout, while the leads are witty, fierce, bighearted, and easy to love.... A successful and thoroughly enjoyable mix of mystery and romance."

—*Kirkus*

A Lady's Guide to Mischief and Mayhem

"A delectable mystery that reads like Victorian *Moonlighting* (with a good heaping of Nancy Drew's gumption).... *A Lady's Guide to Mischief and Mayhem* is wickedly smart, so engrossing it'd be a crime not to read it immediately."

—*Entertainment Weekly*, A-

"This book is proof that a romance novel can only be made better by a murder mystery story."

—*Good Housekeeping*

"Smartly plotted, superbly executed, and splendidly witty."

—*Booklist*, Starred Review

"Both romance and mystery fans will find this a treat."

—*Publishers Weekly*

"Collins blends historical romance and mystery with characters who embody a modern sensibility... The protagonists and setting of this first in a promising new series are thoroughly enjoyable."

—*Library Journal*

"Utterly charming."

—PopSugar

"A fun and flirty historical rom-com with a mystery afoot!"

—SYFY WIRE

"Manda Collins smoothly blends romance and an English country-house whodunit…The twists and turns of the plot will keep readers guessing, but Kate's independent attitude and the interesting friends she gathers around her bring the story to vivid life."

—*BookPage*

"With wicked smart dialogue and incredibly strong characters, Manda Collins reminds me why I love historical romance so much. Witty, intelligent, and hard to put down, you'll love *A Lady's Guide to Mischief and Mayhem*."

—Rachel Van Dyken, #1 *New York Times* bestselling author

"When I pick up a Manda Collins book, I know I'm in for a treat. With compelling characters and a rich Victorian setting, *A Lady's Guide to Mischief and Mayhem* weaves mystery and romance into one enthralling tale."

—Tessa Dare, *New York Times* bestselling author

"[Manda] Collins is a delight! I read *A Lady's Guide to Mischief and Mayhem* waaay past my bedtime, absorbed by its spot-on period detail, the well-crafted characters, and of course the intriguing mystery. Brava!"

—Elizabeth Hoyt, *New York Times* bestselling author

"Mystery, romance, and an indomitable heroine make for a brisk, compelling read."

—Madeline Hunter, *New York Times* bestselling author

A Governess's Guide *to* Passion *and* Peril

A Governess's Guide to Passion and Peril

MANDA COLLINS

FOREVER
New York   Boston

Copyright © 2024 by Manda Collins

Reading group guide copyright © 2024 by Manda Collins and Hachette Book Group, Inc.

Cover design and Illustration by Sarah Congdon. Cover copyright © 2024 by Hachette Book Group, Inc.

Forever
Hachette Book Group
1290 Avenue of the Americas, New York, NY 10104
read-forever.com

First Edition: March 2024

Forever is an imprint of Grand Central Publishing. The Forever name and logo are trademarks of Hachette Book Group, Inc.

The publisher is not responsible for websites (or their content) that are not owned by the publisher.

The Hachette Speakers Bureau provides a wide range of authors for speaking events. To find out more, go to hachettespeakersbureau.com or email HachetteSpeakers@hbgusa.com.

Forever books may be purchased in bulk for business, educational, or promotional use. For information, please contact your local bookseller or the Hachette Book Group Special Markets Department at special.markets@hbgusa.com.

Library of Congress Cataloging-in-Publication Data

Names: Collins, Manda, author.
Title: A governess's guide to passion and peril / Manda Collins.
Description: First edition. | New York : Forever, Hachette Book Group, 2024. | Series: Lady's guide
Identifiers: LCCN 2023040987 | ISBN 9781538725603 (paperback) | ISBN 9781538725627 (e-book)
Subjects: LCGFT: Detective and mystery fiction. | Romance fiction. | Novels.
Classification: LCC PS3603.O45445 G68 2024 | DDC 813/.6--dc23eng/20230908
LC record available at https://lccn.loc.gov/2023040987

ISBNs: 9781538725603 (trade paperback), 9781538725627 (ebook)

Printed in the United States of America

LSC-C

Printing 1, 2024

For my readers.
Thank you for loving these stories as much as I do.

Content Guidance

This book, though primarily a romance, is also part murder mystery. As such, it contains off-the-page descriptions of violence and murder.

There is description of off-page parental death, suicide, and parental estrangement.

The heroine is a governess, and as much as we all enjoy thinking of the profession as just like it's portrayed in *The Sound of Music,* it was, in fact, an often lonely job that subjected the governess herself to sexual harassment and assault at the hands of the master of the house, sons of the house, and other servants. There are some allusions to such things happening to Jane, though never in explicit terms.

All mistakes and unintentional insensitivities are my own.

Author's Note

Dear Reader,

Have you ever wondered what it would be like to get a front-row seat to the kind of behind-the-scenes international dealmaking that usually never sees the light of day? Well, that's what governess Miss Jane Halliwell is facing thanks to her employer's need for one more lady at her dinner party. Not only has Lady Gilford demanded that her daughter's governess attend the first evening's festivities of the week-long symposium being hosted by her husband, British diplomat Lord Gilford, but Jane will also be required to rub elbows with the man who broke her girlish heart years ago when she and her mother lost everything. That's the setup for the London-set mystery that grounds the fourth book in my Ladies Most Scandalous Series, A Governess's Guide to Passion and Peril, *which features unlikely sleuths: diplomat Lord Adrian Fielding and governess Miss Jane Halliwell.*

There will be danger, derring-do, and all the banter and flirtation you could want from a romantic murder mystery. And by the end, you'll have a mystery solved and happy that's well on the way to ever after. I loved spending time with these characters and this story so much! I hope you'll have just as much fun reading about them.

Ever Yours,
Manda

A Governess's Guide to Passion and Peril

Chapter One

London, May 1869

M argaret, do stop staring out the window and pay attention to your geography lessons, please."

Miss Jane Halliwell, governess to the only daughter of Viscount and Lady Gilford, was fond enough of her sixteen-year-old charge, but she was all but convinced that the girl's talents lay in something other than book learning. Jane had been with the family for only six months but in that time she'd grown to like the girl, who was lively and good-natured and would make a splash on the marriage mart when she debuted a few years from now. But she was simply not interested in her studies.

Even so, Jane had been hired to educate her, and she would try her best to do that.

"But how am I meant to pay attention to boring old geography when there is so much going on out there?" sighed Meg, not even bothering to turn away from the schoolroom window. "Come and see for yourself."

Jane hadn't yet succumbed to the temptation to peer out at the statesmen and dignitaries, who, along with their wives, were arriving at the Gilford townhouse in Belgrave Square for a week-long symposium on advances in horticulture around the world. In addition to his illustrious career first as a diplomat, then as an administrator in the Foreign Office, Lord Gilford was also noted for his rose garden and had seen this as an opportunity to bring nations that were frequently at odds together through their love of plants. As the only child of a diplomat herself, Jane was familiar with all sorts of costumes and customs that would no doubt fascinate Margaret. But having traveled with her parents to many different countries before her father's untimely death five years ago, Jane was not quite so eager to watch the arrivals as her pupil was. Indeed, she would much rather finish their lesson so she could check to see if the post had arrived.

Only yesterday she'd received another rejection for the detective novel she hoped to have published. Since she and her mother had been left penniless when her father died, the money she'd earn as a writer would allow her to leave governessing and make an independent life for herself. But that could only happen if a publisher decided to take a chance on her book.

"You've only to finish writing a page about the most profitable agricultural region of Portugal, Margaret, and you'll be free to gaze upon your father's guests to your heart's content," she coaxed, guiding her own focus back to their lessons.

On days like today, Jane wished she felt a true calling for the teaching profession. But as grateful as she was to Lord

Gilford for offering her a job when she needed one most, she wasn't particularly enamored of the occupation when her pupil was a reluctant one.

"But Miss Halliwell, there are probably Portuguese people arriving on our very doorstep this moment!" the girl said with a pout. "Why can't I observe them? Isn't that how scientists work?"

There were far too many ways to object to Margaret's suggestion that she examine her father's guests as if they were animals at the zoo for Jane to possibly find a place to start. So instead, she chose to compromise. "If I come and look out the window with you for a few minutes, will you promise to work on your essay?"

The girl looked mulish for a moment but, perhaps realizing this was the best she was likely to get, she nodded.

Moving over to stand behind the girl, Jane leaned forward a little to gaze down at the parade of carriages pulling into the mews of Gilford House.

"That man there," Meg said, nodding toward a rather short man in a bowler hat who was gesticulating with some great emotion, "has been tearing a strip off of Mr. Griggs for these past ten minutes. I'm not sure what it is he's objecting to, but poor Griggs has had no luck at all in soothing his ruffled feathers."

Jane knew from her own interactions with the man that Josiah Griggs, the underbutler, was slow to anger and did not seem fond of conflict. He was no doubt miserable when faced with such a volatile situation. She was about to say as much when her eye caught another man standing near the gate leading into the back garden.

She could not say just what it was about him that brought him to her attention. Perhaps it was the excellent tailoring of his suit, which marked him as a gentleman in a crowd of servants. Or maybe it was something about the way he clasped his hands behind his back, as if purposely trying to keep from fidgeting. Though in truth, she suspected it was the way the afternoon sun glinted off the gold highlights that threaded through his close-cropped light brown hair. She gasped as recognition rang through her.

She might have known Lord Adrian Fielding—whom she was well acquainted with from his time working alongside her father in Rome—would turn up sooner or later. He was Lord Gilford's protégé, after all.

"What is it?" Meg asked, turning to Jane with a start.

"I thought I saw Lord Adrian Fielding," Jane said with a frown. "But surely I was mistaken. I cannot imagine he has any interest in gardening."

The hobby seemed far too tame an activity for a man of Lord Adrian's vigor.

"You may be right about his opinion of gardening," Meg agreed, "but Lord Adrian is a good friend of Father's. I daresay he'll be here for the whole of the symposium. He's quite good-looking, don't you think?"

"I can hardly tell from this distance," Jane said primly. "And you'd better not let your mama hear you speaking thusly. Well-behaved young ladies do not comment on the looks of gentlemen. No matter how handsome they might be."

She saw Meg open her mouth to object to the reproval, but Jane interrupted whatever the girl was about to say.

"Even so, why attend a symposium on a subject of little interest to him?" Of course, it had been half a decade since she'd spent any substantial amount of time in his company. For all she knew he'd spent the intervening years elbow deep in freshly tilled soil.

"Oh, he always comes to these gatherings," Meg said with a shrug. " It's too bad he's so old, otherwise I'd set my cap at him."

Jane bit back a laugh at the girl's assessment. At Meg's age, Jane, too, had suffered a severe case of calf love for her father's young colleague. Adrian had been everything her young heart could have conjured in a perfect beau. He had been friendly, but he'd clearly considered her a child. And then after the disaster that befell her family upon her father's death, he'd disappeared from her life completely, which had put paid to any of her romantic notions about him. All these years later, despite what she'd said to Meg about not being able to tell from their window vantage point, he was still devastatingly handsome.

At least she needn't worry about having to cross paths with him this week. Lady Gilford had already made it clear that she and Meg were to keep themselves scarce while the symposium was in session. As governess, Jane hadn't been expected to be invited to mill about with the esteemed guests, and yet, the directive had still stung.

Jane reminded herself that the banishment worked in her favor today, and that she could hardly be surprised by Lady Gilford's chilly treatment. The woman had made it clear upon Jane's arrival that she was against adding Jane to her household, an attitude that could doubtless be attributed to the unflattering portrait Jane's previous employer—Lady Carlyle—had painted of her. The woman had accused Jane of casting out lures to the master of the house and had no doubt told her good friend Lady Gilford all about her suspicions. Since Jane found Lord Carlyle unappealing at best, the claim couldn't have been further from the truth.

Nevertheless, Jane had been dismissed without a reference and if it hadn't been for Lord Gilford, her father's longtime friend and colleague, she'd have been destitute. Lord Gilford had even suggested she stay with the family as a guest rather than as Meg's governess but knowing that Lady Gilford was close to Lady Carlyle and would therefore make staying as a guest unbearable, Jane had insisted on working for her keep.

And thinking about the parcel containing her manuscript hidden away in her bedchamber, Jane sent up a little prayer that the next editor whose desk it crossed would make an offer for it. That was the only way she was going to make enough money to live on her own, with no fear of importuning employers or false accusations.

"We've done enough gawking at your father's guests, now, Meg," she said aloud. "Let us get back to—"

She was interrupted by a sniff from the doorway. Turning, she saw Lady Gilford scowling at them, and for a moment Jane felt as guilty for her gawking out the window as if she were Meg's age instead of three and twenty.

"I might have expected such behavior from a schoolgirl like Margaret, Miss Halliwell," said Lady Gilford, her mouth twisted in disgust, "but you are meant to be setting an example for her rather than enacting ill behavior by her side. And I will remind you that her name is Margaret. Meg or any other shortened form of her name is beneath her as a viscount's daughter."

"You mustn't scold, Mama," Meg said with an answering frown. "Miss Halliwell was only—"

Touched by the girl's defense of her, though knowing it was inappropriate, Jane placed a staying hand on her arm. "You are correct, Lady Gilford. My apologies." She offered a deep curtsy, the kind Lady Gilford expected from Jane in an acknowledgment of her lowered station.

Meg looked as if she'd like to argue but held her tongue.

"See that it doesn't happen again," Lady Gilford said, seeming only slightly mollified. "Now, though it goes against the grain to offer you a reward after such lax performance of your role, it can't be helped."

And like catching the scent of rain on the air before a storm, Jane felt a prickle of warning on the back of her neck, and she knew suddenly what the "reward" her mistress spoke of would be before she spoke.

Oh, Fate, haven't you played enough havoc with my life already?

"One of the ladies we were expecting for dinner this evening is indisposed and has sent her regrets," Lady Gilford said, sounding as if she viewed it as a personal failing on the unnamed lady's part that she'd succumbed to whatever ailment had assailed her. "You'll need to come down to dinner to make up the numbers."

Then without waiting for a response—and really, what response could there be but "Yes, my lady"?—she continued,

"Make sure to wear one of your more flattering gowns. However far you may have come down in the world, I do not wish you to make it seem as if we are stingy with your wages, nor do I want you to embarrass me at table."

Jane did not point out that the more flattering gowns dated from her time as a wealthy gentleman's daughter and could never have been purchased on a governess's wages.

Instead, she gave another curtsy, grateful she had learned to keep her face from revealing her thoughts. It was a skill she'd needed to hastily acquire while working for the Carlyles and had served her well in the Gilford household as well.

"The gong will announce when to come to the drawing room," Lady Gilford said as she walked to the door. "Don't be late."

Chapter Two

"Has all been made ready?" Viscount Gilford asked from his position near an arched arbor in the rose garden.

Since most of Lord Gilford's guests were either still traveling or busy settling into their rooms, Lord Adrian Fielding had chosen this brief interval, when he and his mentor could speak uninterrupted, to finalize their plans.

Adrian had spent the majority of his time in the Foreign Office reporting to Gilford, and even after the man had permanently returned to England while Adrian remained abroad, they'd kept in touch. Now that he was back in England to stay, it had been unthinkable to imagine he'd work for anyone else. Even if it meant pretending a fascination for roses this week that he didn't feel.

Now, in response to the viscount's question, he nodded. "Everything is in place," he said, gesturing to a branch of cabbage roses drooping under the weight of its heavy blooms so that anyone watching might assume they were discussing the garden. "Payne and Henning are prepared to distract the guests after dinner so that Prince Maxim and the foreign secretary can slip out to the library for the meeting."

Though the world at large believed this house party to be a symposium on the cultivation of roses, it was in fact a highly orchestrated diplomatic meeting between the British foreign secretary and the crown prince of the kingdom of Roskovia, a tiny country in Eastern Europe that was an important trading partner for Great Britain. More importantly, Prince Maxim was the inventor of an electronic, long-distance talking machine, a piece of technology that nations all over the world were in competition to win from the small kingdom.

"Excellent," Gilford said with an approving nod. "I knew you were the right man for the job, Adrian. I have little doubt that once this is over, you will have no trouble making a case for yourself as the right man to succeed Ramswool when he leaves his position at the end of the year."

"Thank you, sir." Adrian hoped the other man was right. Sir Lionel Ramswool, who headed up his own specialized and little-known division of the Home Office that investigated politically sensitive crimes on British soil, was set to retire soon. Having conducted investigations for the Foreign Office abroad for some years now, Adrian hoped to succeed Ramswool. He had enjoyed his work abroad, but he no longer wished to be so far away from his family for years at a time. "I hope you're right."

"Of course I'll put in a good word for you," the viscount

said, clapping him on the shoulder. "Though I expect your brother's recommendation will go far and above my own to ensure your success."

Gilford said it as if it were a foregone conclusion that Adrian would ask for the duke's help. It had been this way his entire life. As the son—as well as the younger brother—of a duke, it was assumed by most people that he relied on his brother the Duke of Langham's favor to garner him whatever he might want in the world.

It was one of the reasons he'd gone to work in the Foreign Office against Langham's wishes, he supposed. He'd spent his entire life under the shadow of the dukedom. For once he'd wanted to do something that was entirely separate from the family name.

The rift between the brothers that had come about as a result of Adrian's defiance had only in the last year or so, since Langham's marriage, been smoothed over. He had little doubt now that if he were to ask, Langham would recommend him for the Home Office position, but for now, Adrian was doing what he could to bolster his record so his brother's assistance would not be necessary. The planning and background operations for this meeting between the foreign secretary, Lord Ralston, and Prince Maxim was a means to that end.

"If there's nothing else, sir," he said to Lord Gilford, "I'd better go make one last check of the meeting room while there's still time."

To his surprise, rather than waving him off as Adrian had expected, Lord Gilford looked pained. "Before you go, there's something I need to tell you."

Adrian felt a frisson of alarm run through him. Had something gone wrong with the arrangements for Prince Maxim's travel from Claridge's to Gilford House?

"Nothing to do with the operation," the viscount assured him, as if reading Adrian's mind. "It's of a more personal nature."

Puzzled, Adrian frowned. "You have in me a captive audience."

Gilford looked uncomfortable. "You will perhaps be angry that I've kept it from you—especially since you explicitly asked me if I knew of her whereabouts—but it's not to be helped."

And suddenly, Adrian knew exactly who his mentor was speaking of. He set his jaw, knowing that whatever Gilford had to say about Jane Halliwell, it would not be anything Adrian would be happy to hear.

"Miss Halliwell is in residence here and is acting as governess to Margaret." Gilford clasped his hands behind his back and rocked on his heels. "I know you were looking for her, but she asked me not to put it about that she was here. After what she went through with the Carlyles I didn't have the heart to defy her. Even for you, my trusted friend."

Adrian was, indeed, annoyed with Gilford's revelation. Not so much that Jane was safely residing here in the viscount's household. He'd known Gilford had helped Jane find a position once she and her mother had returned to England. In point of fact it had been through Gilford's assistance she'd become governess to Adrian's cousins, the Carlyles. Though from what Adrian knew of Carlyle and his wife, and from what he could discern after seeing Jane at Langham Abbey almost two years ago, the position hadn't been a pleasant one.

That Jane had been forced to take a position as a governess at all still made him furious both at himself and on her behalf. In the aftermath of her father's suicide, which he knew the Foreign Office had worked to keep quiet, he'd been required by his own position to leave for Madrid almost immediately. And by the time he was back in England he'd realized the diplomatic community had shamefully turned its back on Charles Halliwell's wife and daughter.

It seemed the rumor that the man had taken his own life out of guilt over losing his fortune at the gaming tables had been stronger than any cover story about a heart seizure the foreign secretary had put about. Both Jane and her mother had been shunned, and Adrian hadn't learned of it until it was too late to do anything about it.

"I can understand why she'd go to you for help," Adrian said now. "After all, you were close to her father and among the only ones in diplomatic circles who didn't turn your back on Jane and her mother. But why as a governess and not as a guest? I wouldn't have thought you to be so—" Then understanding dawned on him. "Of course, what was I thinking? She would remain here no other way, I take it?"

"Of course she wouldn't," Gilford said with a shake of his head. "Stubborn chit was turned off without notice by Lady Carlyle but still informed me that the only way she would accept a room in this house was as Meg's governess.

And so she has been acting in the role for the past six months."

Knowing Lady Gilford, who was bosom bows with Lady Carlyle, Adrian suspected that in the schoolroom with Meg was a far more pleasant place for Jane to spend her days than in the drawing room with her hostess.

Thrusting a hand through his hair, Adrian sighed. "I don't understand why she was so determined to hide herself from me after our chance meeting at Langham Abbey. It isn't as if she has any reason to fear me, for God's sake. I simply wished to ensure she was comfortable and safe in the years since the loss of her father."

"I suspect it had something to do with shame, my boy," Gilford said gently. "When you knew her in Rome, she was the beloved daughter of a respected diplomat. Word spread of the scandal within hours of the man's death. She's had to endure the pitying looks from former embassy friends and acquaintances, as well as society in London. You were a handsome young man who no doubt inspired flights of fancy in her during your time in Rome. Perhaps even a schoolgirl crush. It's little wonder she had no wish for you to see her in her much-humbled state."

Gilford wasn't the first person to suggest this to him. Langham had told him more or less the same thing when he'd complained at their grandmother's birthday house party about how Jane had avoided him. It wasn't entirely out of the question that Jane had been enamored of him in Rome. They'd even been friends of a sort. But he'd been one and twenty and hadn't thought of her as a romantic possibility. She was a child, for pity's sake. Not to mention he'd had his hands full with the temperamental Italian widow who'd been warming his bed at the time.

Even so, his recollections of their interactions in Italy had been pleasant ones until he'd run into her at his family's estate and begun questioning everything he remembered from that time.

He'd been present at the Halliwell residence that disastrous day, and the memory of Mrs. Halliwell's scream still haunted him. A search of the man's desk had revealed evidence of staggering gambling debts, which pointed to suicide rather than any kind of foul play.

Adrian had wanted to delay his departure for his next posting to Spain, but the Foreign Office had denied his request. It was thought that the least said about Halliwell's death, the better. Could it be that Jane had taken his leaving so soon as a slight against her and her mother?

"You may be right that it's shame that made her reluctant to see me at first," he said to Gilford, though he was beginning to think it might be something more. "But it's been years and she is no longer a schoolgirl. I'd have thought she'd have overcome it by now. Even so, I promise not to seek her out while I am here if you think my company would upset her. I certainly doubt our paths will cross since I have no expectation that Meg will be attending any of the meetings."

He expected Gilford to laugh, but instead the man looked sheepish. "I'm afraid that's not quite the case. Not that Meg will be attending the symposium of course, but that your path won't cross with Jane's. You see, one of the ladies who was meant to attend dinner this evening sent her regrets this afternoon and—"

"And," Adrian finished for him, "Lady Gilford asked Jane to take her place so that the numbers would be even."

"Indeed," Gilford said with a shrug. "It couldn't be helped."

Thinking of the lengths to which Jane had gone to avoid him, Adrian said, "I rather think it's Jane you should be explaining that to rather than me."

"I'll try to pull her aside before dinner and inform her of your presence, though I don't know if I'll have time given the number of guests I'll need to speak with."

"If you aren't able to do so, I'll try to find a moment to have a word." Though Adrian suspected he might find it just as difficult to find a way to speak with Miss Halliwell.

Which, all things considered, she'd probably prefer.

Chapter Three

Despite Lady Gilford's order that she wear one of the gowns from her former life, Jane was sensitive enough to her mistress's mercurial temper to choose the most understated of her remaining frocks. Purchased in preparation for her planned season that had never happened, the unembellished blue silk by Worth would be noted as being out of fashion by any lady who followed current trends, but it was one of Jane's favorites because of the way it flattered her dark hair and pale complexion.

She'd had to sell the pearls she'd been given for her sixteenth birthday, and possessed no other jewelry to speak of, so her neck and ears were bare. She dressed her hair in a simple up-swept style with face-framing curls that brushed her cheeks.

The transformation from her usual staid appearance back to the girl she'd been was so stark that when she caught a glimpse of herself in the pier glass in the hallway just outside the drawing room, she felt as if she were looking at a ghost.

For the barest moment she wished that instead of living hundreds of miles away with a cousin in Scotland, her mother was here with her tonight. But the reasons she'd chosen to go to work as a governess were just as valid now as they'd been when she and her mother had parted ways, no matter how difficult her path had turned out to be.

As if to remind her of just *how* grinding her journey had been, Lady Gilford appeared at the other end of the hallway and hurried toward her.

"Is that Worth?" she asked, her mouth tight with disapproval. The viscountess's own gown had also been crafted by the renowned Parisian designer, but sported what Jane assumed must be this year's fashionable details.

Before Jane could confirm the lady's suspicion, Lady Gilford continued, "Never mind. I suppose we're lucky you have anything suitable at all. But I will warn you, my girl, before we go into company, that you aren't to cast out lures to any of the gentlemen present. I have been warned by Lady Carlyle, so I will be watching. You are here to even out the numbers and that is all. Don't forget that."

Leaving Jane to follow in her wake, Lady Gilford swept past her toward the drawing room. The idea that Lady Gilford thought so ill of her gnawed at Jane, but she pushed those feelings aside as she steeled herself to face the task that had been appointed her.

Many of the guests had already gathered in the spacious chamber, which boasted ornately frescoed ceilings, and an eclectic mix of paintings and objets d'art that Lord Gilford had collected over the years in his various postings as a British ambassador. Even for Jane, who had grown up in the often-palatial residences afforded her father and his family in foreign countries, this particular room was awe-inducing.

All the same, she was mindful of Lady Gilford's admonition and despite the friendly smiles directed her way from some of the guests as she entered, she limited her interactions to brief smiles and found a secluded corner where she could wait for the dinner gong without calling attention to herself.

But she hadn't been there for more than a few minutes—having turned her attention to a wonderfully elaborate painting by an old master whose name escaped her hanging in the corner—when she heard a familiar male voice behind her.

"Miss Halliwell, well met," said the Honorable Mr. William Gilford, son and heir of Viscount Gilford. "I didn't expect to see you at this deadly dull affair."

With his father's height and his mother's good looks, Will, as he was known to his intimates, was an attractive man. But Jane hadn't been in the Gilford household above a week before he'd tried to kiss her.

Fortunately, though her father was negligent in other ways, he'd been smart enough to recognize that a beautiful daughter might one day have need of a way to fend off importunate men, and so had taught her how she might use a well-aimed knee to dispatch any male foolish enough to ignore the word "no."

The knee to Will's tender parts had delivered the message Jane intended, and the two had formed a friendship of sorts. Inasmuch as a young man about town and a governess could be friends, that is. There was no question of him courting her, of course, and since Jane had no intention of offering the only other sort of relationship that he might desire from her, friendship was all he could hope for.

"I could say the same for you, Mr. Gilford," she said after offering him the deferential nod owed him as her employer's son. "I would not have thought this to be the sort of entertainment that would draw a young man about town." Especially, she thought cynically, one who could usually be found in houses of ill repute and gaming hells if the gossip sheets were to be believed. "Never say you have developed a passion for cultivating exotic plants. Your father must be pleased."

The golden-haired young man gave a guffaw of laughter that drew more eyes than Jane was comfortable with to their corner of the room. "Hardly," he said once he'd regained his composure. "The pater might hold out hope that one day I'll join him in his obsession with roses, but on that he's doomed to disappointment. I prefer blooms of another sort."

At this last he gave her a broad wink that made Jane raise her eyes heavenward. "So if it isn't gardening," she said, "then what has brought you here this evening?"

Will picked a bit of fluff from the sleeve of his black evening coat. "The same thing that's brought you downstairs looking a sight more fashionable than you do for days in the schoolroom with Meg, I imagine."

Perhaps realizing that hadn't been the most gallant thing

to say to a lady—even one who was employed as the governess of one's sister—he added, "Not to say that you're not lovely in your usual rig, of course."

Biting back the urge to tell him to spit it out, Jane made do with raising her eyebrows expectantly.

"No, of course it was a note from Mama," Will continued with the kind of exasperation that only a put-upon child can wield, "informing me that, horror of horrors, she needed another man for the table tonight lest the numbers be uneven. I ask you, has there ever been another cause to which more young men—and ladies, I suppose, if truth be told—have been sacrificed than the almighty numbers?"

Jane might have remarked that she suspected more men had been lost at Waterloo had she not been struck by the oddity of Lady Gilford calling on Will to come even out the numbers when she'd already requested Jane's attendance for the same reason. If Jane was brought in to replace a lady who had cried off, and if a gentleman had also cried off, Jane could simply have been informed she was no longer needed. There was no point in pointing this out to Will, however. They were both already here, and it was entirely possible that Lady Gilford had wanted her son in attendance for entirely other reasons. Jane had no wish to embroil herself in a matter that was really none of her affair.

Aloud she said, "I'm sure you'll find a way to make it up to whichever companions to whom you were forced to send your regrets, Mr. Gilford. Perhaps some roses, the cultivation of which you are so determined to turn your back on?"

"I doubt Gilford's allowance can afford the cost of posies for every member of Jenner's Gaming Club, Miss Halliwell."

Will broke into a grin as he turned to clap the newcomer on the shoulder. "Adrian, I knew you'd be around here somewhere. Though God knows why a man of your intelligence would wish to play dogsbody to m'father for this gathering when you already spend so many of your days working for him at Whitehall."

Adrian had exchanged the sack coat and trousers she'd spied him wearing that afternoon in the Gilfords' garden for the black tailcoat, white bow tie, and black wool trousers that were de rigueur for gentlemen at evening affairs. Despite her reluctance to see him, Jane had to admit that though most men managed to look if not handsome then distinguished in evening attire, Adrian was almost breathtakingly handsome. Of course, she imagined that even in rags, with a three-day beard and his light brown hair in dire need of a cut, he'd still manage to draw her eye.

The look he gave her now, which seemed to guess the direction of her thoughts, made her want to run away, but Jane stood her ground. Raising her chin, she said, "My lord," before dropping into a curtsy that bordered on mocking.

"Miss Halliwell." His bow was pitch-perfect, though she noted a spark in his blue eyes that said her disrespect hadn't gone unnoticed.

"Ah, good, you know one another," Will said, looking from one to the other, somehow missing the undercurrent that Jane had feared was in danger of igniting the drapes with its energy. "Miss H has the unenviable task of educating my sister, Adrian."

Jane saw Adrian's brow rise at Will's words.

"I learned of it just this afternoon from your father," he told the younger man. "Imagine my surprise, Miss Halliwell, when I learned you'd been residing here at Gilford House for the past several months. The last I'd heard you were in the employ of a different family altogether."

That he didn't name the Carlyles aloud seemed to indicate to Jane that he was aware of the ignominious way in which she'd been dismissed from his cousin's employ. Did he believe the story Lady Carlyle had no doubt given out as a reason for her dismissal? It wasn't true of course, but Carlyle was family. Surely Adrian would be more disposed to believe his own relatives than Jane.

Mindful of the story Lord Gilford had told her to tell should it become necessary to explain her reasons for leaving the Carlyles, Jane said, "When such a dear friend of my father's came to me in need of a governess for his daughter, I could not deny him, of course."

She made no mention of regretting the need to leave the Carlyles' employ.

Jane was not above telling the occasional fib, but she had no wish to ruin Lord Gilford's symposium by getting struck by lightning in his drawing room.

"Of course you couldn't," Adrian agreed with a cordiality that Jane could tell was entirely feigned.

"I suppose you know each other from one of your father's postings, eh, Miss H?" Will asked.

"We met in Rome," Adrian answered, before turning to look at Will with a frown. "Do you speak to all young ladies of your acquaintance by such inappropriately informal appellations?"

If, like his brother the duke, Adrian carried an old-fashioned quizzing glass in his coat pocket, Jane rather thought he'd be surveying the Honorable Mr. Gilford through it right about now.

To her reluctant amusement, the young man who she'd begun to believe was entirely unflappable began to redden under Adrian's scrutiny.

"I," he began, running a finger under his collar, "that is to say . . . dash it, she doesn't mind. Do you, Miss Halliwell?"

Adrian let out a sound of exasperation.

"I don't mind it, sir."

At that one little word "sir," understanding dawned on the young man's face.

"Dash it all, Miss Halliwell, I am sorry. I didn't think."

Though being addressed as Miss H hadn't particularly bothered Jane, if Lady Gilford overheard her son behaving so familiarly with his sister's governess, it would be Jane and not Will she blamed.

Even so, Jane didn't appreciate Lord Adrian's interference in the matter. If she'd realized when she'd been mooning over Adrian in Rome just how high-handed he'd later become, the knowledge would have gone a good way toward dampening her ardor.

"I see my mother gesturing to me from the other side of the room." Will gave a quick bow and absented himself with the speed of a criminal pursued by a policeman.

Perhaps he'd seen the imaginary storm clouds hovering over Jane's head.

Mindful to keep the bland expression on her face, she lowered her voice and hissed at her companion, "What was the meaning of that, Lord Adrian?"

When, upon his arrival in the drawing room, Adrian had spotted Jane in conversation with the handsome—and it must be admitted good-natured—Will Gilford, he'd felt an unfamiliar stab of jealousy. He'd noticed when he'd seen her nearly two years ago at Langham Abbey that Jane had grown into a beautiful and delightfully curvaceous woman. But he'd hardly lost his heart—he hadn't had a real conversation with her in years. Even so, he felt an urge to warn the younger man off.

What he should have done—after all, he was at Gilford House to oversee the gathering of some of the most important foreign dignitaries to ever set foot on British soil—was ignore the chatting pair and turn his attention to the group of guests conversing near the fireplace. Instead, he'd made a beeline for the tucked-away corner where Jane and Will stood. And promptly raised the lady's hackles.

He was sorry that he'd no doubt embarrassed her, but he wasn't sorry for Will's departure.

"What was the meaning of that, Lord Adrian?" she hissed, her expression bland with the exception of her eyes, which were narrowed with fury. "Are you so high in the instep now that you must embarrass me before the son of my employers? Lady Gilford thought me enough of a lady to mix with her guests this evening, but perhaps that isn't good enough for the son and brother of a duke?"

Ignoring the way her anger heightened the color in her cheeks in a most becoming manner, he instead turned his attention to her words. Feeling another pang of regret, he said, "I had no intention of embarrassing you, Miss Halliwell. Indeed, my words were intended to rebuke only Mr. Gilford, who, though he no doubt means well, was making you uncomfortable."

Her small sigh told him he hadn't guessed wrong about her unease at the casual way the young man had addressed her. "Perhaps he was," she admitted, "but that wasn't an invitation for you to embarrass us both by rebuking him. I have few enough friends these days. Now one of my only allies in this family will no doubt avoid me the next time we are in company together."

"Lord Gilford said he offered to let you live with the family as a guest," Adrian said with a frown. "Why would you choose to work as their governess when you don't have to, for pity's sake?"

For a moment, Jane let her irritation show. "Perhaps you've never been around a family with a poor relation living with them, but I have. If I am going to live with another family that is not my own, I will do so as a paid employee rather than as an unpaid one."

He opened his mouth to object, but she continued before he could speak. "You've met Lady Gilford. Do you honestly believe she would take kindly to having an unmarried young lady of no relation to either herself or Lord Gilford living as a permanent guest? She is contemptuous enough of me as Margaret's governess. I can only imagine how much worse it would be if I were not an employee. At least having an occupation means she cannot accuse me of sponging."

There was a great deal he wanted to ask her about how Lady Gilford treated her, but at that moment, he saw the American attaché, Benjamin Woodward, approaching them. "Lord Adrian," the dark-haired man said with a hearty clap on Adrian's shoulder, "I might have known you'd find the most beautiful lady in the room and hide her from the rest of us. I insist you must introduce me at once."

It wasn't that he disliked Woodward, Adrian thought grimly. He'd known the man for some years since they had both been working in their respective countries' embassies in Paris when Adrian first went to work for the Foreign Office. Adrian also suspected that like himself, Woodward did some type of work for his government that was of the covert variety. Even so, they were friends of a sort and under different circumstances he might have been happy to introduce the man to Jane. Circumstances in which the fellow—who was a bit of a lothario—was safely married and so in love that he would never think of straying. Alas, those circumstances were not present today.

Biting back his frustration, he told himself to stop being an ass and made the introductions. "Miss Jane Halliwell, allow me to present Mr. Benjamin Woodward, attaché to the American ambassador."

He watched with resignation as Jane curtsied to the American, who bowed smoothly and pressed a kiss on the back of her gloved hand.

"If all English ladies are this charming, Miss Halliwell," Woodward said with a smile, "I am surprised my ancestors were so eager to revolt against your country."

Jane's lips twitched in amusement. "I believe it had something to do with taxation without representation, Mr. Woodward. Though far be it for me to educate you about your own national history. I have a feeling it's rather a requirement for one in your occupation."

"A lady of education as well as beauty." Woodward turned to Adrian and drawled, "I am now doubly annoyed at your failure to introduce us sooner, my lord. When I think of the time we might have spent discussing the political reasons for the revolution, I am positively livid." His eyes twinkled with mirth despite his words and Adrian could tell from the way she smiled that Jane was charmed.

Damned Woodward and his flirtations.

"So sorry to have disappointed you, Woodward," Adrian said dryly.

He was saved from listening to more of his American friend's repartee with Jane by the lady herself.

"I see Lord Payne is here," she said with a smile that Adrian knew wasn't meant for him or Woodward. "He was a dear friend of my father's and I remember him fondly from our time in Rome. I hope the two of you will excuse me so that I may go greet him."

After a curtsy that was meant for both men, she hurried to the other side of the room.

Once she was gone, Adrian turned to the American.

"You are not to attempt to add her to your list of conquests, Woodward," he said in a low voice to the other man before he could think better of it. "She is not that sort of—"

Woodward raised his hands as if in surrender. "No need to raise your hackles at me, old sport. I would never poach on your territory."

"She's not a damned game preserve, Woodward," Adrian said scowling. "And she's not mine. I was a colleague of her late father, and we know one another a little from that time, and I simply do not wish her to be trifled with."

The sound Woodward made indicated just what he thought of that assertion. "I wasn't breeched yesterday, friend. I know what it sounds like when a man is warning me off of a woman he's interested in. But if you wish to protest again I won't argue with you."

It was just like Woodward, who considered himself an expert at sussing out what secrets others may be harboring, to see some romantic connection between Jane and Adrian. But in this instance, the man was simply wrong. In truth, Adrian had forgotten Jane Halliwell existed until he'd run into her at Langham Abbey. Her attitude toward him then had been his first clue that she held him in contempt for some reason. And for the life of him he couldn't recall what he might have done to give her such a strong dislike for him.

That was a mystery to be solved later, he reminded himself. For now, he needed only to ensure that she wasn't treated like fair game by men like Woodward, who was known for his discreet but plentiful affairs.

"Believe what you want regarding my reasons for telling

you to leave her alone," he said now to Woodward. "But I am deadly serious. She's had enough trouble in the past few years to last a lifetime. And if you aren't afraid of my wrath, there is Lord Gilford's to consider."

Woodward's brow furrowed. "Is she some relation of his?"

"She's his daughter's governess, in addition to being the daughter of an old friend."

At that, the American's eyes widened. "His daughter's governess? That explains her knowledge about American history."

"Or," Adrian said acidly, "it could simply be that she's well read and paid attention to her lessons as a girl herself."

Ignoring Adrian's rebuke, Woodward continued with obvious regret, "It's really too bad. I suspect she'd appreciate my American disregard for the kind of class distinctions you English hold on to so dearly. Besides, I've never kissed a governess before."

Clapping Woodward on the shoulder with a bit more force than necessary, Adrian said dryly, "You'll have to learn to live with the disappointment, I'm afraid."

And with that the two men separated to go in to dinner.

Chapter Four

To her surprise and pleasure, Jane found herself seated next to Mr. Woodward, the handsome American. The elderly gentleman on her other side hailed from one of the tiny principalities of the Germanic states that made up Central Europe, and claimed to speak little English. Though from the way he devoted himself to the soup course, Jane suspected he was simply more interested in his dinner than conversation with an undistinguished English lady.

"Lord Adrian tells me you are governess to Lord Gilford's daughter, Miss Halliwell," Mr. Woodward said as Jane lifted her own soup spoon. And just like that her pleasure in the seating arrangements evaporated.

Of course Adrian had told the man about her position in the household. It wasn't as if it were some sort of state secret, after all. And no doubt the duke's son wished to warn his friend that she was not an appropriate object of any kind of flirtation. Not that she wished for a flirtation.

She would have settled for a single evening in which she was allowed to forget for one moment just how far she'd fallen socially since her father's death.

Still, it wasn't Mr. Woodward's fault she was enjoying only a temporary visit to the elevated world of polite society once more.

"I am," she replied, not ashamed of her position, but wishing they could discuss something else. "Margaret is a dear girl, and I enjoy teaching her, though she is less than enthusiastic about geography lessons when there are exciting happenings right here in her own home. And lest you think," she added, "that I am imparting the knowledge of the ages to her, at this point we primarily discuss how to behave in company and which topics of conversation to avoid. Such as anything that might remotely be of interest to a young lady of intellect who has more than a passing interest in politics."

Mr. Woodward gave a soft laugh, and Jane noticed that there were lines around his eyes that suggested he did so frequently.

"I imagine she objects to this tutelage?" he asked wryly. At her nod, he continued, "I wish I could say that society back home was better at cultivating intelligence and good sense in its young ladies, but I'm afraid that the powers that be in New York society are just as intent on keeping them ignorant and sweet as they are here."

Jane leaned back to allow Geordie, one of the footmen, to remove her soup course. His presence reminded her of her own privilege at even being downstairs this evening. Mindful of that, once Geordie was farther down the table, she told the American, "I shouldn't complain, especially when my employer has generously invited me to sit at the table with such illustrious company. Pray forget I said anything."

"My dear girl," Mr. Woodward said, tilting his head to look at her more closely, "I can find no fault with what you've said and if there is any chance that you will be chastised for speaking your mind, I will be more than happy to come to your defense. Though I suspect a certain Englishman of our acquaintance will be there before me."

Now it was Jane's turn to laugh. "Lord Adrian, do you mean?"

Against her best judgment, her eyes darted over to where the gentleman in question was in spirited conversation with an elegant lady whom Jane had heard introduced earlier as the wife of the French foreign minister. As she watched, Madame Dulac pressed a long-fingered hand on Adrian's arm. Jane felt a stab of jealousy at the gesture, and when Adrian looked up and caught her staring, she felt her face heat and quickly returned her gaze to her plate.

This, she reminded herself, was precisely why she would never set her cap at Lord Adrian Fielding. He was clearly drawn to ladies of far more sophistication than Jane could ever boast of. And she was happy to leave him to them.

Swallowing, she forced herself to remember what she'd been talking about with Mr. Woodward, then said, "I assure you that he has far more important things to occupy his time than to plead my case to Lady Gilford. Besides, I would not wish for him or you to intervene on my behalf. So I will simply be more discreet for the rest of the evening."

"I am sorry to hear you say so, Miss Halliwell, for I have

enjoyed hearing the unvarnished truth from a sensible lady."

The next few courses passed in spirited, if less controversial, conversation.

They had just been served the fish course—a delicious filet of sole in a rich sauce that was one of Chef Henri's most celebrated dishes—when the low hum of conversation around the table was punctured by the sound of raised voices at the other end of the table.

"I suppose I should not be surprised," said a distinguished looking gentleman with a luxurious moustache and flashing dark eyes—Jane thought she remembered him from her days at the British embassy in Rome, where he was a Russian delegate of some sort, but she could not remember his exact title—"that the nation which has never met a sovereign country it did not wish to colonize would be so unwilling to give up even a small part of its wealth—even for a friend."

"There's no need for us to brawl, is there, Dimitri?" Lord Gilford said in a calm voice that Jane recognized from the few times she'd seen her employer attempt to talk her father down from a bout of temper. For a diplomat, Papa had been surprisingly volatile—though she supposed in retrospect it should have foretold his downfall. "Come now, my friend, let us save this conversation for later when the ladies aren't present, and we can speak freely."

"I can see no reason why we ladies should not hear about what you discuss," said a handsome blonde lady—the wife of the Swedish ambassador, Jane believed. "It is foolish to exclude us from the important business of governance. Your own queen would not stand for such a thing, surely?"

"Of course not, Mrs. Lindholm," assured Lord Payne. "But this has nothing to do with the topic of this gathering Gilford has organized. We don't wish to bore you with matters of state when you are here to discuss the endlessly fascinating topic of cultivating roses."

Was it Jane's imagination or was Payne's voice laced with irony? Though she knew Lord Gilford was indeed a dedicated rose gardener—especially now that he lived in England year-round thanks to his position at Whitehall, she'd been surprised to learn that this gathering of important personages from around the world was to focus on roses rather than diplomacy.

Now she suspected that she'd been right to be suspicious. Though if she was right, that meant whatever the Russian had been arguing with Lord Gilford about was far more important—and possibly more dangerous—than which fertilizer worked best to produce the heartiest blooms.

"I think perhaps it's time for the ladies to retire to the drawing room," said Lady Gilford before Mrs. Lindholm could object to Lord Payne's words. "That way we can leave the gentlemen to their heated discussion of their beloved roses."

Jane stood, and before she could get away, Mr. Woodward bowed over her hand. "It was a pleasure dining with you, Miss Halliwell. I hope I will see you again this week. You can share more of your unconventional ideas about the educating of young ladies."

Feeling her cheeks heat at the compliment, Jane thanked him and hurried to follow the other ladies to the door leading out of the dining room.

"I hope you weren't a bore for your dinner companions, Jane," said Lady Gilford in an undertone as she took Jane by the arm and walked with her toward the drawing room. "Though I suppose Herr von Humboldt was not bothered by your lack of conversation. The man only attends these kinds of functions for the superior food. He's from a noble family but is poor as a church mouse. No, it is of Mr. Woodward I speak. I did you a favor by seating you beside him, and I hope you are grateful for it. He's quite handsome, as I am sure you noted. But he is also quite wealthy if the gossip is to be believed."

Not knowing how she was supposed to respond to such revelations, Jane merely nodded, which seemed to be all Lady Gilford expected from her.

"I thought because he's an American," the viscountess went on, "he would not be bothered by your frank way of speaking and lack of refinement. Though he seemed happy enough to hurry away from you, so I suppose you were unable to charm even him. It's a shame really. Your mother was such a dear friend of mine. It pains me to see how different you are from her."

Since Lady Gilford hadn't, so far as Jane was aware, made the slightest attempt to contact her *dear friend* since she'd been forced by her husband's death to remove to Scotland, Jane found it difficult to take the other woman's lament at face value.

"You cannot say I haven't done my duty by you," Lady

Gilford continued with a shake of her head before she broke away from Jane and hurried to take a seat where she could preside over the tea tray.

Grateful to be spared any more of her employer's interest, Jane found a seat in a corner where she might observe the rest of the ladies without bringing attention to herself. As the daughter of a diplomat—even an only marginally successful one—she could have held her own among the wives and daughters of the delegates to this odd symposium if she'd needed to. But as Lady Gilford was so fond of telling her, it was no longer Jane's place to speak to these women as if they were equals. So, she used the free time to think about which publishers she would send her novel to next.

She had just finished drafting a cover letter to Ferrar and Sons in her mind, when she heard her name.

"Jane," Lady Gilford barked. "Drat the girl, can she not hear me? Miss Halliwell!"

Reluctantly, Jane rose and hurried to the viscountess's side.

"Finally," the woman complained, giving Jane a pinched look. "You should pay closer attention when you are in company in case you are needed."

"Yes, my lady," Jane said, curtsying deeply. If in her mind the gesture was laced with multiple layers or disrespect, that was for Jane's knowledge only.

"I need my shawl, you know the one I mean," Lady Gilford said. "I left it in my husband's study this afternoon. Go and fetch it for me."

Aware that being sent to fetch was a job for a housemaid

and not a governess, Jane would have liked to object, but she knew that if she were to cause a scene in a room full of prestigious ladies from across Europe, Lady Gilford would make her life miserable.

With an obedient nod, she hurried from the room, grateful that she was at least allowed to leave the space for a bit.

She had been in Lord Gilford's study only a few times since she'd moved into the household, but it was easily one of Jane's favorite rooms in the house. With its book-lined walls and faint smell of tobacco from his lordship's pipe, it reminded her of happier times before her father had succumbed to his passion for gaming.

When she reached the hallway outside the study, she saw that the door was ajar, gaslight streaming from the open doorway onto the thick carpet ahead. Thinking that Lord Gilford might have brought one of the delegates here for a one-on-one discussion, she hesitated outside for a moment, listening for voices. But save for the faint murmur of chatter from downstairs, it was eerily quiet up here.

Even so, she knocked briskly on the paneled door, just in case. "Lord Gilford, I don't wish to disturb you, but I've come to fetch her ladyship's shawl," she called, even as she pressed on the door and stepped inside. The room was thankfully empty. Wrinkling her nose, she noted that instead of tobacco, the room had an unpleasant, metallic odor. And something else that made her wonder if one of Lord Gilford's dogs had been sick in here. She'd mention it to one of the footmen when she got downstairs.

Spying the shawl draped over the arm of a large leather sofa against the far wall, she hurried forward to pick it up.

When she turned to leave, she could now see behind Lord Gilford's massive mahogany desk. And what she saw made her give an involuntary cry of alarm.

Lord Gilford, a dagger protruding from a bloody wound in his chest, lay awkwardly on the floor behind his desk.

And he was quite dead.

Chapter Five

Once the ladies had left the dining room, as was often customary, the men broke into smaller groups to enjoy their cigars and port and individual conversations.

Adrian wanted desperately to insert himself into the quartet that included Lord Gilford and Dimitri Antonovsky, the Russian foreign minister, but he knew Gilford was well able to calm the Russian's pique. And in any case, Antonovsky wasn't the only diplomat in attendance riled by the British government's attempt to acquire the much-coveted talking machine. The device would revolutionize communications in the same way the telegraph had done twenty years earlier.

When word had spread among the governments of Europe that such a machine was in the works—and had been invented by a member of the Roskovian royal family no less—the various governments had immediately begun pressuring Prince Maxim for the rights to the machine. But the future ruler of Roskovia was no fool. He'd refused to sell the machine without milking every last drop of profit from the deal.

"I would have thought Dimitri would have learned how to hold his tongue by now," said Woodward from his place beside Adrian, where he was clipping the end off a cigar. "But he's always been a hothead. Which makes his position in the diplomatic corps that much more amusing."

Since Adrian and Woodward had both encountered the Russian frequently in their years in their own respective countries' governments, they'd both become familiar with Antonovsky's temper.

"It's difficult to prevent a tsar from appointing his beloved nephew a coveted government position, I would wager," Adrian said, sipping his port. "Though I'm surprised you didn't join him in his condemnation of Britain's methods. I believe the French would also agree with him."

"I would not be so rude as to criticize my host country," the American said blandly. "Besides, if a certain European royal has not yet figured out that the best prospect for his invention lies on the other side of the Atlantic in the New World, then my joining in with Dimitri's tirades won't help."

"May the best government win." Adrian raised his glass and when Woodward did the same, the two men drank to the notion.

Though he was confident that Britain had the best odds of winning the contract with Roskovia, Adrian wasn't so bold as to believe the Americans didn't have a chance. The United States, despite the recently concluded war that had occurred between its slaveholding south and abolitionist north, had played midwife to any number of world-changing inventions of late. It made sense that the former British colony would wish to lure Prince Maxim and his talking machine to its shores.

"Speaking of winning," Woodward said into the silence that had followed their toast, "I see why you are so charmed by Miss Halliwell. I knew from our little conversation that she is capable of intelligent conversation, but after an entire dinner spent in her company, I am even more impressed. If I were a different sort of man, I'd attempt to steal her away from you, but alas..."

Adrian shook his head. He knew Woodward was attempting to rile him into confessing to some sort of tendre for Jane Halliwell. Which was a ludicrous notion. Yes, with her dark hair and eyes that put him in mind of lapis lazuli, she was lovely, but he'd met any number of beautiful women over the years—and even enjoyed the occasional affair—but he hadn't lost his heart to any of them.

And as intelligent as Jane was, she was also as stubborn as a mule. Just look at how she'd intentionally refused to meet with him at Langham Abbey when they'd both been there two years ago. He'd only intended to ask after her well-being since he hadn't seen her since her father's death. He had little doubt she'd have avoided him at all costs this week as well, if not for the happenstance of Lady Gilford needing Jane to make up the numbers at table this evening.

No, as lovely and intelligent as Jane Halliwell might be, she was the sort of lady one took to wife. And with his hopes to shift positions from the Foreign Office to the Home Office, he was not looking for a wife. The work was dangerous and having lost his parents as a child, he would not wish that sort of loss on anyone, much less his own wife and children. There would be plenty of time when he was older to settle down. His brother hadn't married until he was well into his thirties. Why should Adrian behave any differently?

"There is no question of your stealing her from me," he told Woodward with a shrug, "when she doesn't belong to me in the first place. I don't know how many times I have to tell you. I merely warned you off her because of my connection with her father. Not to mention she's employed by my mentor. Anything else you might surmise is simply nonsense conjured by your fanciful imagination."

"If you insist." Woodward's eyebrows indicated he was not convinced, however.

But even as he smirked at Adrian, his expression changed abruptly from amusement to wariness.

"Dimitri and Lord Gilford are gone," he said in a low voice that only Adrian could hear.

Adrian glanced over to where the Russian and their host had been seated. The two men were indeed no longer there. Lord Payne, the other British delegate at the symposium, was also not in his seat. And a glance around the gathering indicated that the three men hadn't simply shifted positions to another conversation group. They were no longer in the room.

Likely Lord Gilford had decided soothing Dimitri's ruffled feathers required a private conversation in his study and Payne had gone with them to offer Gilford his support. But generally, Adrian would have been invited along as well. If only to take notes.

Payne had been against the notion of the symposium from the start, had even attempted to go around Gilford to press the prime minister to invite Prince Maxim for a solo meeting with the queen in order to convince him to sell his invention to Britain—Payne had deemed the very notion of offering Britain's competitors a chance to potentially undercut Britain at their own gathering ridiculous, whereas Adrian wished to adhere to a sense of fair play. As the most powerful nation in the world, it went without saying that Britain already had an advantage over the other countries vying for the talking machine. They didn't wish to look like bullies to their allies.

Had Payne accompanied Gilford and Antonovsky in order to warn the Russian off altogether?

"If anyone asks," he said to Woodward in an undertone, "I've gone to check on something for tomorrow."

"Check what exactly?" the American asked with an arched brow.

"I don't know," Adrian hissed. "Make something up."

With that, Adrian slipped from the dining room and headed to Lord Gilford's study, where he suspected the man would have taken Antonovsky for a private chat.

He'd just reached the east wing, where the family quarters were located, when he heard a feminine cry coming from the direction of the study.

Was that…?

Breaking into a run, Adrian tried and failed to guess why Miss Halliwell's voice would come from the viscount's study. He only knew his heart was pounding out of his chest as the thought of her in danger compelled him to get to her as fast as he possibly could. Whoever had caused her to cry out in alarm would soon regret it.

When he pressed through the open door of the room in question, however, it was to find Miss Halliwell was alone.

"Adrian, thank God." She threw herself into his arms and with something like relief, he pulled her against him. Physically, at least, she seemed unharmed.

But just as he was fishing out his handkerchief to press into her hand, he noticed the metallic tang in the air. It was an odor once encountered, would never be mistaken for anything else. It was the scent of death.

For the briefest moment he was transported back to a similar study in Rome, and before Jane spoke, he knew what she would say.

"It's Lord Gilford," Jane continued, trembling against him. "He's been murdered."

Ignoring the stab of shock her words sent through him, he ran a soothing hand over her back as he tried to think.

First, he needed to get her out of this room.

Slipping an arm around her back, he led her out into the hallway, closing the door behind them.

They only had a few moments before the rest of the household learned what had happened. Lord Gilford had been not only his mentor, but also a dear friend. And Gilford might have been murdered by one of the delegates Adrian had invited here. The notion was enough to make his blood boil. He would find out who had done this and make sure they were brought to justice.

But first—though he had no notions of Jane having been the one to kill Gilford, he needed to know why she'd been the one to find his body.

"What were you doing in here?" he asked in as gentle a voice as he could manage. "Why weren't you in the drawing room with the rest of the ladies?"

Jane blinked, as if coming to herself after a bad dream. "I…Lady Gilford sent me to fetch her shawl. She said she'd left it in the study earlier this afternoon."

As if she couldn't stop herself from speaking once the tale had begun, she continued, "I thought the room was empty at first, though the lamps were lit and the door was ajar. And I saw the shawl at once on the sofa. But there was a bad smell. I meant to tell one of the footmen later so that they could clean it. But when I turned around from picking up the shawl, I saw…"

Her dark blue eyes pooled with tears, and unable to stand seeing her so overset, Adrian pulled her against him again. He'd do just about anything to have prevented her from seeing Gilford like that. He'd seen her father's death scene all those years ago and he knew all too well how difficult it was to erase such a sight from one's memory.

"Well, well, well." Lady Gilford's voice intruded from the quiet of the hallway. "I suppose I shouldn't be surprised you would take advantage of the opportunity to throw yourself at an eligible gentleman, Jane, given how you behaved with Carlyle. But really, Lord Adrian, I thought you had better sense than to—"

At the first sound of her employer's voice, Jane had

removed herself from Adrian's arms and, having no choice but to let her go, he turned to face the viscountess.

"Lord Gilford has been murdered," he interrupted the now-widowed lady. "Miss Halliwell, whom you sent to fetch your shawl from the study, was the one who found him. So I would suggest you find a way to explain why your shawl was there in the first place."

There was little chance the viscountess would be blamed for her husband's murder, Adrian knew, but having seen her hateful antics enough times over the years, he wasn't overly worried about the plausibility of his words. He simply wanted her to be quiet before she started accusing Jane of killing Lord Gilford.

But that didn't mean Lady Gilford had discounted his words.

Faced with the possibility she'd be accused of murder, the viscountess fell to the floor in a dead faint.

Chapter Six

When Jane made it back downstairs after seeing Lady Gilford safely tucked into her bed with a sleeping draught from the physician who'd been called to attend her, it was to find the hallway outside the study teeming with servants, police, and a few gentlemen she recognized from her father's time with the Foreign Office.

She'd been able to get her own shattered nerves under control fairly quickly after realizing that someone would need to speak to Meg about her father's death, and considering that Lady Gilford had proved to be far more fragile than Jane would have imagined, that duty would fall to either Will—now Viscount Gilford—or Jane. And if it proved necessary for Jane, who well knew what it was like to lose a parent, she wanted to have her own wits about her.

Looking about her for some sign of Adrian or Will, she finally saw them both, in the sitting room directly across the hall from the study, engaged in what looked to be a heated conversation with another man who looked familiar, though she couldn't place him.

When she crossed into the chamber, however, her progress was halted by a frowning police constable who held an arm up to block her from entering. "Sorry, miss, but we've been told to stop any guests from coming into this part of the house. You'll need to return to the drawing room and wait for his lordship to explain what's going on."

She was puzzled for a moment at his mistaking her for a guest, but then remembered she was wearing one of her gowns from her life before going into service. "Oh, no, I think you've misunderstood," she said hastily, "I'm not—"

But the young man's expression grew annoyed at her words. "Miss, I think you are the one who's misunderstood. I know your kind thinks you're entitled to do whatever you want but in this case you're going to need to do as I say and go back to—"

With every word the man was adding another log to the fire of Jane's annoyance. But before he could finish, he, too, was interrupted, by the man she'd seen speaking with Will and Adrian. "Let her through, Rushing; she's the one who found the body."

"Yessir, Mr. Eversham," Rushing said quickly, though it was clear from the tightness of his mouth that he disliked being corrected. "Apologies, miss."

"Miss Halliwell," Eversham—whom Jane now recalled she'd seen in passing at Langham Abbey, where he'd been called upon to investigate a murder—said, his expression somehow grave and pleasant at the same time, "Lord Gilford and Lord Adrian wished to speak to you. May I accompany you?"

Grateful for his escort, she gave a nod and took his proffered arm. As the assembled crowd parted to let them through she realized that his politeness had likely been as much a function of expediency as good manners. She would likely have been met with several more Rushings on her way to where Adrian and Will stood watching their progress.

When they finally reached the other two men, she offered her hands to Will. "My lord, I am so very sorry for your loss."

She watched in sympathy as he swallowed and got control of his emotions, even as he clutched her proffered hands like they were a lifeline stopping him from being washed out to sea. "Thank you, Miss Halliwell," he finally said. "Your words mean a great deal to me."

"If there is anything I can do, you must let me know. Your father was very kind to me. As you have been as well." She felt her own feelings of loss threatening to overcome her, and she, too, fought to keep them in check.

Deciding to focus on the details of maintaining the household, she continued, "I left your mother upstairs sleeping soundly after taking the sleeping potion Dr. Barnes left for her. And I am happy to go up to Meg since you are occupied with other matters here."

But the young man shook his head at her last words. "No, I appreciate your offer, but I'll tell Meg first thing in the morning. There's no sense waking her to tell her. Let her sleep while she may."

If he hadn't been waiting to instruct her on what to tell Meg, Jane wondered, then what had he and Adrian wanted from her?

She glanced at Adrian hoping for some clue, but his expression was inscrutable.

"Then, if you'll pardon the impertinence," she said cautiously, allowing her puzzlement to show, "why am I here?"

Adrian cleared his throat. "I'm afraid it was I who wished to speak with you, Miss Halliwell, and since the viscount is your employer, I thought it best for him to be here while we discussed the details of what we wish of you."

"Who is 'we'?" Jane asked.

"The government," Adrian said, looking deadly serious. "The reason for this symposium was not for those assembled to discuss their favorite methods for cultivating roses. Instead, the gathering was an attempt to convince Prince Maxim of Roskovia to sell the plans for a certain machine he's invented. I've only just learned that this afternoon, before the symposium was even fully underway, Lord Gilford was successful at convincing the prince to give the contract to Great Britain. A fact he kept private, I presume, because so many of our guests had traveled for days, and in some cases weeks, to be here."

Jane stared at him, stunned. "You think one of the guests is responsible for killing Lord Gilford," she said, feeling her gut clench at the idea that one of the people she'd only hours ago sat down to dinner with had plunged a knife into their host.

"We don't know that yet, Miss Halliwell," said Mr. Eversham gravely. "But given the likelihood he was killed by someone in this house it stands to reason that it was either one of the servants, a member of the family, or one of the guests. And it seems to me that the servants and family, if they wished to do in Lord Gilford, would choose to do so when the house wasn't being watched by dozens of armed police officers."

"Or they would choose exactly that moment since the house is teeming with other likely suspects," countered Adrian wryly. At Mr. Eversham's raised brow, the other man shrugged. "We cannot discount the possibility, surely."

"But what do you want with me?" Jane interrupted before the detective could argue the point. "I'm happy to help but I'm hardly an investigator. Unless one counts being an avid reader of your wife's *A Lady's Guide to Mischief and Mayhem* column, Mr. Eversham."

"We don't need you to solve the murder, Jane," Adrian said, his blue eyes trained on her with an intensity that told her whatever he was about to ask was serious indeed.

"Miss Halliwell," Will said after exchanging a look with Adrian, "you know as well as anyone that my mother isn't an even-tempered woman at the best of times."

Thinking back to the viscountess's harsh words to her multiple times that day alone, Jane nodded.

"We need someone to act as hostess while we conduct the investigation into Lord Gilford's murder," Adrian said, his expression deadly serious. "Someone who can maintain a cool head and isn't likely to inflame the tempers of the guests. As soon as they learn of their host's death, they will wish to return to their own countries and we must stop that from happening until we're able to learn who killed Lord Gilford."

Jane didn't bother hiding her astonishment. "I'm the governess. Not one of the guests who has been introduced to me as such is going to take me seriously as their hostess. I'm not even married. Surely that—or at the very least widowhood is a requirement for such a role?"

The three men exchanged a glance. Finally, Mr. Eversham spoke. "Your birth and upbringing are that of a lady. The fact that you've worked as a governess does not negate that. As for your unmarried state, that doesn't matter if you are of a certain age."

"Not that we're saying you're old," Will said hastily, giving a beseeching look to Adrian. "You don't look a day over twenty—"

Before she could tell the younger man to stop, Adrian cut in. "What Lord Gilford is attempting to say, Miss Halliwell, is that despite your youthful appearance you are of an age that will make it unremarkable if you begin acting as hostess once we are able to remove the dowager from the premises."

Good Lord, Jane thought. She hadn't considered what Lady Gilford would think of this plan. "She won't just leave her own home without a by your leave. And if she learns I'm the one to act as hostess in her stead she will have an apoplexy. Lady Gilford isn't fond of me to begin with."

"You leave my mother to me," said Will grimly. "Though I suspect she will be more malleable than we'd generally have cause to believe. The fact that she fainted on learning of my father's death leads me to believe she was fonder of the pater than she ever let on to the rest of us."

Jane rather thought his mother had fainted out of surprise as much as any overwhelming grief but didn't say as much.

"And much as she might not like to hear it," Adrian added, "Lady Gilford will have no choice. You are the one both Scotland Yard and the Foreign Office wish to see in the role of hostess this week and that's the end of it."

Jane felt as if her head were spinning. She'd awakened that morning with nothing more in her mind than that day's lessons for Meg.

Meg!

"What of your sister, my lord?" she asked Will. "Surely she'll need me with her right now."

"I'm going to send for our aunt Thea and she will stay with both my mother and sister at our house on the south coast," the new viscount said. "Once we are able to hold a funeral—after my father's murder has been solved, I suppose—we'll figure out what the living arrangements will be. And if you wish to return to your duties as Meg's governess, I dare say we can see about that. Though I can't imagine I will be able to see you as an employee after you do this for our family, Miss Halliwell."

Jane felt the heat of unshed tears well in her eyes as she realized just how much change this was going to introduce into their lives—Margaret's and Will's especially.

"I suppose I don't have much of a choice," she said slowly after realizing the three men's silence indicated they were waiting for some sign of assent or denial from her.

"There is always a choice," Adrian said softly. "If you don't wish to do this, you have only to say so."

She felt a rush of gratitude for his words, though she knew very well that they were lip service. She would do as they wished. Because she'd been fond of Lord Gilford. And she would do whatever she could to help find his killer. Even if it only meant watching over the distinguished guests who were gathered in Gilford House.

"I will do it," she said with more decisiveness than she felt. "Though I have never yet had need to use them, my mama ensured that I had the training in the skills needed to run a household and preside over social events that is de rigueur for young ladies of my class."

But it had been years since she'd thought she'd ever have need of those skills. Years when she'd become accustomed to her in-between status, where she belonged neither downstairs where the servants dwelled, nor upstairs with the family she served. A knot of anxiety formed in her stomach at the thought of returning to the station she was born to—even temporarily. How much harder would it be to go back to being a governess after she'd had a taste of what it was like to be a lady of the house?

Detective Inspector Eversham nodded, then cut into her reverie. "Excellent. If you're clear on what your duties will be, Miss Halliwell, I have a great deal to accomplish here, so I'd best get to it. Thank you again."

Jane returned the man's nod of thanks with a confidence she didn't feel and stood for a moment watching him stride over to confer with another member of the Metropolitan Police.

Perhaps sensing her unease, Adrian took her arm. "I'll see you to your room so that you can get some rest. Tomorrow will be a difficult day."

She didn't argue at first, but as they made their way past the policemen milling about in the main hallway, Jane pulled away from him.

"You may leave me here," she said as they approached the hidden door that led to the servants' stairs. "It will only cause talk if you come upstairs with me."

Adrian looked as if he would like to argue, but said only, "You're likely correct. But at times like this I really do despise the rules of propriety. I simply wish to ensure you get to your room safely in the aftermath of a great shock."

"I'm hardly a shrinking violet to succumb to a fit of the vapors, my lord," Jane said tartly. Then, still smarting from her memories of the time after her father's death when Adrian had simply disappeared, she added, "It is five years too late for such gallantry in any case."

As soon as the words were out, she regretted them, but once she'd said them, she felt as if a weight had been lifted from her. The resentment had been festering inside her for years now, and it felt good to have finally voiced it.

Adrian, on the other hand, looked as if she'd slapped him. "What does that mean?"

She gaped at him. "Exactly what I said. Papa died and then you were gone. I know I was barely out of the schoolroom and beneath your notice, but it never occurred to me that you wouldn't be there to assist Mama. You were as familiar a face in our household as Lord Gilford or any of the others from the embassy. But one day you were there and the next you were gone."

The anger that had fueled the beginning of her words had, by the end, been replaced with a profound sadness. The sadness of a girl who had lost her father and the object of her, admittedly unrequited, adoration in the space of a day. But more than that, the sadness of one who'd desperately needed a friend, and had no one to turn to.

To her embarrassment she felt tears welling, which she hastily brushed away.

Adrian, she saw, looked stricken, but also as if he understood. "This is why you've avoided me. Because you thought I abandoned you and your mother."

This last was not a question, but Jane nodded. "I had no reason to think of you kindly after what transpired. And aside from that, I was busy with my duties when we ran into one another at Langham Abbey and had no time for meaningless chitchat."

A muscle in his jaw tightened at the mention of "meaningless chitchat" but she held her head high.

Finally, he sighed and thrust a hand through his hair, which had begun the evening perfectly tidy. "I had no say in when I left Italy. I thought you knew that if it were up to me I would have made my farewells to you and your mother. But at the time I was not much better than an underling and I was in no position to dictate my own travel arrangements."

Before she could respond, he continued, "But looking at it from your perspective I can see how you might have thought I was indifferent to what you and your mother were going through."

His brow creased in concern as he reached for Jane's hand, which she let him take in his.

It had never occurred to her that he'd had no say in his departure from Rome. At the time, she'd seen him as a very important person in the embassy. But in retrospect, she could see that he'd been a good decade or more younger than the others, including her father, in the British delegation. As a girl she'd had no interest in the hierarchy of her father's workplace. But with the understanding of maturity, she realized she'd been holding on to resentments that had been built on the scaffolding of false assumptions.

"I did ask after you both," he said now, still looking troubled. "But I didn't learn about how you'd been treated by the rest of society, and indeed the families of the other diplomats, until much later. And even with a bit of seniority I was still in no position to change things."

"I doubt you could have made a difference," Jane conceded, feeling abashed at how she'd misunderstood things so badly. "Mama retreated to live with a cousin in Scotland not long after we returned to England and saw which way the wind blew."

"But why didn't you go with her?" Adrian hadn't let go of her hand yet, and he gave it a gentle squeeze as he spoke. "Why become a governess?"

"The cousin she went to live with made it clear that she would prefer to accommodate only one of us, though she was never explicit in her wishes," she said, pulling her hand free despite the comfort she'd gained from the simple human contact. It would do well for her to recall that there was a chasm of social standing lying between them that could not be erased by a few days of her acting as hostess. "I had no wish to live on sufferance, which was just as well because I prefer to be on my own. Now, if you'll excuse me."

Adrian looked as if he wanted to press her, but must have thought better of it. Thrusting his hands into his pockets, he nodded. "Yes, there will be a great deal to do tomorrow, so I'd better leave you to your rest."

She moved to open the hidden door once more, but then turned, seeing he was still standing there, watching her.

"I am sorry for accusing you—" she began, but before she could finish, Adrian spoke up.

"You weren't entirely wrong," he admitted with a twist of his lips. "I might not have been able to control when I left, but I could have done more." He shook his head in self-disgust. "I was upset by what happened to your father, but I was also a foolish young man puffed up in his own importance. I didn't consider how you and your mother might have felt about my leaving so soon after what happened. And for that, I apologize."

Feeling as if whatever remaining burden had been left after she'd said her peace had been lifted, Jane gave him a smile. "Thank you."

And when she turned to leave him, she felt a hand on her arm.

"Before you go, Jane," Adrian said when she turned to

him, "there might well be a murderer lurking among us in this house. Please look after yourself."

His words sent a shiver of alarm through her. Catching his eye, she said, "I will, so long as you promise to do the same."

Not waiting for him to respond, she disappeared through the hidden door.

Chapter Seven

O nce Adrian and Will, along with Eversham, had done what they could to assure the assembled guests that they were in little danger of being murdered in their beds, he made his way toward his own room to pen a note to his brother, the Duke of Langham, to request his assistance with the assembled guests during the coming week.

It might be cynical to assume that the presence of a duke—the highest rank in the English aristocracy below the royals—might suitably impress the gathered foreign dignitaries enough to convince them to comply with Eversham's orders, but Adrian was willing to risk it. Joshua would no doubt despise every minute he'd be required to interact with their guests but he was loyal enough a brother to come to Adrian's aid. At least Adrian hoped so.

It was the other person he'd asked to step in this week that was troubling him at the moment, however. Though he knew it was necessary for both diplomatic and practical reasons to have Jane act as hostess for the remainder of the gathering, some primal, protective part of him wanted her far away from here. He trusted that Eversham would not put her in a position where she would be in imminent danger, but he was well aware that in the absence of her parents, Jane had no one watching out for her interests. Especially now that Gilford was dead.

Her accusation earlier, that he'd purposely abandoned her and her mother after Halliwell's death, had hit him like a fist to the jaw. Not only because it had never occurred to him that she would have interpreted his leaving for an assignment so soon after her father's death in that way, but also because he'd been so self-absorbed that it *hadn't* occurred to him. But now, he realized, it should have.

At least now he knew why she'd been so keen to avoid him when he tried to speak to her at his grandmother's house party. And again later at Joshua and Poppy's wedding. She must have despised him for his defection. And he couldn't blame her, however misguided her interpretation of his actions might have been.

But knowing how hurt she'd been by his disappearance only meant he was even more determined to ensure that her acting as hostess for this misbegotten house party didn't cause her any further harm. Whether it meant ensuring her reputation was rehabilitated from any damage that might remain from his cousin Lady Carlyle's gossip or keeping her from any physical harm the unknown murderer might wish to do her, Adrian would protect her.

It was perhaps not his place to be that person—and he

suspected she would not thank him for it—but he was aware now of how he'd failed her after the death of her father and he wanted to atone for his earlier mistakes.

If Jane ended up resenting his vigilance, then so be it. There was an unknown killer who might not yet be finished with Gilford House, and he was damned if he'd stand by and let Jane go unprotected. He owed it to her father, if not to the friendship with Jane that he'd betrayed all those years ago.

Once he'd finished the letter to Langham, he made his way back downstairs to find a footman to deliver it—tonight if possible. He'd just handed his letter to the stern-faced butler, Reed, when the sound of the knocker on the door below rang out.

Reed winced at the sound. "I apologize, my lord. I will have the knocker removed at once."

Knowing how many tasks were involved in draping a house with all the markers of mourning, Adrian didn't doubt the man and the housekeeper, Mrs. Parker, had their hands full.

Before he could reassure the butler, however, one of the footmen came hurrying toward them. "Lord Adrian, your brother, the Duke of Langham, has arrived and would like a word."

Surprised, Adrian took his missive back from Reed and slipped it into his pocket, then followed the footman to the Blue Room, one of the many extraneous chambers that could be found in a house this size, for which no particular purpose had been designated.

He found Langham standing with his back to the fire, his hands clasped behind his back, rather like a military man, though Adrian knew the posture had been drilled into the duke at school instead of on the battlefield.

"I see you've heard the news," Adrian said without preamble, though he did step forward to clasp his brother by the hand. "I must admit to a bit of surprise at the speed of the servants' gossip network, though I suppose that's naive of me."

"Though I would never rule out listening to servants' gossip if there were something I truly needed to know," Langham drawled, "in this case, it wasn't necessary. I received a note from Eversham, who indicated you might have need of my assistance this evening. It was only once I arrived that I was informed that the household was at sixes and sevens because his lordship had been killed."

Despite their sometimes contentious relationship, Adrian was gladder than he could have imagined at his brother's presence. Moving to the sideboard where he knew Gilford had kept a store of Irish whisky, Adrian poured a glass for each of them—his own slightly less full since he needed to keep his wits about him.

Once they were seated before the fire, Adrian related the evening's events, grateful that Langham only interrupted for a couple of clarifications. When Adrian reached the plan to have Jane act as hostess for the gathering, however, his brother made a snorting sound.

"What?" Adrian demanded with a frown. "You doubt Miss Halliwell's ability to manage a houseful of guests for a week or more? I can assure you she is quite a capable lady."

"Oh, I have little doubt as to Miss Halliwell's skills at commanding any number of dignitaries. She did govern our cousin's children for the better part of a year, and that can have been no small feat."

"Then what?" Adrian demanded, suddenly not quite so grateful to have the one person in the world who knew him better than anyone here to query his actions.

Langham contemplated his whisky for a moment, as if searching for the right words. That he was being careful with how he spoke said as much about the rift that had kept them at odds with one another as it did about the man himself. Clearly the duke was as eager to maintain their relatively recent detente as Adrian was.

"Though you might have guessed that I was only slightly aware of your connection with Miss Halliwell at Grandmama's house party two years prior—I was, after all, chasing a killer with my now wife—you would have been wrong. Indeed, I was approached by the dowager herself inquiring after what I knew about your inappropriate familiarity with a governess when there was a household of very eligible young ladies in attendance for you to choose from."

Adrian listened with increasing horror at his brother's words. Though he'd complained to Langham about his conversation with Jane the afternoon of the picnic—and really that had been their only conversation given that Jane had found some excuse every time thereafter he'd attempted to speak with her—he hadn't thought they'd been so conspicuous as to catch the dowager's notice.

He muttered an imprecation. "Why am I only hearing of this two years later? I can only assume you were able to

---

calm Grandmama's fears, for which I find myself in your debt."

"It is, rather, Poppy to whom you owe your thanks," Langham said dryly. "I'm afraid I was so happy to have my wife safely out of harm's way that I told Grandmama I didn't care if you wished to court one of the scullery maids so long as she left me in peace with my own betrothed."

Imagining just how well that suggestion must have gone over with their formidable grandmother, Adrian stifled a laugh.

"Exactly," Langham said with a rueful look. "Fortunately, Poppy is far more canny about handling the dowager than I am. She assured Grandmama that you were acquainted with Miss Halliwell in one of your previous postings and there seemed little danger of you marrying her—or anyone—for several years yet. Then, knowing just how determined the dowager is for great-grandchildren, with a truly masterful stroke of distraction, Poppy made some mention of refurbishing the nursery and Grandmama was so diverted she never mentioned the matter again."

Diverted for a moment, Adrian looked sharply at Langham. "Poppy wasn't—I mean to say there was no—"

"Of course not," Langham said with a roll of his eyes. "We'd only met earlier that week. Even I am incapable of impregnating a lady with merely a glance at my stunningly handsome face."

Glad he hadn't been taking a drink at that particular moment, Adrian shook his head at his brother's words. "As interesting as this is, perhaps you'll tell me what any of this has to do with Miss Halliwell?"

"I simply find it interesting that the young woman with whom you were so taken at the house party is not only a member of this household, but you've found a way to install her as hostess for the duration of this symposium." Adrian was about to object but Langham raised a staying hand. "I know that diplomatic circles are nearly as cliquish as the aristocracy, so it isn't terribly surprising that the daughter of a diplomat should find herself employed in a diplomat's household, but I simply find it interesting that it is Miss Halliwell whom you've chosen to act as hostess."

Feeling his face heat, Adrian said coolly, "She happened to be here, and as Lady Gilford and her daughter are going out to the country where they might grieve in private, Miss Halliwell was available."

That he might just as easily have requested some other, older, lady of good reputation to act as hostess for the duration of the house party and Eversham's investigation, he didn't bother admitting to his brother. It had galled him to see Jane at the beck and call of people like his cousin Lord Carlyle and his wife, as well as the venal Lady Gilford. Jane was a lady born and bred. She deserved to be treated as such.

Langham's telltale brow rose once more, but he only said, "If you are content to tell yourself that, then I can hardly argue."

Grateful that his brother didn't press the issue, Adrian changed the subject to Jane's need for attire for the week ahead.

Once Langham promised to send his wife in the morning, he rose to take his leave. "If there is anything you need of me during this hell-bound gathering, you have only to let me know."

Adrian squeezed Langham on the shoulder. "Be careful what you offer. I might take you up on it. If nothing else a visit from a duke might pacify them that they are not being fobbed off on a mere younger son."

Chapter Eight

The next morning Jane said her goodbyes to Meg, who seemed nearly as crushed by being sent away to the country with her mother as she was by her father's death—and really Jane could hardly blame the girl. Though Lady Gilford was notably quiet during their departure, she had been angry at Will for sending her away and made sure to tell him so loudly enough that Jane could hear it from where she stood with Meg in the hallway outside.

When the new Viscount Gilford emerged from the room, Will's eyes were shadowed and though he gave Meg a warm smile, Jane could tell that the responsibility of his new position was weighing on him.

Once they were downstairs, and Will had led Lady Gilford out to assist her into the carriage, Meg hugged Jane one last time. "Promise me that you will write as soon as there is any news," the girl said with feeling. "I should be able to rely on information from Will, but he insists on treating me like a child, just as he's done by sending me away. Just because Mama is volatile does not mean that I should be lumped in with her."

Jane wanted to tell Meg that Will's sending her to the country had more to do with wanting his family out of a house where a killer was running loose, but she knew that would not sway the girl.

"I promise," she told Meg. "And do not worry. Inspector Eversham is quite good at his job, and I have no doubt that he'll find whoever did this to your father." She didn't say that if the murderer was part of a foreign delegation, then whether the person would be brought to justice would very likely be a matter for the Foreign Office to decide. But Meg was the daughter of a career foreign diplomat—she knew well enough how these things worked. "Now be a good girl and go with your mama. She will have need of you, no matter how much she might push you away."

Meg's gray eyes, so like her father's, took on a world-weary look that gave her a maturity beyond her years. "I know," she said quietly. "Thank you, Miss Halliwell. You turned out to be a much better governess than I'd expected."

And with that mixed compliment, the girl hurried down the stairs and allowed her brother to hand her into the carriage that would take them to the train station.

Dabbing at her eyes, Jane was grateful to have a moment to herself before Will—Lord Gilford, she reminded herself—came back inside.

"She'll be better off at the country house," said a familiar voice from behind her, and Jane bit back a yelp of surprise.

"Lord Adrian," she said, tucking her handkerchief into her sleeve before turning to look at him.

Unlike everyone else she'd seen so far that morning—which admittedly had been only a few of the servants and the Gilford family—Adrian looked almost as if he'd rested. Though Jane knew that he had very likely been up until the wee hours discussing how the foreign guests should be handled over the course of the investigation.

"Not to mention the fact that you have more important things to do than teach a girl who won't be in the school-room for much longer about ancient Rome or sums or what-ever it is that you were educating her about." He smiled kindly, and to her dismay she found herself entranced by the glints of gold in his light brown hair shining in the weak sunlight. He was far too handsome for his own good.

And Jane was reminded yet again that she needed to lock away the part of her that noticed such things. She wasn't here to moon over handsome gentlemen. She was here to do her part to help find Lord Gilford's killer.

Still, that didn't mean she couldn't also correct Adrian about his misperception of what a young lady's education entailed. "In fact, my lord, ancient Rome is considered far too scandalous a subject for young ladies to study—as I'm sure you would realize if you took a moment to recall some of the more salacious poetry of Catullus or the Emperor Caligula, perhaps?"

But if she'd hoped to put him on the defensive, Jane was mistaken.

"Of course I didn't think you would have the chit reading

Catullus." Adrian raised a brow at her, as if he were wondering what she knew of the poet's ribaldry. "I only meant to ask—"

Fortunately for Jane's peace of mind, Will chose that moment to come back inside. Though his words nearly made her wince. "Who is reading Catullus?" Then with a frown in Adrian's direction, he said with a censorious tone, "And, really, my lord, I am not your nursemaid, but is Catullus a proper topic of conversation for a lady?"

"Oh, for pity's sake," Jane said, only barely able to stop herself from rolling her eyes. "Do I need to remind you, William, that I am nearly three years your elder? Not to mention that I have, in a great shock to your sensibilities I feel sure, read a great deal of Catullus's poetry thanks to the library in my family's house in Rome. And while some of it is, indeed, vulgar, some is quite good and would be entirely unobjectionable for any young lady to read."

Giving both gentlemen her best forbidding governess glare, she continued, "Now, might we go to the breakfast room? I have little doubt that many of the guests have asked for trays in their rooms, but whoever has come down will no doubt need some reassurance from the new Lord Gilford, and for better or worse, their new hostess."

Looking abashed, Will gave her a sheepish nod and indicated that she should precede them down the hall.

As she stepped into the breakfast room, however, she felt as if her gown might have gone up in flames, so intense was the scrutiny the nearly full table of houseguests greeted her with.

"Good morning, everyone," she said, then taking the coward's way out, she made her way, with as much haste as she could manage without making herself look foolish, to the sideboard where she took her time loading her plate with more food than she'd ever eat in a week.

"You are fond of kippers, then?" Adrian asked in an undertone from beside her, and as she noted the amusement in his voice, she realized she had placed three pieces of the smoked fish on her plate.

In fact, she did not like kippers at all. Not wanting to reveal her blunder to Adrian, she said with a pleasantness she didn't feel, "I am quite fond of kippers, as it happens. And everything looks so delicious this morning, I simply had to have a bit of everything."

Then, remembering that she was meant to be keeping him at arm's length, she said, "I hope you aren't one of those men who thinks badly of a lady because she has the temerity to eat sensibly, Lord Adrian."

They'd nearly reached the end of the table and when he placed a hand on her arm, careful to do so while they were still facing the wall—where the gesture would not be seen by those at the table— she nearly leapt out of her skin. That was twice today he'd startled her, she thought with annoyance. She would need to work on desensitizing herself to him.

"You have nothing to worry about," he said to her patiently, entirely ignoring her jibe about ladies and their eating habits. "You are your father's daughter. However he met his end, he was one of the most skilled diplomats I've ever met. And that includes Gilford, though he was also very good. You will have this group eating from the palm of your hand within the hour."

Feeling a lump rise in her throat, she turned to look at him, to gauge in his eyes the sincerity of his words. And was startled for a moment by the admiration in those silver-blue eyes that could conceal just as much as they revealed. But he was also a skilled diplomat. Could she trust what she saw there?

The sound of someone clearing their throat on Adrian's other side reminded her that they were not alone, and with a nod to him, she turned and crossed to the table where she took a chair next to Mr. Woodward.

Before she could greet him, however, from across the table, Madame Dulac, the wife of the French envoy, said with a speaking look, "I realize last night you were needed to, how do you say, 'invent the numbers,' Miss 'alliwell, but such things are not needed for breakfast?"

Her words ended with a questioning note and Jane didn't miss the way the older woman's eyes looked from her to Adrian, who had taken the seat on her other side.

"It's 'make up the numbers,' Madame," he told the French woman as he indicated to Geordie that he would prefer coffee to tea. "And in light of what happened last evening, Lady Gilford and her daughter have retreated to their country estates for the time being. Miss Halliwell has kindly agreed to act as hostess in her absence."

At this news, a chorus of murmurs and sounds of annoyance rose up from those gathered around the table.

"And yet we are expected to remain here," Dimitri

Antonovsky said in an aggrieved tone, "as if we are criminals? Who is to say that Lady Gilford is not the one who killed her husband?"

"I can say it," Jane said, imbuing her voice with more calm than she felt. "Lady Gilford didn't leave the drawing room once the ladies retired to it after dinner. At least not until later, after I found his lordship's body."

"There is also," said Mr. Woodward from beside her, "the fact that Lady Gilford's home is only a train ride away. If the rest of us were allowed to return home only to be found guilty of murder later—well, wars have been started for less, Mr. Antonovsky. As I'm sure you're well aware."

The Russian still looked cross, but he didn't argue the point.

"Since the topic has been broached," Adrian said into the silence that followed, "Detective Inspector Eversham of Scotland Yard will be here soon to interview each of you, so I ask that you make yourselves available for him."

Jane was watching to see who would argue the point, but she felt a presence behind her. Turning, she saw that Reed was there.

"I apologize for interrupting your breakfast, Miss Halliwell," he said, "but the Duchess of Langham has called for you."

"I—" She was at a momentary loss. She counted Poppy as a friend, but a governess was hardly in a position to accept callers. Certainly Lady Gilford would have discouraged it even if it were allowed. Reed stood awaiting more of a response from her than astonishment, so she nodded to him. "I'll go to her at once."

She rose from her chair and excused herself to the rest of the table, though they didn't seem to notice or care.

Once they were in the hallway, when Reed didn't move and continued to stare at her in the manner of a cat who wished she would feed him, she asked, "What more do you need to tell me?"

"It's just that the duchess is in your bedchamber, Miss Halliwell," he said quickly. "That is to say, your *new* bedchamber. It's the Rose Room in the family wing."

Before she could ask what was wrong with her old bedchamber, he added, "It's on Lord Gilford's orders, Miss Halliwell. He said if you're to be acting as hostess you shouldn't be up in the attics with the schoolroom."

That didn't explain why Poppy was in her new bedchamber, but Jane supposed she'd find out once she got there.

"Thank you, Mr. Reed," she said firmly. "Please have some tea sent up to us." Remembering her uneaten plate of food—not all of it had been kippers—she added, "And please ask cook for some scones as well."

As she hurried upstairs to the family wing, Jane couldn't help but breathe a sigh of relief at having—even momentarily—escaped what had been sure to be a thorough interrogation from the assembled guests. Though she hadn't expected Poppy to visit, she would be happy to accept any advice her friend might have about how best to manage a houseful of guests.

And if the duchess had any suggestions on how best to manage her brother-in-law, Jane would welcome them. Recalling the frisson of awareness that had run through her at the mere touch of his hand on her arm, she knew it would be best to nip any revival of the tender feelings she'd had for him as a girl in the schoolroom. Especially now that he was no longer her social equal.

And if Poppy, who had some experience with their ilk, had some tips for finding a murderer among the guests, Jane would appreciate those as well.

After Adrian had finished breakfast, he strode toward the small room Gilford had set aside for his use during the symposium. Will had offered to let him set up in his father's study, but neither of them was ready to spend much time in the room where the viscount had been murdered.

Adrian had requested that the dignitaries gather later that day in order to reassure them that every precaution was being made to ensure their safety. And given that at this point Scotland Yard still considered everyone in the household a suspect—no matter how reluctant Adrian was to tell them so—he was certain there would be some pointed questions for him. As such, he wanted to be prepared with any bit of information that might help him soothe any ruffled feathers.

He was going over his notes for the meeting when he heard a brisk knock on the door, and before he could respond, it opened to reveal Eversham.

"Do you have a minute?" the detective asked, even as he lowered himself into the chair beside Adrian's desk.

"By all means," Adrian said dryly, "have a seat. Shall I ring for tea or would you prefer coffee?"

Not looking at all chastened, Eversham nodded. "Coffee would be fortifying. Though I was able to break my fast with Katherine at home, I fear there was no time to finish my tea before I was summoned to the office of the coroner."

This made Adrian frown. "Is that usual for a case like this?"

The footman, Geordie, must have been standing right outside the door because almost as soon as Adrian pulled the bell, the young man appeared and was soon on his way to the kitchen to fetch coffee.

"Only if there is something unusual or unexpected about the manner of death," Eversham responded once they were alone again. "In this case, Dr. Barnes found something in Lord Gilford's pocket that might have some bearing on the investigation."

As Adrian watched, the detective reached into his own breast pocket and withdrew a folded page that looked to have been torn from a book. He opened it carefully and revealed a flower that had been pressed within—the sort which a young lady might save as a keepsake by flattening it within the pages of a heavy tome. "Does this mean anything to you?"

"No. What book is the page from?" he asked, his mind trying to remember if any of the countries Lord Gilford had interacted with was known for sending covert messages like this. "I don't recognize it."

Wordlessly, Eversham handed him the page and the pressed flower that had been tucked inside. One glance told Adrian the page had been cut from a volume of Machiavelli's *The Prince*. Underlined in ink on the page were the words "If an injury has to be done to a man it should be so severe that his vengeance need not be feared."

"You don't recognize it." Eversham's words were not a question.

"No," Adrian said with a slight shake of his head. "That is to say, I am familiar enough with *The Prince* but I have no notion why this particular page or quote should be found on Lord Gilford's body. I've known the man for a decade and don't recall him ever speaking of Machiavelli. Though, of course, this particular work is familiar enough to any man of education."

"So you don't believe this was something Gilford would have chosen on his own. As a remembrance of sorts?" Eversham asked, his gaze intent. "The rose might indicate a woman is involved."

"If you're wondering whether Gilford had a mistress," Adrian said dryly, "then I can't really help you. As far as I know, he didn't but you know how these things are. Some men flaunt their affairs and don't give a damn who knows. But Gilford was discreet about most things given his position in the government."

Eversham sighed. "It was too much to be hoped that he'd have boasted of an affair. And I don't suppose you can tell me if this kind of thing is common in your line of work? Perhaps as a not-so-hidden message?"

"I was wondering the same thing, actually," Adrian admitted. "I don't know of any particular cases but it's not out of the question."

He stared down at the underlined words. "The thing is, the words in this passage read like a threat. Could it be that it was a warning that he failed to heed and was killed for it?"

The detective looked troubled. "It's possible. It's also possible that these tokens were left on his body as a sort of calling card by the murderer. I had a case several years ago in which the killer left biblical quotes with the bodies."

Adrian felt a chill run down his spine. Could they be dealing with the same sort of killer? It was bad enough knowing someone had broken into Gilford House and murdered the master of the house. The notion that they'd also brazenly left a clue to their identity felt worse somehow—the arrogance of the act making them more terrifying.

"You were able to catch this other murderer, though, weren't you?" Adrian was grateful his voice sounded calmer than he felt.

"We were," Eversham said thoughtfully. "My wife and I worked on that case together in fact. And without her assistance, I'm not sure I'd have managed it."

Adrian couldn't help his gasp of surprise. "You allowed your wife near such a dangerous inquiry?"

Eversham laughed. "There is no *allow* with Kate. And in truth, she was not my wife at the time. But I have since learned that ladies can be of great help during investigations. They often catch nuances that we men miss. That is why I am glad Miss Halliwell agreed to assist us by acting as hostess."

At the mention of Jane, Adrian felt the chill return. "What do you mean? She is merely going to be overseeing the guest activities, leading the ladies to the drawing room after dinner, that sort of thing."

If he'd had any notion that her taking Lady Gilford's place this week would mean putting her in harm's way, he'd have made his objections known immediately.

"And so she will," Eversham agreed, "but that doesn't mean she will not be interacting with the guests and observing their reactions to their fellow guests. A great deal can be learned in the guise of drawing room conversation. And I believe Miss Halliwell is an intelligent young woman. I plan to speak to her later today about what to be on the lookout for."

Adrian felt his ire increasing as Eversham continued speaking. Sitting up straighter in his chair, he glowered at the detective. "Now see here, Eversham. I don't intend to let you put Miss Halliwell in danger. She's an innocent in all this and doesn't deserve to be put at risk simply because you fellows at Scotland Yard can't do your jobs."

If he expected Eversham to look abashed, he was sorely disappointed. "I don't believe there is any danger for her in the Gilford drawing room, no matter how vicious the gossip might be. And that fear aside, I believe it is up to the lady to decide whether she wishes to give this bit of assistance to us. Is it not?" He asked the question as if he truly wished to know, though Adrian suspected it was rather rhetorical.

"You know what I mean, damn it," Adrian ground out. "What if whoever it was that killed Gilford learns she's asking questions?"

"I can assure you that anyone who is fool enough to attempt anything while this house is teeming with officers from the Metropolitan Police will be met with swift and harsh measures," Eversham said, looking grim. "Miss

Halliwell will be safer here than she would be anywhere else in London at the moment."

Adrian nodded. Trying to get their discussion back to the subject at hand, he asked, "If the Machiavelli quotation and the pressed rose are akin to the notes left in the other case you mentioned, then what does that mean?"

Looking relieved to no longer be discussing Jane, Eversham said, "If that is the case, then there will be more murders to come. Or, if this isn't the first, then there will have been others in the past. Perhaps murders that were not recognized as such."

"What do you mean?"

"Perhaps a death that was thought to be an accident, or perhaps a suicide," Eversham said. "Any death of a colleague in the Foreign Office that left you with an uneasy feeling that there was something not quite right about it. That sort of thing."

As the detective spoke, Adrian felt an increasing sense of dread. He could think of several such deaths, including that of Jane's father. But surely there could have been no foul play in Charles Halliwell's death—he'd seen the man's gambling vowels himself the day his body had been found. And hadn't Attingly been killed by footpads? It had been murder, but not the sort Eversham was speaking of.

Halliwell, Attingly, and Gilford had been close friends as well as colleagues. And if they could find evidence of the same types of tokens among the dead men's belongings? Well, Adrian hadn't felt this kind of unrest since Halliwell's body had been found five long years ago.

"I know of two others in the Foreign Office who died under suspicious circumstances," he said to Eversham. "And one was Miss Halliwell's father."

Eversham raised a brow. "Then I believe we need to speak to Miss Halliwell as soon as possible."

Chapter Nine

Because she'd been waylaid on her way to her new bed-chamber by Mrs. Parker, who'd wanted clarification on the menu for luncheon, by the time Jane stepped into the light and airy room decorated in a pale rose (which could have fit three of her attic room inside with space left over), Poppy was already sipping a cup of tea.

On seeing Jane, however, she set the steaming cup down and came forward to envelop her friend in a surprisingly strong hug. "My dear girl, what an ordeal for you," the duchess said without waiting for Jane to greet her. "And Lord Gilford was the one who came to your rescue when your father died as well, was he not? I am so sorry, Jane."

For the first time since Mr. Eversham and Adrian had enlisted her the evening before to play hostess, Jane felt her body relax and she allowed her friend to take care of her for a bit. Poppy led her to the sitting area where the tea tray had been set out on a small table and pushed her into a lovely but comfortable chintz-covered chair there.

"Did you get a wink of sleep?" Poppy asked, taking her own seat and surveying Jane with a sharp eye. "I do not mean to indicate you are looking less than your usual lovely self but—"

"But the shadows beneath my eyes are large enough to have been cast by both Houses of Parliament as well as the clock tower?" Jane asked wryly. At Poppy's wince, Jane waved her off. "No, do not apologize, it is only the truth. It was difficult to close my eyes last night without seeing poor Lord Gilford's body on the floor of his study again."

Poppy reached for her hand. "It was the same for me after my ordeal in the caves at Langham Abbey. It will fade in time—at least it has for me. And I hope it will for you as well."

Jane hoped her friend was correct. Because given how tired she was at the moment, if she was unable to sleep tonight she would be dead on her feet by the end of the week. And it was only her first day acting as hostess.

"Thank you," she said to Poppy, grateful her friend had come, but not quite sure why she had done so. "Now, please do not take this amiss, but what brings you here? For I know it is not to glean gossip for the tea table, as it would be for some other ladies of the *ton*."

The duchess set the teapot down and gave Jane a rueful smile. "I should have known you would not simply accept my presence without question. If you must know, as soon as Joshua informed me of what had happened and of your being recruited to act as hostess, I had my maid set to work altering a few of my gowns for you."

Jane felt herself coloring at her friend's words. "I don't understand," she said stiffly. Though in fact she understood all too well. Poppy knew that Jane's wardrobe was likely to be filled with the sorts of dresses that were meant to fade into the background. Certainly not anything that would pass for acceptable among the well-born guests at Gilford House.

But she should have known Poppy would not let her feigned ignorance pass without challenge.

"My dear Jane," Poppy said with a shake of her head. "Pray do not think that icy look will stop me from speaking my piece. I am familiar with the tactic from the dowager and if she cannot cow me then no one can."

Jane sighed. "I suppose I should have known better. But honestly, Poppy, I will not accept charity from you no matter how kindly meant." Even as she spoke, she felt tears threaten. It was bad enough that she had to demean herself before the likes of Lady Gilford. Must she swallow her pride with someone she counted as a friend as well?

The duchess grasped her hand and said sharply, "It is not charity. It is a loan of a few dresses that I have never worn and will never be likely to wear. The fact that I'm required to purchase far more gowns than I need is shameful, really, but apparently there's nothing I can do about it. And believe me, I've tried."

Their eyes held for a moment, and Jane felt her objections evaporate in the face of Poppy's implacable gaze. "Oh, very well," she said, accepting defeat. "I suppose it is silly for me to be so high in the instep when I've lost any bit of social standing I once had."

At that, however, Poppy scolded her. "Do not let me hear you talk about yourself in that way. I had no intention of making you prostrate yourself before me. Goodness, are you forgetting that before I married Langham I was working as a lowly assistant to a newspaper editor?"

Now Jane felt her cheeks heat for a different reason. "Of course I haven't forgotten. But you are a duchess now and that is all that matters."

"I wish you would explain that to the ladies who look down their noses at me behind the dowager's back whenever we pay social calls." Poppy's brow was raised in an imitation of her husband. She needed only a quizzing glass to replicate the full effect.

Before Jane could reply, the duchess continued, "You would have no way to know it, but when Joshua brought me to Langham Abbey as his betrothed, it was a charade meant to keep the other young ladies at bay. I had been away from my family for two years and had no appropriate gowns to my name. And his sisters very graciously loaned me several of theirs."

Jane stared at her in shock. "I had no notion that was the case. But you seemed so elegant. And your gowns looked as if they'd been made for you."

"Yes, well, one of the maids at the gathering was a very skilled needlewoman," Poppy said with a wink. "And I was grateful for it. Without the costumes I may not have played my part so effectively."

"So effectively you ended up betrothed to the duke in earnest," Jane said with a grin.

"Exactly. So you must allow me to repay my debt by coming to your aid in the same way that Joshua's sisters came to mine."

Thinking over her friend's words, Jane nodded. "I am sorry for being so prickly. I thought I'd got past those prideful feelings that were such trouble for me when I first started governessing, but it seems I still had some left that needed exorcising."

"Do not apologize," Poppy told her softly. "I may have worked for my living in the past, but my employers were Lady Katherine and Caro. I suspect any amount of time having to kowtow to Lady Carlyle or Lady Gilford would turn me into a snarling beast."

Jane laughed and they sat smiling for a moment before Poppy spoke up again. "I came to bring the gowns, but I also came because I know what it is to feel like a fish among fowl. And I thought you might need an ally who has dealt with a similar situation."

At her friend's words, Jane felt herself near tears again. Goodness, when had she become such a watering pot? *When you found the dead body of a man who was like a second father to you*, her tart inner voice reminded her.

"I am so grateful you came," she said with sincerity. "I know everyone else here is equally overset but from the moment Mr. Eversham asked me to act as hostess, I've felt at sixes and sevens. Mama taught me well how to manage a household like this one—and if our lives had gone a different way I would very likely be married with my own house to run by now, and she'd be living abroad with my father instead of living in penury with a cousin in Scotland. But it has been some time since I even dared dream of such things, and I fear I might make some stumble that reveals me to be a charlatan."

"Oh dear." Poppy's brow creased with concern and understanding. "I well know how that feels. But you must remember that you were born to preside over just this sort of house party. There is nothing that any one of the guests can do that will erase that fact. You have just as much right as anyone else among the guests to be here. Indeed, more right because Eversham and Adrian requested you specifically to oversee this gathering."

At Poppy's reminder that this was her birthright, Jane felt some of her nervous energy dissipate. "Thank you," she told the other woman with a smile. "I think that these last years with the likes of Lady Carlyle and Lady Gilford reminding me constantly of my lowered station have taken a larger toll on my amour propre than I'd realized. There is a certain freedom in no longer being held to the same standard as other ladies of the upper class, but at the same time, one must be vigilant about not stepping a foot outside of the parameters of your new station. It can be quite exhausting."

Poppy nodded with understanding. "I know precisely what you mean. I had much the same struggle when I lived in London. But you must not let your self-doubt stop you from the task Eversham and Adrian have set for you. There could be lives at stake."

At the mention of Adrian, Jane felt her chest constrict. She wished she weren't so conflicted about how she felt about him. One moment she was still angry with him over his disappearance after her father's death and the next she was in danger of falling into her same old infatuation with him. She was no longer a girl of eighteen, however, and she needed to behave like the adult woman she was now.

As if she'd been able to see into Jane's thoughts, Poppy said, "I have reason to believe he thinks very highly of you. Adrian, I mean. I suppose you're unaware of just how distressed he was when he'd found you working at the dowager's house party not only as a governess."

"You've never said anything about it before," Jane said, frowning. The two women had been exchanging letters from the time they'd met at that same party. Indeed, Poppy had even arranged for Jane to meet her former employers, Lady Kate and Caro, so they could lend their assistance in helping Jane add authenticity to her novel. And she was quite sure Poppy hadn't mentioned Adrian more than twice and then it had only been in passing. "Why didn't you say anything?"

"For starters," Poppy said with a look of exasperation, "because I was annoyed on your behalf. You'd found yourself in straitened circumstances and had found a way to put a roof over your head and food in your belly. Who was he to approve or disapprove of the way you'd gone about it? I knew you were already overwhelmed with Lady Carlyle's harsh attitude toward you, and I did not wish to add to your burden."

Since Jane *had* been at her wits' end over the way her mistress had been criticizing her every action with the children, she was grateful for Poppy's discretion. It had been one of the reasons why she'd not wished to get into a discussion about the past with Adrian at the time. She'd been having enough trouble dealing with the present.

And yet...

"You're telling me this now," Jane said aloud. "Why?"

"My husband was struck by how much Lord Gilford's death has affected his brother," Poppy said with a sad smile. "As the older of the two, Langham feels some responsibility for Adrian and does not wish to see him hurt."

Jane was taken aback. "And he thinks that I have some way of helping him?"

Poppy shook her head. "No, no. I am sorry, I've bungled this. Langham said nothing about you at all. I simply heard his concern and thought that since you and Adrian are both grieving for Lord Gilford that you might agree to keep a watchful eye over him. Just to ensure that he doesn't become maudlin."

"You do realize that Lord Adrian is a grown man who holds a very important position with the Foreign Office, do you not?" Jane tried to make her question sound neutral but wasn't sure how well she succeeded.

Now it was Poppy's turn to redden. "I know. I sound just as meddlesome as the dowager, don't I? It's just that I know how happy Joshua has been over his reconciliation with his brother and I do not wish for this incident with Lord Gilford to put that at risk."

Considering that she was going to be in proximity to Adrian for at least the coming week, Jane supposed it would not be too difficult to watch for signs of melancholy in him. Though she suspected that if he knew Poppy was seeking such surveillance he'd have a few choice words for her. And, if he suspected Langham had had a hand in the scheme, he would not be best pleased.

"Very well," she said to her friend after a moment. "If I see any signs that Lord Adrian is dwelling overmuch on the loss of Lord Gilford I will let you know. Though I have no expectation that there will be anything to report."

"Thank goodness," Poppy said with a smile. "You are a dear to accommodate me in this, Jane. I know the duke may seem to the outside world as if he is a bit prickly, but he does care very much about his family. And since he and Adrian got past the rift between them he's taken a special interest in his brother's welfare."

This was the first that Jane had heard of a quarrel between the brothers. Remembering how fondly Adrian had spoken of his elder brother back in Rome, she suspected the coolness had been painful for him.

But the last thing she wished for now was to have Poppy draw her into further discussion about Adrian, so she turned the subject back to the reason Poppy had felt the need to come here in the first place. "Lord Gilford's death has affected everyone in the household, I should imagine."

At the mention of the viscount, as Jane had hoped, Poppy's eyes sharpened. "I wonder if the killer is among them. You know that most murders are committed by someone who is close to the victim. That means that it's likely someone Lord Gilford knew—perhaps even a loved one—who killed him."

Jane tried and failed to imagine a member of Lord Gilford's immediate family plunging a knife into his chest.

Even Lady Gilford, for all of her cruelty to Jane, had clearly been fond of her husband. And aside from that, given the viscountess's inability to abide a mess, Jane could not imagine she would choose a method that would lead to a stain on the carpets. And there was also the fact that Lady Gilford had been in Jane's presence while the earl was being killed.

"I know it was not Lady Gilford because she was with the rest of us, and I cannot imagine Mr. Eversham would not have investigated Will—that is the new Lord Gilford—if he believed him to be the killer." Jane had seen firsthand how devastated Will was about his father's murder. She'd known him long enough to know that it wasn't an act.

"And that leaves only Margaret," Poppy said with a sigh. "And as much as I like to think ladies are just as capable of anything a man might do, I cannot imagine she has the physical strength to plunge a knife into a man's chest."

At Jane's shocked look, Poppy shrugged. "I had to do a bit of research for Kate once on the force needed to stab someone in the chest. It's surprisingly difficult, it turns out. Which is why so many stabbings occur in the belly. Or so I suppose."

Jane shuddered. "I am just as intrigued by a mystery as anyone who reads the *Mischief and Mayhem* column, but some details are simply too much even for me."

"It does help when the details are not something you imagine happening to a loved one." Poppy gave her hand a sympathetic squeeze. "Now, if it wasn't a member of his family who killed Lord Gilford, then it could have been a member of staff, or heaven forbid, one of the foreign guests."

She didn't have to say why the culprit being one of the visiting dignitaries would be especially bad. Jane knew that if one of the guests was found to have killed Lord Gilford, there would, without question, be a diplomatic disaster.

"That would be a very bad thing, indeed," she agreed aloud. "I hope that all of the foreign guests are accounted for during the time in which Lord Gilford was killed."

"The possibility that one of the servants has murdered the master of the house is no more comforting," Poppy said with a shake of her head. "Either way you are living under the same roof with a murderer. A murderer who might well feel the need to kill again before all this is over."

Though the fire in the Rose Room was burning merrily, Jane couldn't help but shiver at Poppy's words. She hoped it was not an omen of things to come.

For everyone's sake.

Chapter Ten

J ane and Poppy were headed toward the drawing room
when they were waylaid by one of the footmen.

"Beg your pardon, Miss Halliwell, but Lord Adrian
would like to see you in his office," Geordie said with a
bow, before hurrying away down the hall.

"Oh dear," Poppy said with a raised brow. "I hope this
does not mean you are in for a scolding."

"Since I've done nothing to warrant a scolding, then I
can't think it's that," Jane returned absently as she stared
after the footman. She suspected she was being summoned
by Adrian for a completely different reason.

Though Will had asked her to stay on as hostess, his
mother had not. And Jane very much feared Lady Gilford
had left some sort of dismissal letter before she'd departed
for the country that morning.

"Something has you looking as if you've been stuck
with a hatpin," Poppy said, frowning. "Do you wish me to

accompany you? I am more than happy to stand up to my brother-in-law on your behalf. Though I cannot imagine he would be so rude as to say anything cruel to you after what you went through last evening. I have never seen him in his professional capacity, however, so perhaps I am wrong."

Jane was so lost in her own thoughts she only heard the latter half of her friend's words. Emerging from her reverie, she gave Poppy a smile and squeezed her hand. "I cannot think he will be cruel in the least. I was merely thinking he might have news about Lord Gilford's murder."

Which wasn't a lie, she realized, feeling selfish for worrying about her position when there was still a murderer to catch. "I had better go before he comes looking for me himself. Will you return home or would you like to wait in my sitting room?"

"Oh, I believe I will go have a seat in the drawing room, if you don't mind," Poppy said. "I am friendly with Lady Payne and Lady Ralston, who I believe are here."

Leaving her friend to find her own way to the main drawing room, Jane went in the opposite direction to the small chamber that was Adrian's temporary study.

Reaching the door, she squared her shoulders, then knocked briskly on it before entering.

A quick scan of the chamber showed that Adrian was standing behind the desk, and to her surprise, Eversham was also in the room, standing before the window.

Giving a brief curtsy, Jane said, "My lord, Detective Inspector, you summoned me?"

Since Eversham was there, she no longer suspected

Lady Gilford had anything to do with Adrian's reason for requesting her presence.

"I did, Jane," Adrian said, something about the somberness of his gaze putting her on alert. "Eversham has come with some news this morning and we'd like to discuss it with you. Please have a seat."

There were a pair of comfortable looking armchairs facing the desk and Jane took one of them, but only perched on the edge. Eversham took the other and Adrian settled behind the desk. Quickly, Eversham explained about the pressed rose and the page from Machiavelli that had been found on Gilford's body.

As he spoke, Jane felt the blood drain from her face and her ears began to ring. *It couldn't be.* The rose and quotation that had been found among Papa's things were simply mementos he'd saved. He was forever collecting bits and bobs from their travels. Hadn't Mama scolded him about it more than once?

"Get her some brandy," she heard Adrian say from beside her as she felt his hand press gently on her back so that she was leaning forward. "Breathe, Jane. In and out, that's it. Just concentrate on your breathing."

For several minutes she did just that, all thoughts of roses and quotes and her father gone as she worked on regaining her composure. After a few moments, she sat back up and watched as Adrian went to his haunches before her chair and pressed a small glass into her hand. "Drink," he said gruffly. She brought the glass to her lips, and the first sip made her cough a little. After a few minutes, the fiery liquid had warmed her from the inside and she was feeling calmer.

He must have deemed her recovered because Adrian pulled his chair from behind the desk to sit facing her and Eversham. "You went quite white," he told her, his expression grave. "What was it about Eversham's words that upset you?"

"I wasn't upset," she began but Adrian was having none of it.

"Cut line," he said with an edge in his voice that she wasn't accustomed to. "You almost fell out of your chair in a faint. That wasn't a normal reaction."

She felt her cheeks flame at his words. It had become second nature over her years in service to make the best of things—to lock away any alarm she might feel over anything because all that mattered were the feelings of her employers and their children. But Adrian was right. She had almost fainted. With good reason.

Looking down at her clasped hands, she said, "I apologize. You are right, of course. I was overset because the items you described, Mr. Eversham, sound nearly identical to the rose and underlined quotation found among my father's things after his death."

Adrian swore. "Are you sure?"

"Of course I'm sure," Jane said with irritation at the question. "I've carried them with me from house to house in the five years since he died. I keep them in my portable writing desk and see them every time I write a letter."

"I apologize." Adrian ran a hand through his disordered

locks. "I was expecting we'd have to go searching through his things."

"Mama was too distraught to look at the cache of personal items that were brought to us from the pockets of his clothes when he died." Jane took a calming breath before she continued. "I went through them for her and chose a few keepsakes from among them. The rose, the quotation, and a couple of pretty stones that I assumed he'd picked up while walking through the city."

"Perhaps you could show the rose and the quotation to us, Miss Halliwell?" Eversham asked gently.

Jane looked up at the detective and something in his expression made her clench her fists. "You believe my father was murdered, don't you?"

"We don't know," he told her, and she couldn't doubt the sincerity in his gaze. "But if the pressed rose and quotation you found are a match for the ones found with Gilford's body, then it's a possibility."

"Why don't you show me the ones you found with Gilford and I can tell you if they are the same?" she asked, looking over to where Adrian had gone back to sit behind the desk.

Both men hesitated and Jane felt her heart sink. "You don't trust me."

It wasn't entirely unexpected. She might be, as Poppy had reminded her, born to a station that made her qualified to preside over a house party like this one, but there had been a murder in this house only yesterday. Everyone was a suspect.

"It's not that," Eversham assured her, and she was

impressed that he didn't shy away from looking her in the eye. "It's just that I'll need to see the items side by side in order to tell if they're the same. And if we'll need them to present in court, I'll have to take them to Scotland Yard."

Oh. It hadn't occurred to Jane that he'd need to take them from her. But of course he would need them.

She was surprised when a knock sounded before Geordie stepped in. Adrian must have pulled the bell while she was conversing with Eversham, she realized.

After she'd instructed the footman to ask her maid for her writing desk to be brought here, she turned to face the two men again, feeling slightly awkward. But the detective, for all that he seemed focused entirely on the job at hand, was actually quite adept at conversation. "My wife tells me you are quite an excellent novelist, Miss Halliwell. I hope you have had some success in finding a publisher for your crime novel."

Jane was startled by the man's question, but she supposed it wasn't so odd that Kate had spoken to him of her book given that she and Caro had been assisting her. "Not yet, I'm afraid. Though I am expecting to hear back from one this week. 'Hope springs eternal' as Keats said. Thank you for asking."

"You have written a novel, Jane?"

She wasn't sure whether to be offended by the shock on Adrian's face or amused.

"I have, my lord," Jane told him with a smile—she'd decided to go with amusement. "Though I don't know when I should have told you."

He gave a sharp laugh. "I suppose our conversations have been dominated by other topics."

Jane was saved from further discussion by the arrival of Geordie with her compact desk. She took the highly polished wooden box covered in brass scrollwork from the footman, set it on Adrian's desk, and used the tiny key she kept on a chain around her neck to unlock it. After lifting the lid, she pulled open one of the small drawers and removed a folded and well-worn page that had been cut from a volume of *The Prince*.

Carefully, she opened the folded page and saw that the pressed rose was just where she'd left it. Over the years since her father's death, she'd taken out the page and the pressed flower any number of times, thinking to glean some insight into the father she'd adored. But the translated words—especially the underlined ones—had rung cold to her. And now she suspected why.

Handing the items over to Eversham, she watched as he carefully let the pressed flower fall into his left palm while he held the page in his right and scanned the words.

"Did the quotation hold any particular meaning to you, Miss Halliwell?" the detective asked once he'd handed the items over to Adrian.

"'Whoever believes that great advancement and new benefits make men forget old injuries is mistaken,'" Jane recited from memory. "For all these years I've thought it was given to Papa by one of his friends in the Foreign Office. As a reminder that no matter how cordial relations between another nation and ours seem, there are always old resentments lurking beneath the surface. But now, well, it sounds like a warning."

"It does," the detective agreed solemnly. "And given that both your father's quotation and Gilford's were found on their bodies when they died, it isn't beyond reason that they were left by the killer."

"So, you believe this same person killed both my father and Lord Gilford," she said flatly.

"I cannot say for certain just yet," Eversham told her. "But that seems to be the case. And there may have been others."

"Others from the Foreign Office who died suspiciously, you mean." Jane could think of at least one of her father's friends who had died not long after him but she couldn't recall what had happened. "Could it be one of Great Britain's enemies? We have certainly done enough to make them angry."

She saw Adrian wince at her assertion but didn't amend her statement. While she was proud of being a Briton, she wasn't blind to all the harm they'd done in the world.

"That is a possibility," Adrian said dryly. "It's safe to say that everything we once thought to be true is now in question."

Jane felt her head spin as another prospect rose in her mind. "Including Papa's suicide," she whispered. As if too afraid to say the words aloud.

Could her father have truly been everything she'd ever thought him to be? The flicker of hope that lit within her now felt selfish in the light of the other murders, but she clung to it like the life rope on a ship crossing the channel.

One thing was painfully clear, whether her father's culpability in his own death had changed or not.

The entire situation had just become a thousand times more complicated.

Adrian relied on years of policing his emotions to stop himself from pulling Jane against him to offer her comfort. But she was a grown woman now and that kind of easy familiarity was forbidden, no matter how much the circumstance might warrant it.

He settled for his most well-honed diplomatic skill, words.

"It would seem so," he said, taking her hand in his—surely hands were not off limits, he rationalized, though well aware the most stringent society hostesses would strongly disagree. "I know it's a great deal to take in."

At his words, Jane's eyes welled, and Adrian handed her his handkerchief.

"There's another death that may be connected. Lord Attingly, another colleague of both your father and Gilford," he continued, "was stabbed and robbed on the way home from his club a few years ago. He was ambassador to France at the time but was in England for his daughter's wedding."

Having wiped away her tears and regained her composure, Jane gave a nod of recognition. "He and Papa were good friends. I knew he'd died but couldn't recall the circumstances. Do we know if a rose and quotation were found among his things?"

"We do not know." Adrian wondered if there had been any sort of attacks on Attingly's reputation as there had been with Halliwell. He certainly didn't know of any that had been brought to his attention. But it was possible his family had been able to cover them up. For both Will's and Margaret's sakes he hoped that there would not be any such assaults on Gilford's good name. They had enough to deal with already.

As if conjured by his thoughts, the new Viscount Gilford opened the door to Adrian's office, and he looked as haggard as a man of twenty could.

"Good, you're here," Will said with relief as he shut the door behind him. "Have you learned anything new?"

Then, as if only just now realizing Jane was in the room, he stopped in the middle of striding toward Adrian's desk. "Miss Halliwell, I apologize. I didn't see you there."

After bowing to her he crossed to one of the empty chairs and lowered himself into it. "I take it you have learned something new or you wouldn't be looking so grim."

Quickly, Adrian told the younger man about the roses and the lines from Machiavelli that had been found on both his father's and Halliwell's bodies. He also mentioned their suspicions about Attingly's death.

Will swore under his breath. "So someone has been killing representatives of the Foreign Office for years and no one has caught on?"

Adrian felt the need to defend his fellows at the Foreign Office. "In Halliwell's and Attingly's cases, their deaths were disguised as something other than a simple murder.

For Halliwell, it was suicide. For Attingly, murder in the course of a robbery. And we're not yet certain there was anything suspicious at all about Attingly's death. We'll need to question his family to see if they found a rose or quotation with his things."

' "Because he was a man of some prominence, the local authorities in Cornwall called in Scotland Yard, and as it happens, I was the one who investigated," Eversham interjected.

"I take it you didn't find the culprit?" Will asked with a frown.

"No," said Eversham. "If I'd known I should have been looking for similar cases among representatives of the Foreign Office I might have made more headway."

"And before you ask, I don't know if a rose or quotation was found on his body. By the time I arrived, the body had been removed from the scene," the detective continued. "But I will send one of my men to question the family. We should know something soon enough."

"No."

There was a thread of steel in Jane's voice that made all three men turn to her in surprise.

"What I mean to say," she continued in a softer tone, "is that someone with an acquaintance with the Attingly family should go there to speak to Lady Attingly. Learning that her husband's death might be part of a larger scheme is bad enough without the news coming from a stranger."

Adrian nodded. It wasn't a bad idea. And he could extend the condolences of the Foreign Office to the widow.

"Thank you, Miss Halliwell. You make an excellent point. I have some acquaintance with Lady Attingly and she is rather formidable. I'll go at once."

"If Lady Attingly is as difficult as you say," Eversham said, glancing meaningfully at Jane, "perhaps it would be a good idea to bring a familiar face with you."

Before Adrian could object, Jane spoke up. "Lady Attingly was one of the few ladies of my acquaintance from Papa's time in the Foreign Office who did not cut Mama and me after his death. I should like to see her again and thank her for her kindness. And as I said earlier, this news is not something to be conveyed by an underling."

He couldn't argue with her logic, but even so, Adrian was not happy with the notion of having Jane accompany him on a visit to Lady Attingly. Now that they suspected that whoever had killed Gilford had killed Halliwell and possibly Attingly as well, the danger surrounding the investigation had intensified by leaps and bounds. The only reason he would allow her to come along on this visit was that he'd have her in his sights the entire time.

"Fine," he said, sounding disgruntled even to his own ears. In a more measured tone, he added, "If you wish to change your gown or any of those other frippery things ladies do before they pay calls, you'd better go do so before I change my mind."

Jane raised a brow at his words and looked as if she wished to object but must have thought better of it because she said only, "I'll just be a few moments."

Once the door shut behind her, Adrian heard Will laughing softly. "What?" he demanded of the younger man.

"If that is how you speak to a lady, it's a wonder to me you have any experience in diplomacy at all." Will shook his head, as if truly baffled.

"I suspect the reasons for Lord Adrian's gruffness over being maneuvered into spending time with Miss Halliwell have nothing to do with his diplomatic experience, Gilford," said Eversham thoughtfully.

Adrian had been ready to take his leave but at the man's words, he stopped in his tracks on the way to the door.

"Yes, Adrian," said Will, crossing his arms over his chest. "Do tell us about the reasons you might have for wishing to avoid Miss Halliwell."

To Eversham the young man said, "He nearly took off my head and then later—from what Payne told me—that of Mr. Woodward, the envoy from America, last night for merely speaking to her. And yet, he seems not to want her for himself. Dog in the manger if you ask me."

Annoyed that he'd been the one to put the notion that there was something between himself and Miss Halliwell in the other men's minds, Adrian bit back an oath. "Last evening, I was merely reminding you that Miss Halliwell deserves your respect," he said through clenched teeth.

"I have the utmost respect for Miss Halliwell," Will retorted. Then, a sly gleam coming into his eyes, he continued, "I have need of a wife now that I'm the viscount. I wonder how she would feel about becoming the next Lady Gilf—"

"That's enough."

Adrian's words cut through the air with the sharpness of a steel blade. He was willing to accept a certain amount of wit from the younger man, but he would not have Jane's name bandied about, even if Gilford were only jesting.

At Will's stunned look, Adrian said only, "You have made your point. But whatever you think might be between the lady and me, that doesn't give you leave to talk about her disrespectfully. I'll thank you to remember that."

Adrian turned his gaze to Eversham. "I'll go have the carriage brought round. I will speak to you both once our errand is complete."

Inclining his head to both men, Adrian went off in search of Jane.

He hoped like hell this visit to Attingly's would be worth the trouble it was causing.

Chapter Eleven

J ane was coming down the stairs from the family wing when she saw Lord Payne climbing toward her.

"Miss Halliwell," he said warmly, a smile softening the harsh lines of his craggy face as they stopped on the landing. "I had hoped to speak more to you last evening but the unfortunate business with Gilford prevented me. But I am happy to see you now, however unhappy the circumstances."

His kind words gave Jane a pang of nostalgia for the days when her father had still been alive and respected, and their house had been a frequent meeting place for his friends and colleagues. Lord Payne had been a particular favorite of hers from childhood because of his insistence on speaking to her as if she were a sensible being and not an ignorant child. He'd also been a reliable supplier of peppermint sweets, which he always seemed to have hidden in the inside pocket of his coat.

"It's been a long time since whatever ailed you could be cured with a sweet, hasn't it?" he asked with a rueful smile, as if he'd read her thoughts.

"I'm afraid so," Jane said sadly. "I miss those days more than I can say. You were a good friend to Papa. And Mama and me. I was never able to thank you properly and—"

The older man waved off her thanks. "I only wish I'd been able to do more. When I learned from Gilford that you were working as a governess, I was quite angry on your behalf, let me tell you. But by the time I learned of your reduced circumstances it was too late to intervene."

His mouth was tight with anger and Jane felt a mix of gratitude and injured pride at his words. She was not ashamed of her work as a governess over the past few years. It was a respectable occupation, however it might signal to polite society that she was unable to live a life filled with parties and leisure as other young ladies of her class did. Still, she'd learned from her time in service that it would not do to correct an elder's errors.

She took his proffered hand and squeezed it. "I do thank you, but I have been happy here at Gilford House." Then, realizing that he was quite familiar with Lady Gilford, she amended, "Well, mostly happy. Until what happened to poor Lord Gilford last evening."

"A terrible business," he agreed, his bushy brows furrowed. "That someone had the temerity to do such a thing in the man's own home is truly shocking. I am not surprised that Lady Gilford fled to the country with her daughter, but why did she not take you with her, my dear?"

Given how unpleasant Lady Gilford had been to her,

Jane was quite happy she hadn't been required to accompany them, though she could hardly admit that aloud—even to someone she'd known as long as Lord Payne. "I believe she wished for some private time with Margaret considering what a blow Lord Gilford's death was to both of them. I do not mind acting as hostess in her absence at any rate. It gives me something productive to do with my time."

"Indeed, I suppose you have been longing for a household of your own these past years." Lord Payne's words stung, though Jane knew he meant them kindly. "Pray forgive me and my unruly tongue. I did not mean to remind you of your changed circumstances."

"There was no harm intended, I am sure," Jane said with a brief smile. "But I mustn't keep you from your destination. I am sure Lord Adrian is waiting for me downstairs."

At the mention of Adrian, Lord Payne's gaze sharpened and Jane mentally cursed herself for speaking so thoughtlessly. She'd only meant to extricate herself from a conversation that had turned awkward. Now Lord Payne would be making assumptions about her relationship with Adrian.

"Oh, it's nothing like what you must be thinking," she assured Lord Payne with a laugh. "We are merely going to pay a call on Lady Attingly. You were a friend of her late husband's, along with Papa and Lord Gilford, were you not?"

At the mention of Attingly, Lord Payne's expression grew troubled. "Another colleague who was cut down too soon. Pray send my regards to Lady Attingly. She remains a dear friend of Lady Payne's."

Jane promised to do so and had thought she'd taken her leave of him when she heard Lord Payne's voice behind her.

"Jane, my dear," he called. When she turned, he gave her a fond smile. "I know it is not my place to do so, but please may I give you a bit of fatherly advice since your own dear papa isn't here to do so?"

Her heart warmed at his kindness. "Of course, my lord."

"Lord Adrian is an ambitious man and in the Foreign Office, and that will likely mean a life of traveling from continent to continent for years at a time." Payne gave her a tight smile. "I remember from one of our talks years ago that growing up in that life has given you a wish to put down roots. Pray do not let yourself become attached to a man who will require you to give up the chance to settle down as you have long wished."

And with those words, he turned and continued his ascent to the upper floors.

Jane stared after him for a long moment. Wondering how a man she hadn't interacted with in years had been able to see so clearly into her most closely held anxieties.

The skies opened just as Adrian and Jane stepped outside to begin their journey to Attingly House. Despite the luxury of the coach, the muddy roads made the ride a bone-rattling one. More than once a rut sent Jane hurtling off the front-facing seat and into Adrian's arms, the feel of her soft curves against him sending his senses reeling. That she seemed not at all affected as he resettled her in her own seat was a fact he'd rather not dwell on.

"Lady Attingly was one of the few acquaintances from

Papa's time in the service who sent a note of condolence to Mama after he died," she said, turning away from the carriage window and giving him a sad smile. "I hadn't heard of her husband's death until months after it happened and I'm sure Mama didn't hear of it or she'd have told me. I know we would both have written to her otherwise."

"I'm sure she won't hold that against you," Adrian said smoothly. "In my experience she is a genuinely kind person. Hopefully, she will not find it too odd that we're asking about items found among Attingly's things after his death."

As if a cat had walked over her grave, Jane shivered. "It's disturbing to think of the killer slipping a page from *The Prince* and a pressed rose into his victim's coat after he's killed them. What would make someone do such a thing?"

"Perhaps to send a message?" Adrian had been racking his brain for answers from the moment Eversham showed him the page found on Gilford's body. "As you said earlier, the quote found with your father's things seems to be suggesting his killer had old resentments he was avenging. And Gilford's quotation, 'If an injury has to be done to a man it should be so severe that his vengeance need not be feared,' mentions vengeance outright."

"And murder is certainly the most severe act of vengeance," Jane said thoughtfully.

"I find it difficult to imagine Gilford doing anything so awful as to warrant his murder," Adrian said, trying to recall those moments in his mentor's career that could have triggered such hatred. "As a representative of the government, of course, he was forced to make unpopular decisions a time or two over the years. But that isn't unusual in our line of work. He always made it a point to keep things as cordial as possible. As did your father, for that matter."

"Perhaps it's not so much that a single matter itself was handled cruelly in any way." A pucker appeared between Jane's brows as she considered her words. "But, as my father's quotation suggests, there were old injustices that had not been forgotten. Or forgiven for that matter."

"It definitely smacks of long festering wounds," Adrian agreed. "And given that all three of these men spent decades working for the Foreign Office there are innumerable actions to be looked into before we settle on the correct one." His mind balked at the amount of paperwork that would need to be gone through over the next few weeks.

"I don't like to think of someone hating my father so much," Jane said softly, frown lines bracketing her lush mouth. "Even when I thought gambling debts had caused him to take his own life, I never stopped believing he was a good man."

Unable to stop himself, Adrian reached across the carriage and took Jane's gloved hand in his. "He was a good man. Even if he harmed this unknown person in some way, he didn't deserve what happened to him. Any more than my own parents deserved to die in a carriage accident."

She looked at their joined hands for a moment and he wondered if he'd overstepped, but she made no move to pull away.

"You were a child when they died, weren't you?" she asked softly. "That must have been difficult."

"I barely remember them," he admitted, realizing he must have told her about the late Duke and Duchess of

Langham during one of their long-ago conversations in Rome. "It's more impressions than actual memories. Mama was pretty and soft and smelled of lilacs. I remember the feel of her arms around me. Papa was dark—though I suppose that was his suits—and smelled of cigars and faintly of the stable. Langham and my sisters were older when our parents died and so have more fleshed-out memories. It's harder for them because of that, I suspect."

The carriage hit another bump and they were forced to drop each other's hands, but Jane merely transferred hers to his arm. Even if she didn't intend it to be comforting, Adrian found he liked the feel of her touch. Perhaps a little too much if his body's response to it was anything to go by.

"Do not discount your own grief," Jane chided lightly as she settled back into her seat when the carriage righted. "Even without having known them beyond an infant's view, your loss is perhaps the worse since you not only lost your parents but also any chance to truly know them."

"I suppose," he admitted. "Though I was lucky enough to be shielded from the acuteness of grief. I know your own pain has been exponentially worse than my own."

"And now we are all joined in our grief over the loss of Lord Gilford," she said, brushing past her pain at losing her father. "Unfortunately, I fear grief is a part of the human condition that cannot be shirked. No matter how we might wish to do so."

Realizing that they were very likely nearing the Attingly townhouse, Adrian changed the subject slightly. "I will leave it to you to question Lady Attingly. If her son is in residence, I will make it a point to leave you ladies together and go speak to him. I suspect he is most likely to have seen the contents of his father's study."

Jane nodded. "If we have no luck with either of them, we might ask to speak with the late Lord Attingly's valet. There is a tendency among the upper classes to discount servants as if they are invisible, but I've learned from my own experience that they observe far more than they are given credit for."

It was a good point, and the fact she had firsthand knowledge as one of the nameless, faceless serving class angered him anew that the murderer they were after had engineered her social downfall, as well as her father's death. He'd always disliked the biblical notion that the sins of the fathers should be visited upon their children, and even if Halliwell's death had been the suicide it was purported to be, it had been wrong to make Jane pay such a heavy price for it. But knowing her father had been murdered made the way she and her mother had been treated in the wake of Halliwell's death even more shameful.

Jane had shown herself to have a strength of character that he could only have guessed at even a couple of years ago when he'd first seen her again at his grandmother's birthday party. Now, having seen her patience, kindness, and dignity over the past couple of days, he realized she'd matured into just the sort of woman he'd always hoped to have as a w— The carriage began to slow just then, and Adrian was glad not to have completed his previous thought. He needed to keep his attention focused on the investigation into the murder. Besides, he'd already decided his position in the Home Office as an investigator would mean delaying marriage for several years. Jane would be wed, and with a passel of children, by that time.

He scowled at the idea of some nameless, faceless interloper marrying Jane. Then, schooling his features into something less fearsome, he watched as Jane set about straightening her hat and gloves and stiffening her spine in preparation for their arrival.

"There is no need to be nervous," he reassured her, unable to keep the softness from his voice. "You look lovely and every inch the lady that you are."

She looked startled, but quickly masked the emotion behind a wry smile. "You are kind to say so. Poppy told me much the same thing earlier. But it's been some time since I've felt deserving of being treated as such. And like in one of the Grimm brothers' tales, I will turn back into a governess once this is all over."

He would have argued but the vehicle came to a stop just then and the carriage door was opened by a waiting footman.

And then they were disembarking, and Adrian was handing their cards to an unsmiling butler before they were shown into a light and airy drawing room. But instead of the dowager Lady Attingly, it was her son, Lord Attingly, who came to greet them nearly a quarter of an hour later.

"Miss Halliwell," the ruddy-faced young man, who was dressed for riding, said as he bowed over Jane's hand. "It is good to see you again. You may not remember but we met years ago when my father visited yours in St. Petersburg.

You spent more time with my sister, as I recall, but it was a memorable trip all the same."

"I remember it well," Jane replied. "I always enjoyed meeting other diplomatic children. How is your sister?"

They spent a few minutes speaking about past acquaintances before Attingly turned to Adrian sheepishly. "My apologies, Lord Adrian," he said, offering his hand. "It is so rare I run into those who know what it is to grow up in an embassy that I forgot myself."

"Not at all," Adrian assured him blandly, though he couldn't fail to note the hint of color in Jane's cheeks. "Miss Halliwell was hoping to have a word with your mother. We were told she now lives here with you and your wife."

He didn't mean to emphasize the word "wife" but somehow that was what happened when he spoke.

At the mention of the dowager, Attingly looked apologetic. "I'm afraid Mama is in Lincolnshire visiting her sister at the moment. Are you here about Gilford? I read about his death in the papers. Shocking business. Who would have thought he would be gone so soon after your father and mine, Miss Halliwell? And I once thought diplomacy was a rather dull occupation."

Before Adrian could say anything, Jane spoke up. "It is troubling, isn't it, my lord. I am so sorry that we missed your dear mama, for it was about those deaths that we came. But perhaps you will be able to help us? Might we call for some tea?"

At the mention of tea, the other man winced. "I fear both my wife and my mother would be aghast at my poor hosting. Please, both of you do have a seat and I will ring for some refreshments."

Almost as soon as he pulled the bell, the door opened to reveal a stony-faced butler with a tray laden with tea service and assorted sandwiches and cakes.

Once they were all seated and Jane had begun to pour, Adrian spoke again. "Lord Gilford's death was indeed shocking for all of us."

"But I'm unsure of how my mother or I could possibly help with the matter," said Attingly, looking from one to the other. "I spend most of my time in the country these days and haven't laid eyes on Gilford in years. Mama might have seen him, though I suspect she would more likely have seen the man's wife a time or two."

Again it was Jane who waded in. "It is not your interactions with Lord Gilford we wish to speak of, my lord. I beg you will forgive me if this is too indelicate a subject to broach with you—but we've come to ask about your own father's untimely death. Or rather, something you may have found when you were going through his things."

At the mention of the elder Attingly's murder, the man's son seemed far less surprised than Adrian would have imagined. He set down his teacup and nodded once.

"There is something. But I didn't think it would be of interest to the Foreign Office." He rose and gestured for them to follow him. As he walked he said over his shoulder, "Come into the study. I've saved all of his things that the police returned to us after his death and to be frank, I'll be glad to have the lot out of this house. I never thought my father had any fondness for Italian literature, but that this page in particular was in his pocket when he was killed has never sat well with me."

At the mention of Italian literature, Adrian looked over at Jane and saw her eyes were wide with excitement. Unable to stop himself, he raised his own brows at her before they both followed their host from the room.

Chapter Twelve

J ane fought the impulse to scream in frustration as Attingly led them into a well-appointed study but did not do so with any degree of urgency. At least, not to her mind anyway. She would have thought Adrian was just as placid as their host, but then she noticed the way his right hand was clutched in a fist at his side.

Perhaps she wasn't the only one seething with impatience, after all.

"Please, have a seat," Attingly said as he stepped behind the desk and went to a landscape painting on the near wall. With practiced movements he slid the artwork aside to reveal a safe. "I found these items in Father's desk drawer a week after the funeral." He lifted out a sheaf of papers from inside the safe as he spoke, then laid them down carefully on the desk before turning back to shut and lock the compartment.

"You'll be wondering why I didn't hand them over to

Scotland Yard or the Foreign Office at once," he continued as he retrieved a book page and a pressed flower from the papers on the desk, "but the truth of the matter is, I thought they had something to do with—beg your pardon, Miss Halliwell—a woman."

Once again Jane found herself staring at a page from Machiavelli's *The Prince*, and she noted that the typeface was the same as the one she'd seen on the page found with Lord Gilford's body. So they'd likely come from the same volume of Machiavelli's most famous work.

"'Everyone sees what you appear to be, few experience what you really are,'" she read the underlined words aloud. "I suppose I can see why you might think this could have come from a lover."

It was clear from the way Attingly rubbed the back of his neck he was uncomfortable by such frank talk from her, and Jane bit back a sigh at the man's misguided chivalry. Still, she could hardly chide him for it if they were to gain any more information from him.

"It was not so much the quote," Attingly said sheepishly. "It was more the combination of it with the pressed flower. My father wasn't much for peccadilloes if you must know. But in a certain context that line can be seen as an attempt to persuade a reluctant suitor as it were."

"Or to persuade a man to betray his country," Jane said thoughtfully.

At her words, Attingly stiffened. "I say, Miss Halliwell, that's uncalled for."

Jane intercepted a look from Adrian that seemed to be a warning of sorts. But she didn't feel cowed in the least.

"I didn't say that your father succumbed to the pressure, my lord," she told their host gently. "I only meant to suggest that someone might have been trying to corrupt him." To Adrian she said, "It is not unheard of for men of Lord Attingly's or Lord Gilford's position within the Foreign Office to face attempts by foreign powers to lure them into spying for them, is it?"

Adrian's expression was grim, though Jane was pleased to note that his frown was not directed at her. "No," he said after a moment's thought, "it is not unheard of. In fact, such attempts are often made using such hidden messages that can be mistaken for other sorts of communications."

"But what has this to do with Gilford?" Attingly asked, looking between the two of them. "Was something like this found among his things?"

"I'm afraid I'm not at liberty to say at the moment," Adrian said smoothly. "But I can say we've begun to look more closely at a number of recent deaths among members of the Foreign Office."

Sagging against the desk, Attingly shook his head. "My father's death wasn't a result of a robbery as the Yard suspected, was it? I suspected as much."

"What made you doubt the conclusion the police came to?" Jane asked.

Attingly crossed to drop into the chair behind the desk, as if he were no longer able to stand upright. "Father was jumpy as a cat the week before his death. He was looking forward to my sister's wedding at the week's end, yet he startled at the least thing. One of the new maids dropped a tray of glasses one afternoon and I thought he would come out of his skin. He assured me it was nothing but I knew he was lying. If this message was a warning of sorts, then I don't doubt my father was afraid."

"We don't know for sure that it was a warning," Adrian told the other man carefully. "But your father's behavior does seem to point in that direction."

Jane made a mental note to ask Lord Gilford's valet whether the viscount had been showing any signs of concern this past week. She'd thought he seemed on edge but had attributed it to nerves over the coming symposium.

"There's also this." Attingly lifted another item from his desk and stood to hand it to Jane. "My father received this letter from Halliwell only a month or so before he was murdered in Cornwall. As you can see, your father was warning mine about someone called E."

Jane was surprised to see her hand tremble as she took the letter from the man. When she unfolded the pages, she saw that it was indeed written in her father's familiar hand. Her heart accelerated as she noted the date on the missive—just two days before he'd taken his own life. "He must have written it just before—"

She felt Adrian's hand on her shoulder and was surprised to see he'd come to stand beside her. Together they read the brief letter to Lord Attingly.

Attingly, E has sent word that unless I do as he wishes there will be hell to pay. I fear once he has got what he wants from me he will set his sights on others—in particular on you. Make haste to protect yourself if that is what you choose. I have told him to go to the devil, but I have had no response as yet. Pray God he is the coward I suspect him of being and will leave my wife and daughter alone. And if he does reveal all, then I will endure it. But I wish to spare you the same. Beware, Attingly. The game E plays is a dangerous one.

"So this E was threatening my father and he suspected would soon do the same to your father," Jane said, her voice sharp with frustration at past dangers she could do nothing about. She turned the page to look at the back, but it was blank.

"That's what it looks like," Lord Attingly said grimly.

"And yet your father didn't take it to the authorities," Adrian said thoughtfully. "I wonder why."

"I thought it was clear that Halliwell had—that is to say—not to be indelicate, Miss Halliwell, but didn't he...?"

"If you are trying to find a more palatable way to say that my father took his own life, Lord Attingly," Jane said in a matter-of-fact tone, "then I beg you will not do so on my account. I have spent the years since it happened trying to wish it away, but unfortunately, there is no way to make it otherwise."

"I suppose it's possible that Attingly would have felt little need to take the warning from Halliwell to the authorities," Adrian said slowly as he took the letter from Jane and scanned it carefully, as if looking for some hidden marking, "if he believed Halliwell had taken his own life. Yet this note complicates that theory."

"It is also possible that whatever the man was threatening my father with was bad enough that he took his own life before it came out," Jane said, not daring to latch on to the bit of hope Adrian had offered her. "We didn't know the extent of his gambling until after his death, remember. If this E person knew of his deep play and threatened to tell all, then that could have been what precipitated Papa's actions."

Adrian came to crouch before her chair, taking her hands in his. "But that is not what this letter suggests. See here, he says, '*I have told him to go to the devil*' then later '*And if he does reveal all, then I will endure it.*' These are not the words of a man preparing to take his own life."

Jane stared down at his strong hands gripping hers. "But that doesn't mean he didn't change his mind once he'd thought better of it. Or perhaps this E contacted him after all."

"I don't think so," Adrian told her. "I think this means that E might be the one who is responsible for your father's death."

Before she could respond, Attingly interrupted. "Are you saying this fellow E is responsible not only for Halliwell's death but also my father's and Gilford's? What the devil, Lord Adrian?"

Rising to his feet again, Adrian stepped back so that he could look at both Lord Attingly and Jane. "I know it's a lot to take in, but you said yourself, Attingly, that you had your doubts about your father's death having been a simple robbery."

"I know," the other man said, rubbing at his chin absent-mindedly. "But that doesn't mean it's an easy thing to think that he was murdered by a blackmailer."

"You have evidence that your father was being black-mailed, too?" Jane asked him with a frown.

"No evidence," the earl said with a shrug. "But it stands to reason if the fellow had a hold over your father, then the same man must have had a similar hold over mine. Other-wise there would have been no reason for Halliwell to warn him."

"True," Jane said thoughtfully. "So now we have three potential murders we can connect to each other through the Machiavelli quotations and the roses. It would help if we could find a blackmail letter from E among your father's things, Lord Attingly."

The earl nodded, his brows drawn. "I had most of his per-sonal papers moved into the attics. I'll have them brought down and begin going through them this afternoon."

"And we'll begin sorting through Lord Gilford's papers to see if there is any sign of a communication from E among them." Adrian looked tense, and Jane knew it couldn't be easy for him to think of his mentor living under the weight of such a threat.

"May we take this letter with us?" Jane asked Attingly as she indicated the page with her father's familiar hand-writing on it.

"Of course," Attingly said with a slight shudder. "I'm

only sorry I didn't give it to you earlier, Miss Halliwell, but I thought since both our fathers were gone there would be no use in dredging up past troubles that no longer mattered."

"Unfortunately," Adrian said as he and Jane followed their host back toward the main entrance hall, "it would seem that these troubles still matter a great deal. And we need to find out who E is before he kills again."

Chapter Thirteen

Seated on the plush velvet seat of the Gilford traveling carriage, Adrian was close enough to Jane to see that she was keeping a tight rein on her emotions. The letter from Halliwell to Attingly had come as a shock to both of them. And despite the current Lord Attingly's assurance that he'd held on to the letter because he thought it was proof that Halliwell had reason to kill himself, Adrian couldn't quite forgive him.

If they'd had this letter sooner, along with an explanation about the late Attingly's odd behavior before his murder, then Gilford's death might have been prevented.

"I had no idea Papa was under such a heavy strain when he died," Jane said, cutting into his thoughts, her voice trembling with emotion. "I was so angry with him, you see. I believed that he had wagered away his fortune on the turn of a card leaving Mama and me penniless. But now I don't know what to believe."

Adrian wanted to take her in his arms to offer comfort, but he knew that way lay madness. Without solid evidence he couldn't offer her answers either, but he did his best to reassure her.

"Once we prove that your father was another victim of this villain who has killed Gilford and it appears Attingly as well, then there is a very good chance that you and your mother can return to your rightful positions in society." He disliked the idea of her marrying some other man but didn't want to be a dog in the manger as Will had accused him of being, so he forced himself to add, "You could marry. Have a home and family of your own."

She shook her head. "Tell me you are not so naive as to think that the *ton* will simply ignore the scandal attached to the Halliwell name. Even if Papa did not take his own life, he was careless enough to get himself murdered. And that is unforgivable in some quarters."

He opened his mouth to object, but she raised a staying hand. "Oh, I know very well it wasn't Papa's fault, but when has society ever cared about the truth? Even if we are able to set up our own household again—and really I do not see how, given that Papa's funds have not suddenly appeared again—there will still be whispers. What man would want to ally himself with such a family? Not to mention marry a lady with no dowry? The very idea is absurd."

Her words were bold, but there was a slight tremor in her voice that told Adrian that however absurd she might think the idea, she also felt a great deal of pain at the way her lack of fortune had ruined her hopes of a decent match.

"Eversham has men looking into your father's banking records to see if there is evidence that his gambling was just as much of a fiction as was his suicide." It wasn't a guarantee of course, but Adrian hated the hopelessness in her voice when she spoke of her lack of dowry. "I know that I had no notion of him ever wagering more than a few pounds at a time. And after his death, the rest of his colleagues at the Foreign Office were just as baffled by the rumors of his losses. It wasn't like him. You know that, too, I'd guess."

Jane sagged back against the seat and sighed. "Yes, I thought it was out of character, too, at the time. But nothing made sense in the aftermath of his death. The father I loved would never have risked his family's future, much less left them to deal with the consequences of his taking his own life. Yet everyone seemed to believe him capable of it. Including you."

He heard the note of betrayal in those last two words. Unbidden came the memory of his last glimpse of her in Rome. Her eyes puffy from tears, looking younger than her eighteen years. He'd wanted nothing more than to wrap her in his arms and tell her all would be well. But he'd been a single man, of no relation to her, and there were rules against such things. Even, or perhaps especially, in times of grief.

"I am sorry I left Rome without having a private word with you." Adrian had apologized during their argument last evening, but he couldn't help but feel as if she were owed more from him. Or perhaps he simply wanted to give her more. It was a perilous line he walked with her, but he could give her the truth at least. "I didn't want to face your sadness."

His words must have surprised her because she tilted her head to one side and looked at him quizzically. Finally, she said, "I can hardly blame you. I doubtlessly would have fallen upon you in the vain hope that you'd soothe my sorrows." She turned her head to stare out the window at the passing scenery.

At her bitter words, he shook his head in exasperation. "You may have jumped at the chance, then, but I can assure you it would have been an unhappy match for both of us at the time."

At this her head whipped over to look at him. "Why you conceited—"

"Oh, come, Miss Halliwell," he said with a laugh, "I was not a simpleton. I knew you had a schoolgirl's crush on me. It was plain from the way you blushed every time we saw one another. But however much you might have thought you wanted me I was in no position to take a wife. Much less one so young."

She gave a huff of annoyance. "I can't believe you knew. I thought I was so clever at keeping my secret well hidden."

"If it's any consolation, I doubt either of your parents would have approved of such a match either. You forget that I was a lowly junior staffer. Your mother said more than once she was hoping you'd land a title once you were launched. She had no intention of letting you throw yourself away on a mere younger son."

"The younger son of a *duke*," Jane said wryly. "Which is nothing to sniff at. But yes, back then Mama would not have entertained an offer from you—no matter how much I would have swooned over it."

She smiled and her eyes danced with mirth. "I daresay she'd be of a different mind now. It's funny how things change in the space of a few years. I would have given my last farthing if you'd but looked at me with one of your charming smiles back then. And now…"

As her voice trailed off, he looked up to see her watching him, her expression arrested. The air between them fairly crackled with awareness as their eyes met.

"And now?" he asked, his voice low with unspoken emotion.

"And now," she began. But before she could finish the thought the carriage jolted to a stop, throwing Adrian across the carriage onto Jane's side and then started up again only to career violently, tossing them both across the interior.

He was able to keep himself from crashing against her by bracing his arms against the seat behind her but when they were slung to the side, Jane's head slammed hard enough against the carriage window to crack the glass and she slumped against it.

"Jane?" Adrian asked once the carriage had slowed to a stop—if he didn't miss his guess, the horses had escaped their traces. Pulling her away from the window, he scanned her face and saw a lump forming on her forehead where it had hit the window. There was also a small cut where a shard had gouged into her skin. "Jane? Miss Halliwell?"

He was cradling her against him when the carriage door was flung open and the coachman, his livery stained with dirt and his hat askew, said breathlessly, "Milord, I'm that sorry. The traces were cut. They weren't damaged when we left Gilford House, I can assure you. I would never have taken out a carriage with—"

But at the moment, Adrian was more concerned about Jane than the carriage. "I'll deal with that later," he told the man. "I need to get Miss Halliwell back to Gilford House. She's been injured."

The coachman's eyes widened, and he nodded. "Yes, milord, right away." He shut the door behind him and left Adrian to use his handkerchief on her wound, which had begun to bleed in earnest.

"Come along, Jane," he said softly. "Wake up now, darling. You don't want to let me have the last word, do you? I vow you must have all sorts of things to chide me over."

To his relief she began to stir, and her lids fluttered as she came back to herself.

"That's it," Adrian said, his body almost weak with relief. "There's a good girl, wake up now."

She muttered something but he was unable to understand her words. "What was that? Tell me again."

"Not-a-girl," she said more clearly, and he breathed out a huff of laughter.

Thank God. "You are entirely correct. My apologies, Miss Halliwell."

He pulled her a little closer all the same.

Someone had cut the traces, the coachman said. If it hadn't happened at Gilford House, then it must have been done while they were inside Attingly's townhouse. Which meant it had been done deliberately to endanger Adrian and Jane.

It was only through good fortune that the carriage hadn't careened off the road or over a parapet.

At the thought of the carnage that might have caused, he held her a little bit tighter against him. They were lucky to be alive.

"What happened?" she asked, trying to sit up, but when he held her firm, she relaxed against him. "Was there an accident?"

"I don't wish you to be alarmed, Miss Halliwell," he said frankly, "but I believe someone has tried to kill us."

Chapter Fourteen

"Stop coddling me, Adrian," Jane said even as the man lifted her into his arms and carried her into the Gilford townhouse. "It was little more than a bump on the head. I am perfectly fine."

"I've sent for the physician, Lord Adrian," said Reed, who had obviously been alerted ahead of their arrival. "And I've had cook prepare one of Lady Gilford's headache potions. Never you worry, Miss Halliwell, we'll take good care of you."

Though Jane was well aware of how close she and Adrian had come to serious harm, she had never been an easy patient and if everyone in Gilford House insisted on treating her like an invalid she was going to well and truly lose her temper in short order.

"This is absurd," she muttered even as she relaxed in her captor's arms. "You know this, do you not?"

"I know nothing of the sort," Adrian argued as he

carried her up the stairs toward the family wing where her bedchamber was located. "You suffered a serious injury and should wait to speak with the doctor before you go off running around at your usual harum-scarum pace."

She would have liked to argue, but Jane knew when there was no point. And she had a hard time remaining angry with Adrian considering the circumstances. She'd felt the fine tremor that had run through him when he'd gathered her in his arms in the carriage. He'd been just as frightened as she'd been.

And in truth, her head did hurt terribly.

When they reached her bedchamber, Jane was surprised to find Poppy waiting there for her along with her maid.

"That will be all, thank you, Adrian," the duchess told her brother-in-law as he carefully set Jane down on her bed. "I sent for Langham not terribly long after you left for Attingly's and he's waiting for you in that tiny closet you've been using as a study."

At the mention of his brother, Adrian swore softly. "But why would you send for him?"

"Because I thought he might come in useful," Poppy said tartly. "And I was right."

Adrian looked as if he wished to argue the point but seemed to think better of it.

Turning to Jane, he tipped her chin up so that he could look more closely at her injured forehead. She felt a shiver run through her at the touch and when he brushed a thumb lightly over her cheekbone, she got the strong feeling that if they were alone he might have kissed her.

But that was silly.

Wasn't it?

"I'll leave you to Poppy's capable ministration," he said finally. "Try not to get into any more mischief while I'm gone."

"Thank you," Jane called after him, belatedly realizing that she'd failed to say anything when he was within earshot. Probably because she was too busy mooning up at him like a goose.

But when he turned to look at her, she saw the way his eyes softened. "Of course," he said in a warm voice. And then he left and shut the door behind him.

"I don't suppose you wish to talk about that, do you?" asked Poppy as she watched Jane's maid assist her into a nightgown and into bed. "Because that didn't seem like the behavior of a man who considers you to only be a friend."

"Poppy," Jane hissed at her friend, with a meaningful look toward the maid.

But the duchess was not to be cowed. "Oh, please. Unless the servants in this house are unlike those in every house in the country, then they've likely got wagers placed on whether or not the two of you will make a match of it. Isn't that right, Tillie?"

But Tillie was no fool. "Oh, no, Your Grace, I would never—"

"It's all right, Tillie," Jane assured the girl with a chiding look at Poppy. "Her Grace is just making a very poor joke."

Looking relieved, the maid took Jane's discarded clothing and hurried out of the room.

"You're incorrigible," Jane told her friend as she reclined against the pillow. Her head had begun to throb and she was feeling slightly dizzy. She must have hit the window harder than she'd at first thought.

"Only because I want you to marry the man you've dreamt of since you were a girl in the schoolroom," Poppy said as she pulled a chair closer to Jane's bedside and took her friend's hand.

Keeping her eyes closed, Jane sighed. "I knew I should never have confided in you."

"I don't know how you would have kept me from finding out." Poppy began rubbing lavender water on Jane's wrists, which felt like heaven.

Jane was saved from further awkward talk about her and Adrian by the arrival of Dr. Barnes. Though she was a duchess, even Poppy wasn't bold enough to get between a physician and his patient.

After pronouncing that Jane would likely have a headache for several days and leaving her with instructions to rest as much as possible for the next week and to take the powder he'd left for her as needed, he left in a rustle of coats.

"You heard the doctor," Poppy told Jane after she'd resumed her seat beside her friend's bed. "You need rest. I'll stay here until you fall asleep if you like."

There was much Jane needed to tell Poppy, but the headache powder Dr. Barnes had insisted she take had begun to work its magic. Not only was her headache beginning to subside, but her eyelids had grown impossibly heavy.

"There now, dear. Just rest," she heard Poppy tell her just before the memory of Adrian's voice saying "Someone has tried to kill us" intruded. But Jane was far too close to sleep to care whether it was real or illusion.

"I want her away from here," Adrian bit out as he paced the perimeter of the room. "She can go to the country with Langham and his wife. He's already agreed to it."

"I have no objection to your plan, Lord Adrian," Eversham said mildly from where he stood near the hearth, watching the younger man with much the same air as a gazelle looks upon a pacing tiger. "Rather I suspect that if she is anything like her friend the duchess, or indeed my wife and Caro, then she will not take kindly to having matters decided for her before she has had a chance to offer input."

But this was neither here nor there in Adrian's estimation. "Jane is a sensible lady," he said with a shrug. "She will not insist on remaining here when there is such obvious danger. I feel sure that as soon as I explain matters to her she will—"

His words were interrupted by the sound of his brother's laughter.

"What's so damned funny?"

Langham, who had been leaning against the desk, stood upright so that he could pull out his handkerchief and wipe his streaming eyes. "My dear boy, if you think that a simple explanation has ever worked to persuade a lady who has made up her mind, then you are not as intelligent as I once thought."

Scowling, Adrian glanced over to see that Eversham was also looking amused. "I suppose you, too, think I'm being an idiot?"

But Eversham shook his head. "I don't think you're an idiot, just a bit misguided."

Some of the wind having gone out of his sails, Adrian dropped into the nearest armchair and let his head fall back against it. "Then what the devil am I supposed to do to keep her safe?"

At his words, Langham and Eversham sobered.

"I understand that you are upset that Miss Halliwell was injured, my lord," said the detective in a measured tone, "but we do not yet know that she was the target of today's accident. We only know that you were both in the carriage that was tampered with. Tampered with after your visit to the Attingly household. Could it be that someone guessed at what you might have learned at Attingly's and wished to stop you from acting on it?"

Eversham's calm penetrated Adrian's frustration in a way that shouting would not have and he took a moment to get his temper under control. Stalking to the window to stare out at the afternoon shadows, he recalled the terror that consumed him when he saw Jane flung against the window by the jolting of the carriage. How pale and still she'd been in his arms afterward. It had been his fault she was even there. He'd known as soon as Eversham suggested she accompany him that it was a bad idea. But he'd thought then that the risk was his growing admiration for her and how it could upend all his plans. It had never occurred to him that there would be danger in the short journey itself.

Finally, he blew out a breath and said, "It's possible someone saw the visit to Attingly's so soon after Gilford's murder as a threat. The killer, after all, knows about the connection among the three deaths. But who the devil is it?"

Eversham crossed his arms over his chest. "Who knew you were headed for Attingly's?"

"Reed. The coachman and grooms, obviously," Adrian said, thinking back to whom he may have interacted with before they set out that morning. "You two, and Will, of course."

"And anyone who might have been lingering while you gave instructions to Reed." Langham's frustration was evident in his tone. "Plus there are all the diplomats both foreign and British who are here for the symposium. Really there is no shortage of possible suspects."

"Thank you for pointing that out, Duke," Adrian said dryly. "But speaking of the symposium, before we knew about the quotation and rose, I wondered if one of the visiting dignitaries might have killed Gilford over England's winning the rights to the talking machine."

"But doesn't the connection between the deaths rule out a murder in a fit of anger?" Langham asked, frowning. "Unless one of them was also in Rome when Halliwell died and London when Attingly was killed."

"That's just the thing, though." Adrian's head was beginning to throb. "I've been thinking back to my time in Rome and I recall Dulac and Antonovsky were in the embassy at some point that year."

Eversham, who'd been listening to the discussion with

interest, whistled. "I will speak to both of them this afternoon. If you have any diaries or notebooks from your time in Rome, Adrian, you might want to take a look at them to see if anything else will jog your memory."

Adrian nodded. "I have always kept journals on my trips abroad. I'll make time to go to Langham House and see if they are in my rooms there."

The detective cleared his throat. "Back to the matter of just who was the target of today's accident. I know you are concerned about Miss Halliwell's safety but as I said before we don't know that she was the intended victim. As far as I know, no one knows she is even involved in the investigation."

"You, however," Langham said with a raised brow, "have been seen meeting with Eversham multiple times since the murder. Not to mention the fact that you share something with the murdered men that Miss Halliwell does not."

"And what is that?" Adrian asked, thrusting a hand through his hair in frustration. "Membership at White's?"

"No, brother," Langham said with a shake of his head. "A position with the Foreign Office."

Chapter Fifteen

Jane awoke the next morning feeling much improved thanks to Dr. Barnes's headache powder. But her dreams had been troubled and she'd awakened multiple times in the night as her mind relived the weightlessness of the carriage careening and the impact of her head against the window.

So too did Adrian's words keep running through her mind: *I believe someone has tried to kill us.*

As Tillie helped her dress, Jane tried to puzzle out what it was about his statement that so bothered her. It wasn't that someone had intended to kill—or at the very least do harm to them. The cut traces were proof of that. No, it was one word that troubled her. *Us.*

So far, this killer had targeted only men, she realized. And what's more, men who were members of the Foreign Office.

Like Adrian.

Hurrying downstairs, she decided to skip breakfast altogether, and headed straight for the room Eversham had been using to conduct interviews with guests and members of the household.

She recognized the fresh-faced young officer standing sentry outside the door from the night of the murder. "Good morning, Mr. Rushing, is Mr. Eversham inside? I'd like to have a word."

"Miss Halliwell," Rushing said with a blush. "If I may say so, I was sorry to hear about your accident yesterday."

Jane thanked him and was soon being ushered into the parlor that had been turned into an office for the Scotland Yard detective.

"Come in, Miss Halliwell. You are looking well for someone who suffered an injury only yesterday," Eversham said warmly. Gesturing to a pair of chairs before the window, he indicated that she should sit. A tea tray sat on a small table, too. "Help yourself to some refreshments. The kitchen has been more than generous in keeping me supplied with food and drink."

After thanking him, Jane poured herself a cup of tea and said, "I suspect the servants are grateful that you are working so hard to find their master's killer. Lord Gilford was well liked among the staff here."

"So I've learned in my questioning of them," Eversham said as he took the chair opposite hers. "I cannot say the same for the viscountess, however. More than one member of staff has suggested obliquely that I should be looking more closely into her whereabouts at the time of Gilford's death."

Jane decided that she had better not say anything regarding Lady Gilford at the moment for fear of dooming the future of her position as Margaret's governess. She might dislike the woman, but a bird in the hand was worth two in the bush, after all.

"It is about the investigation that I wish to speak with you," Jane said, settling her cup and saucer on her knee. "Or rather the carriage accident yesterday. Have you questioned the coachmen and grooms yet?"

If the detective was surprised by her question, he didn't show it. "I did, in fact, speak to them at the scene of the crash yesterday. And afterward I talked to the grooms at the Attingly townhouse."

"And?" Jane asked when he did not continue. "What did you conclude? I know the traces were cut but surely they were able to tell you something about when that might have happened. Or if they saw someone suspicious lingering around the coach either before we left this house or later while we were inside Attingly's house."

Eversham sighed. "Miss Halliwell, I know I was the one who suggested you accompany Lord Adrian to Attingly's, but that was not an invitation for you to become a full participant in the investigation."

"But why would you wish me to go there if not to participate in the inquiry?" Jane asked with a frown.

"Your acquaintance with the Attingly family, with Lady Attingly in particular, as well as the fact that you, too, lost a family member who served in the Foreign Office, meant that you could elicit information that perhaps Lord Adrian could not." Eversham didn't dust his reasoning with sugar crystals, and for that frankness Jane was grateful.

"So, in part, it was the fact that I am a lady that made you think my accompanying Adrian would be a good thing?"

"Indeed," Eversham agreed. "But the fact that you were injured proved that my request was shortsighted. As has been pointed out to me at some length by Lord Adrian himself."

"Even if I was not the one who was the intended victim of the accident?" At Eversham's bland look, Jane made a sound of frustration. "It's quite obvious that as yet another member of the Foreign Office, Adrian is the one whom our culprit wanted to warn off the hunt. As you've already said, *I* am not the one who has been involved in the investigation. I hardly think I've stirred up the killer's fears. Like you, no one expected a lady—especially a governess—to be involved in a murder inquiry. But Adrian has been meeting with you from the start."

The detective gave her a long look, and Jane wondered with alarm if this was the sort of thing he subjected suspects to. She understood why he was so good at his job.

"As it happens, Miss Halliwell," said Eversham, "I have come to a similar conclusion—that is, that the likely intended victim of the accident was Lord Adrian. However, you were the one to find Lord Gilford's body and Lord Adrian followed not long after. Perhaps you both saw something at the scene that the killer did not wish you to see."

"Why wait until we were out of the house before making the attempt?" Jane asked, genuinely curious.

"If you'll forgive the metaphor, the possibility of killing two birds with one stone," Eversham told her with a wince. "And this house has been teeming with the police since Lord Gilford's murder. A carriage accident offered the two of you in an enclosed space where you could both be taken out at once."

The cold calculation that would have gone into that decision sent a shiver down Jane's spine.

"It is entirely possible, however, that you were simply in the wrong place at the wrong time." Eversham sounded almost apologetic. "Short of questioning the culprit we have no way of knowing for sure."

Jane nodded. "So, what will we do to ensure that Lord Adrian is kept out of harm's way?"

To his credit, Eversham didn't laugh at the notion of a lady wishing to keep a gentleman safe. "I have brought in more of my men to watch the house. But Lord Adrian himself is the one who will ultimately be the one to ensure his safety."

Which, Jane thought, meant he would do as he pleased. The thought of him in danger—or worse—made her stomach drop.

The door to the office opened just then and Adrian himself strode in. "Eversham, I was wondering if—" Upon seeing Jane he stopped short.

"What are you doing out of bed?" he demanded with a scowl.

Before Jane could respond, Eversham rose from his chair and said, "I've just recalled an urgent matter I must discuss with one of my men. If you'll both excuse me."

And in almost a blink, the detective was gone.

"Well?" Adrian prompted when Jane didn't answer his query.

The wound on her forehead had been covered with a bit of sticking plaster, which only served to remind him of his terror the day before. She needed to be resting. Not meeting with Eversham, no doubt in an attempt to get even more involved in this investigation.

"I am feeling much improved this morning and came to speak with Mr. Eversham about what he's learned about the cut traces." She didn't appear at all cowed by his ill humor. In fact, there was a decidedly mulish set to her jaw.

It occurred to him suddenly that the confident woman before him was a far cry from the quiet governess he'd encountered on the first day of the symposium. He couldn't say he was sorry for it.

"And what did he tell you?" he asked, his curiosity over whether Eversham had learned anything new since they'd last talked overcoming his annoyance at Jane's being downstairs.

"Nothing," Jane bit out. "Apparently, while, as a lady, I am good enough to be sent along on a visit to the Attinglys to garner information based on my previous relations with Lady Attingly, I am not allowed to participate in the actual investigation.

"I must admit to some degree of surprise at his attitude," she continued in an affronted tone. "Especially given that his own wife rather famously helped him investigate more than one of his cases."

Adrian ran a hand over the back of his neck. He suspected Eversham's insistence that she stay out of the investigation had something to do with his own railing about keeping Jane safe the evening before. While her safety was still paramount in his mind, he didn't think it would hurt to allow her to know what had been learned about the cut traces.

Taking the seat vacated by Eversham's leaving, he said, "After questioning, the Gilford coachman admitted that while we were inside the Attingly townhouse, he left the coach to go play a game of dice with the Attingly coachman, who is a friend of long-standing. The groom he left in charge is a good lad but not the most observant of fellows. And Attingly's butler said he saw a strange man loitering around the carriage. He told the man to move along, but in hindsight by that time it was probably too late."

"Did he recall what the man looked like?" Jane asked, her eyes wide with excitement. "Perhaps we can track him down."

"Unfortunately, the fellow was not particularly memorable," Adrian said hating to crush her enthusiasm. "Eversham sent some men to question around the neighborhood to see if anyone else noticed him, but so far there has been no luck."

Jane's shoulders dipped for a moment at the news, but then she seemed to steel her spine again. "So, what are you planning to do to ensure that no one tries another such ploy again?"

Adrian reached out to take her hand. "I promise you that

no one will get another chance to hurt you. In fact, since you asked, I think it would be a good idea for you to remove to Langham Abbey with Poppy and my brother until—"

"I am not concerned about myself," she interrupted in an exasperated voice. "You are the one who works for the Foreign Office. What are you doing to ensure *your* safety?"

Adrian fought the urge to roll his eyes. Thanks to the lecture he'd received from both Langham and Eversham the evening before, he'd been forced to admit that it was possible he'd been the target of whoever had cut the traces. Even so, it rankled to be in the position of having Jane feel as if she needed to look after him. He was supposed to be the one protecting her.

"I have agreed to refrain from going anywhere outside this house alone for the time being," he admitted reluctantly. "I recognize it would be foolhardy of me to put myself in unnecessary danger. No matter how much it might injure my pride."

Jane's shoulders relaxed a little and she nodded. "Good. I was afraid you would behave like the stubborn male you are."

"Speaking of stubborn," he said with a speaking look, "what of your own safety?"

"If I am not safe in a house that is, as Eversham put it, 'teeming with police,'" Jane said tartly, "then I don't see how removing to your family's country estate will change anything."

Adrian fought to keep his temper. "It would get you out of harm's way, dash it." Was he going to have to bodily remove her from the metropolis?

"It isn't as if Little Kidding isn't a train ride away," she said with obvious annoyance. "He could go there, kill me, then be back in London in the space of an afternoon."

"For God's sake," Adrian said, rising from his chair and stalking over to glare out the window, remembering once again those few moments when she'd been unconscious. "Do not say such a thing, even in jest."

A moment later he felt a gentle hand on his back.

"I'm sorry," Jane said softly. "I let my temper get the better of me. It is only that I am concerned about your well-being."

Adrian turned and when she slipped her arms around him it felt like the most natural thing in the world. "I thought you were gone," he said into her hair, which smelled of citrus and spice. "I haven't been that frightened in a long time."

She lifted her head and looked up at him, her dark blue eyes wide with some emotion he couldn't name. "It was just a bump on the head," she said softly. "I am fine. I promise. If something were to happen to you, though, I . . ."

She didn't finish her thought. Instead, she leaned into him and pressed her lips against his. Adrian knew he should resist—for so many reasons—but it would have taken a strength he was simply not in possession of.

He kissed her with all the passion that had been building in him from the moment he'd traded barbs with her two years ago at his family home. Her mouth was sweeter than he had hoped and she kissed like she argued, with a give and take that spurred him to return each caress with an answering one.

The sound of a brisk knock on the door of the parlor had them both springing apart with a swiftness Adrian would not have thought possible. A quick glance revealed Jane's lips were kiss-swollen, but it was his own physical reaction to their embrace that had him turning to look out the window as if in contemplation.

"Lord Adrian," came the voice of Lord Payne from behind them. "Ralston is looking for you. There have been inquiries from our overseas guest that require your attention."

His colleague's voice, as well as what might have happened if Payne hadn't bothered to knock, was sufficient to dampen Adrian's ardor and he turned to face the other man.

Jane, he noted, had regained her composure and with the exception of a slight flush that remained in her cheeks, she looked collected. Some devilish impulse within him made him want to muss her up a little—as proof that their kiss had affected her as much as it had affected him.

To Payne he said, "Thank you. Where is he?"

"In Gilford's study," Payne said with a glance between Adrian and Jane—a glance that made Adrian suddenly glad Jane wasn't mussed. He knew Payne was unlikely to spread tales, but even so, it had been careless of him to take such a risk with Jane's reputation.

"Thank you for updating me on your recovery, Miss Halliwell," he said to her with a short bow. "I am pleased to see you so improved."

And with a nod to Payne, he left them to go speak to the foreign secretary, who had chosen to take up residence in the room where Gilford had been killed only the night before last.

"Damnation," Adrian muttered under his breath as he stepped out into the hall, deciding the oath could reference any and all of the difficulties at hand.

Lord Payne looked at the door Adrian had just left through and Jane fought the urge to cringe at the older man's obvious disapproval.

"My dear, I hope you do not mind a bit of advice from someone who has known you from childhood," Lord Payne said as he ambled farther into the room, "but you really must be careful how you go on with regard to your reputation. I will, of course, tell no one that I found the two of you alone in this chamber, but what if you had been interrupted by someone without your best interests at heart?"

"I am grateful to you for your discretion, my lord," Jane said with what she hoped was an easy-sounding laugh. "Lord Adrian was simply updating me on the developments in the investigation. There is no need for your concern."

Even to her own ears her excuse sounded weak, but she wasn't going to admit to Lord Payne that she'd just been clinging to Adrian like a garden rose climbs an arbor.

Payne looked as if he'd like to argue, but Jane was grateful when he changed the subject. "Have there been new developments in the case? I must admit I've found the lack of information from Scotland Yard to be most frustrating. We deserve to know who did this. Especially if Eversham will not allow those of us who live in London to return to our own homes."

Jane was unsure how much, if any, of the things that they'd learned so far Eversham would want Lord Payne to know. Especially given that he hadn't wished to tell her what he'd found out about the cut traces. Still, she didn't think it would go amiss to warn the man before her that he should take caution with his own safety.

But before she could caution him, Payne continued, "I know you and Lord Adrian called at the Attingly town-house yesterday. Am I to understand that the late Lord Attingly's death is being investigated as being linked with Gilford's? Is there a reason for those of us who work in the Foreign Office to be on guard for our own lives?"

Jane had hoped he wouldn't put the pieces together between their visit to the Attinglys and the murder of Gilford. "I believe such a connection is being discussed, yes. So it would be prudent for you to keep an eye to your own personal safety until this killer is apprehended."

A flash of anger shone in Lord Payne's dark eyes and for a moment Jane was worried she'd done the wrong thing. But it was gone in the next second.

"I am grateful to you for telling me, Miss Halliwell," he said, placing a hand on her arm in gratitude. "It would have been better coming from Eversham, but I suppose I understand his reasons for keeping the news to himself. It would not do to send an alarm through those of us who work in the diplomatic community."

Relieved that he'd seen reason, Jane gave him a warm smile. "I know given how often all of you move from country to country—thank heavens I no longer have to do so—you are already accustomed to paying close attention to your surroundings. Hopefully this current danger will not last long."

Lord Payne looked as if he was going to say something, then closed his mouth abruptly.

"Is there something amiss?" Jane asked, frowning. "I mean aside from the fact that there is a murderer on the loose?" It was a poor attempt at humor, she knew, but even so, she was surprised not to get even a smile from Lord Payne.

"I know you dismissed my earlier concern for your reputation, my dear," he said, taking her hand in his. "But I must beg you to have a care for your heart, at least. I know Lord Adrian is a charming man. I have known him for many years and I have nothing but admiration for him. But if you are determined to remain in England, then he is unlikely to make you happy. It pains me to say so, but the man has spent years building a career in the Foreign Office, and it is unlikely if he is forced to choose between you and his career that he will choose you."

Jane felt a stab of pain at the man's words. He'd said as much when they spoke before, and she was alarmed that she'd so quickly dismissed his warnings. Now, so soon after her time in Adrian's arms, Lord Payne's cautions regarding their incompatibility hit like a blow.

Still, she would not allow Lord Payne's words to replace the evidence of her own knowledge of Adrian's character.

"I thank you for your concern, my lord," Jane said sincerely. "I will certainly take your warning to heart. Though

I must stress to you that Lord Adrian and I are merely friends, so there is no need for you to worry."

He raised a brow but did not argue. "Then I will bid you good morning, my dear. But not before I ask you to look to your own personal safety. You may be feeling better after your mishap in the carriage yesterday—really, the roads can be so treacherous—but do not think that because you are not a diplomat that you should let down your guard. Who knows which of us this monster might next have in his sights."

Chapter Sixteen

"I t has not gone without notice just how instrumental you were in the organization of this gathering, Lord Adrian," said Lord Ralston from behind the desk in Gilford's office.

Though Adrian knew it was reasonable that the foreign secretary should use the viscount's office while he was, like the rest of them, required to remain in Gilford House, it still struck him as ghoulish. Though he knew the room had been thoroughly cleaned, he still fancied he could smell the copper scent of blood in the air.

"This is why," Ralston continued after a dramatic pause, "I have decided that you should be the one to step into Gilford's position once all of this investigation business has been completed."

A few years ago, Adrian would have given his eyeteeth to be offered such a plum position within the Foreign Office. Indeed, it was the sort of appointment that diplomats spent decades hoping to achieve. And yet, it had been some time since he'd envisioned himself continuing on a path with the Foreign Office. He'd already discussed a shift to working for the Home Office with his brother and if Langham were to be believed, he only needed to accept their offer.

But the carriage accident the day before and seeing Jane lying unconscious in his arms—even if only for a moment— had been a warning that he needed to reassess his priorities. And this morning's interlude had only served to reinforce that notion. Perhaps a position in the Foreign Office, one where he would be able to remain in London for the next several years, was a better choice than the more dangerous one with the Home Office.

"I am honored for your confidence in me, Secretary," he told Ralston now. "May I ask for a few days to think about it? There are matters of some delicacy that I will need to discuss with my family before I can make a decision. I'm sure you understand."

Ralston gave him an approving nod. "Just the sort of careful consideration I would have expected from a man of your caution, Lord Adrian. But do not take too long. There is much work to be done once Eversham gives us leave to quit Gilford House."

"I understand," Adrian replied. "I will give you an answer as soon as I am able."

"There's a good man," Ralston said with a nod. "Speaking of Eversham, you don't have any idea of when he will allow us to leave, have you? I've already been informed by the prime minister that Antonovsky has threatened to write to the tsar and say he's been imprisoned. And I don't need to tell you what sort of havoc that will wreak with the queen."

That was the last thing they needed, Adrian knew. "I will do what I can to persuade him that there is no need for our group to remain in Gilford House for much longer."

After he and Jane had returned from the meeting with Attingly, Adrian had attempted to persuade Eversham that at the very least Ralston could be told what they suspected about the murders being linked. As the foreign secretary, Adrian had argued, the man had a right to know that Halliwell and Attingly had likely been murdered by the same person as Gilford. Eversham, however, had requested more time to keep the news of the connections between the murders quiet. Though he disliked keeping Ralston in the dark, Adrian had reluctantly agreed.

"See that you do," said Ralston, gathering the stack of papers he'd brought with him into the room earlier. It was a clear sign that the meeting was at an end and Adrian was grateful to be given some time to be alone with his thoughts.

"I take it congratulations are in order," said Lord Payne, who had come to stand just inside the door after Ralston had departed.

Adrian gave the older man a sidelong glance. Since Payne had interrupted that incendiary kiss with Jane, he suspected he was in for a lecture on the proprieties from the man. Still, his congratulations were welcome.

"Not just yet, though it is kind of you to offer your

salutations," Adrian replied. "It would be a significant promotion, and I feel the need to give the matter some thought."

"That seems like a wise decision," Payne said with an approving nod. "I know whenever I have been presented with new opportunities, I have always talked the matter over with my wife. Though you are not hampered by the wishes of a wife, are you?"

There was something about the way he said this last that set Adrian's teeth on edge. The other man had almost certainly guessed at what he and Jane had been up to when Payne had interrupted them earlier. Well, he and Jane were both adults and however much Payne might like to think of himself as a father to her, he was not, in fact, Jane's father.

"Not at the moment, no," Adrian agreed with a smile that he hoped didn't show his annoyance. "But that will not always be the case. And I need to think about what the future might hold on that, as well as many other fronts."

He hoped that would close the subject for the time being, but alas, Payne had other ideas.

"I was pleased to find Miss Halliwell looking so much better this morning," Payne said with all the air of a man who was settling in for a long conversation. "I chanced to see her when you were carrying her inside yesterday and she was quite pale. Carriage accidents can be quite dangerous. Have you learned anything more about what caused the traces to break?"

Rather than revealing that the crash had been caused deliberately, Adrian had told the other guests that it had been a case of an accidental tear to the strap holding the carriage horses in place. "I have not, no. Though such things happen from time to time. Horses are quite strong, as you well know."

"I am simply glad that neither you nor Miss Halliwell was more seriously injured," Payne said with seeming sincerity. "It would be too much to bear so soon after losing Gilford. You must both look after yourselves. I have it on good authority that whoever this killer is, he seems to be targeting members of our profession."

How the devil did he know that? Adrian wondered as he watched Payne stride out into the hall beyond.

Chapter Seventeen

"Are you sure you aren't feeling too fatigued after your ordeal yesterday, ma chère Mademoiselle Halliwell?"

Later that afternoon, when all the guests—along with Langham, who had come to support Poppy—were gathered in the drawing room for tea, Jane maintained a pleasant smile for Madame Dulac, though inwardly she was gritting her teeth. This was surely the tenth time the woman had made some comment on how haggard Jane looked and the cuts disguised as solicitude were becoming tiresome. Especially coming from someone as elegantly beautiful as the Frenchwoman.

If Jane still harbored a small niggle of jealousy after the way Madame Dulac had been hanging on Adrian's every word whenever the two of them were in the same room together, well, Jane was only human, after all.

"Thank you, Madame," she said aloud, "but I am quite well. It was merely a bump on the head."

"Here, Madame," said Poppy with a deceptively sweet smile, "perhaps you can shut up your mouth with this delicious macaroon."

With a sniff, Madame Dulac stood up. "There is no need to be rude, Your Grace. I was only concerned for Mademoiselle Halliwell's health." And with that, she crossed to the other side of the room, making a beeline for her bosom friend, the foreign secretary's wife, Lady Ralston.

At the woman's obvious pique, Poppy's brow furrowed with innocence. "Oh dear. I must have got the idiom wrong again. My apologies."

"I think you got it just right, Your Grace," said Mrs. Lindstrom with amusement. "Poor Miss Halliwell, I find Madame difficult to endure even when I am feeling well. You must have a dreadful headache now."

"Please let's stop talking about my head," Jane said with a smile for the Swedish woman—this time a genuine one. "You must tell me something about yourself, Mrs. Lindstrom. Is this your first time to visit England?"

They passed the next several minutes in pleasant conversation around the tea table, while the other guests broke off into smaller groups. From what Jane could tell, the gentlemen were talking about the murder, albeit in hushed tones. She'd overheard Herr von Humboldt's wife chastising a couple of the men earlier for discussing such an unpleasant subject in mixed company. But clearly her admonition hadn't carried much weight. The gentlemen had been trading stories of their interviews with Eversham all evening, and if Jane weren't mistaken, discussing pet theories over the identity of the murderer.

Jane was passing a cup of tea to Lady Payne, when she heard Poppy say to her in a low voice, "Don't look now, but you have an admirer on the other side of the room."

Turning her head to look, Jane saw Adrian was leaning against the fireplace mantel with his arms crossed over his chest, a very un-Adrian-looking scowl on his face while he talked with Mr. Woodward. She hadn't seen him since their kiss that morning. The kiss that set her heart aflutter every time she let her mind return to it—which was more than was wise given the seriousness of their current circumstances.

Still, she couldn't help but admire how handsome he looked, even when his fine-boned face was creased in a frown. Clearly whatever the American was telling him was not something that pleased him.

"He isn't looking at me. And what's more, if that is the sort of expression you interpret as admiring," Jane replied to Poppy, "then I no longer find it so difficult to believe you fell in love with Langham."

Poppy looked surprised. "I thought you liked Langham."

"I do," Jane said with a shrug, "but when he is unsure what to think his face goes grim and forbidding."

Poppy nodded. "That's fair. But I think you misunderstand the way my brother-in-law was looking at you—for he was a moment ago I assure you. I think rather than forbidding, I'd interpret it as hungry."

Jane felt color flood her cheeks. Was it possible that Adrian had been just as affected by their kiss as she had? "You are incorrigible."

"I'm not the one looking at you like that." Poppy smiled behind her teacup.

Clearly, Jane couldn't allow him to continue staring at her in such a manner—no matter how much it might thrill her. Someone besides Poppy would notice before long and there would be talk. She might not know whether Lady Gilford intended to allow her to stay on as Margaret's governess, but even if Jane were dismissed, after the mess with the Carlyles, she couldn't afford another blemish on her reputation.

"Please see to the tea," she told her friend, then rising, she crossed the chamber to where Adrian and Benjamin Woodward stood.

"Miss Halliwell," said Mr. Woodward with a bow. "If you will excuse me, I just recalled a matter of some importance I must discuss with the Duke of Langham."

Jane almost laughed at the speed with which the American fled their company. "I thought you were friends with Mr. Woodward."

"I am," Adrian said, sounding surprised, though his brow was furrowed.

"Then it must have been me who made him flee as if the hounds of hell were after him," Jane said, glancing over to where the American was chatting with Langham.

"I suspect he wished to give us a moment of privacy." Looking a little disconcerted—was it Jane's imagination or did his eyes linger on her lips for a long moment?—Adrian thrust his hands into his pockets. "How are you feeling?"

"I do wish everyone would stop asking me that," Jane said tartly, infusing her tone with annoyance in an effort to mask the way his very presence made her breath catch. "I know you mean well, but truly I feel almost fully recovered."

He looked skeptical but nodded. "I could quibble with 'almost,' but I won't presume to tell you how you feel."

Then, perhaps aware that a change of subject was needed, he continued, "Woodward said you appear to be a favorite among the embassy wives. I saw that you even have Lady Payne deferring to you. And she has been to more afternoon teas of this sort than anyone but Lady Ralston."

Jane felt a color creep into her cheeks at the compliment— had she ever been more apt to go scarlet than she had in the past few days?—but she would not be deterred from her purpose in approaching him. "You are kind to say so, but there is another matter which I need to discuss with you."

Frowning, Adrian glanced at the other side of the room where the guests were gathered, and straightened. "Has something untoward happened? There are times when the customs of other countries conflict with English ones. Just tell me who has insulted you and I will—"

Alarmed at how quickly his mind had leapt to such a conclusion, Jane raised a hand to cut him off. "Of course not. And if someone did give offense, I should take care of the matter myself. I am a grown woman, for heaven's sake."

His usually expressive expression shuttered for a fraction of a second. It happened so quickly she almost missed it, but the next moment he pulled a face.

"You wouldn't believe I'd spent nearly a decade in diplomatic circles, would you?" Adrian ran a hand over his hair, and Jane noted it didn't appear to be the first time he'd done so in the past hour. "I apologize. Of course you are able to fight your own battles. I fear that despite knowing that, my first instinct is to protect you. Especially after what happened yesterday."

Despite her earlier annoyance, Jane felt herself soften. "Very well. But if you insist on protecting me, then I will simply do the same with you. And Mr. Eversham has assured me that so long as you are in Gilford House you should remain safe. Especially given the number of police officers who are here."

She thought she heard Adrian mutter an imprecation beneath his breath but was unable to hear what it was. "You may curse as much as you like," she said primly, "but that does not mean that I will back down any more than you will. We are at point nonplus and that is all there is to be said on the matter."

He looked as if he would like to argue but must have seen the resolve in her expression because he only nodded before asking, "You came over here to discuss something besides my safety, surely."

For the second time in this conversation, Jane felt herself blush and mentally cursed her fair complexion.

"Yes, I did," she said, feeling her heart beat faster as she looked down at the floor for a moment. "I wished to ask you to desist from . . . well . . . looking at me."

His brows raised almost to his hairline. "Stop *looking* at you? What does that mean, exactly?"

She risked glancing up at his face and the amusement she saw there was exactly what she'd needed to stiffen her backbone. "Yes, looking at me. Like you were a short while ago." She pursed her lips and assumed her most forbidding air—the one that had Margaret leaping to do her bidding.

"Poppy said you looked— Well, never mind what Poppy said. Suffice it to say, that it was not the sort of proper look a gentleman gives a lady. Especially not in public."

As she spoke, she saw understanding begin to dawn on Adrian's face. "Ah, I think I know what you mean."

Before she could object, he reached for her hand and began to stroke the back of it with his thumb. "I am sorry, my dear. It was not my intention to embarrass you. But I fear that"—he lowered his voice to a level that only she could hear—"I fear that I was remembering what happened between us earlier. And my face reflected that, I suppose."

Jane felt her pulse jolt at his words and swallowed. She suddenly found herself unable to recall her reason for objecting to his look in the first place. "Oh, I see."

"I thought you might," he said, giving her hand one last gentle stroke before he let it go. "But I will, of course, endeavor to keep a tighter rein on my *looks* in future. I have no wish to upset you."

The spell between them was broken by Poppy hurrying forward, her smile bright but there was something about the pucker between her friend's brows that told Jane all was not well.

"What is it?" Adrian asked, his posture straightening.

"Do not show alarm," Poppy said through clenched teeth. "We've only just managed to settle down our guests and make them more comfortable given the fact that their host was murdered night before last. I've forced your brother to employ his most amusing stories for the gentlemen and I have it on excellent authority—his own—that if

Madame Dulac pinches his bottom once more he will tell Monsieur Dulac to keep her on a leash."

Looking pained, Adrian nodded.

"What has happened?" Jane asked her friend. Though she knew Poppy was trying to be amusing, she felt no impulse to laugh.

"Mr. Reed has just informed me that we have an unexpected visitor."

"Why didn't he inform Lord Gilford?" Jane asked. She knew that Will was still adjusting to his new position, but if the servants didn't begin to treat him as the master of the house, then he would never really settle into the role.

"That's just it," Poppy said with a pained expression. "This guest is for you."

Jane was flummoxed. "For *me*? Who would call upon me here? As far as anyone knows, I'm the governess. Servants don't accept callers. Tell whoever it is to call on Thursday, which is my free day."

"You are living as one of the family," Adrian reminded her. "As a favor to Will. I can see no reason why you shouldn't have a visitor."

Jane was about to argue, but Poppy cut in. "I really think you should see this guest, Jane. In fact, I insist."

Seeing that she was outnumbered, Jane sighed. "Very well, if you insist. I suppose I'll see them in the small sitting room. Who is it that has set the cat among the pigeons?"

Poppy took her by the hand and smiled. "Jane, it's your mother."

At the news of her mother's arrival, Jane's face lost all its color.

"My mother? Here? But why?"

"I'm sure I don't know, dearest," said Poppy as she shot Adrian a questioning look. "But she's here and she wishes to see you."

Jane shook her head, and Adrian had the urge to wrap her in his arms to give her some of his strength. But he knew that would not be welcome. In part because Jane didn't need anyone's strength but her own.

Hell, she'd just offered him *her* protection. Some men would take that as a blow to their pride, but Adrian found it strangely alluring.

"If you wish me to accompany you," Poppy was saying to Jane, "I am happy to do so. Indeed, I should like to meet your mama. If you'll just give me a moment to speak with Langham, then I'm sure I can—"

But Jane shook her head. "No, thank you. I do appreciate your offer, but she is my mama. I do not need someone to protect me from her."

"You did seem a bit—" Poppy searched for the right word but must have had difficulty finding it.

"You went pale," Adrian said softly. "As if you'd seen a ghost. Is all well between the two of you?"

Jane looked as if she would argue, but then she must have realized it would be futile. "It's just that I haven't seen her in quite some time. And the last we spoke, well, to be frank, we quarreled."

Adrian saw a flicker of what looked like remorse in Jane's eyes before she went on. "My mother was against the idea of my becoming a governess, if you must know, and now I must… I have to tell her the truth about what happened to Papa, don't I?"

He was about to suggest they consult with Eversham before sharing details with her mother when Eversham himself appeared in the doorway and indicated that both Adrian and Jane should step outside the room to speak to him.

Jane gave Poppy a little hug. "I'll be fine. Thank you for your offer. But do go rescue the duke from Madame Dulac. She's eying him like a particularly appealing slice of cake."

Poppy made a scowl and crossed the room to protect her husband's virtue.

Without conscious thought, Adrian slipped Jane's arm through his and they stepped out into the hallway beyond the drawing room, where Eversham stood waiting for them.

"Miss Halliwell," the detective said with a nod. "No doubt the duchess has informed you that your mother is here. I believe she's been living with a cousin in Edinburgh?"

Adrian felt Jane stiffen beside him before she said, "Yes, after my father's death and our financial situation, she went to live with a distant cousin. But I haven't spoken to my mother in some time, and this visit is a surprise."

Then, as if expecting an argument from Eversham, she added mulishly, "Although I do believe she has a right to know what we suspect about my father's death."

The detective's mouth tightened. "I didn't come here to stop you from telling her the truth, Miss Halliwell. Quite the contrary. I want you to tell her, but I would also like to question her about that time. Because she may recall something that might give us some clue as to who threatened, then very likely killed your father."

"Oh." Adrian heard the relief in her voice and gave her arm a gentle squeeze of reassurance. Though she didn't say anything else, he felt her relax slightly against him.

"I simply wished to ask you whether you believe she will be able to emotionally withstand such questioning." Eversham's sincere gaze was not without kindness and Adrian was grateful there would be no need for him to upbraid the man he'd begun to think of as a friend. They all wanted to learn who was responsible for the murders, but Adrian wouldn't stand for anyone to ride roughshod over Jane.

"I do not know," Jane said from beside him. "We have not discussed my father's death in some time."

Eversham nodded. "If you do not mind, I would like for Lord Adrian to accompany you in to see her."

"Why?" Jane's tone made clear she was offended by Eversham's request.

"I am perfectly capable of speaking to my own mother without needing a chaperone," she continued, pulling her arm from Adrian's in order to place her arms akimbo in the time-honored stance of annoyed women everywhere.

Adrian gave the other man a raised brow, glad her ire was for the detective and not for him.

"I meant no disrespect, Miss Halliwell," Eversham said with an air of apology, after a bland look in Adrian's direction. "Indeed, I have come to value your good sense during this investigation, but your mother has arrived with a gentleman. And since I suspect your own feelings about the man might be affected by his relationship to your mother, I would like Lord Adrian to make an assessment of him as well. That way I can have a fuller picture of this person's character."

"What?" Jane asked, her voice ringing with shock.

At the same time, Adrian demanded, "What gentleman?"

Eversham handed Jane a visiting card which she studied carefully before handing it to Adrian. The card was made from finely woven stock, inscribed with the name *Sir Ross MacIvor*, and its corner was folded down to indicate the man had called in person.

Who was the man? Adrian wondered. And why had Halliwell's widow brought the fellow with him to visit her daughter after staying away for so long? "Have you ever met this man before?" Eversham asked Jane as he took the card back from Adrian.

Jane shook her head, her lapis blue eyes wide with alarm. "Do you think he has something to do with the murders? Could he have tricked Mama into bringing him here in order to—"

But the detective was quick to allay the worst of her fears. "I have no specific suspicions about the fellow, Miss Halliwell," he assured her. "I confess to a certain wariness, however, regarding his arrival on the arm of your mother so soon after Lord Gilford's murder. We cannot discount the possibility that he's been sent by the killer to gain access to the house given the current state of heightened security."

"You truly think…" She didn't finish the question, as if repeating Eversham's suspicions would make them true. Unable to stop himself from offering her some of his strength, Adrian slipped an arm about her waist. The way she leaned against him was proof of just how rattled she was.

"As I said, it's only a concern. I have no proof," Eversham assured her. "And I would prefer to have Lord Adrian go in with you, as an old friend of the family, so as not to raise the fellow's hackles."

As Adrian had seen her do so many times when she wished to give herself a burst of courage, Jane squared her shoulders before saying, "Very well, Adrian may accompany me."

Eversham gave her a solemn nod. "My thanks, Miss Halliwell."

After exchanging a speaking look with the detective, Adrian led Jane out of the room. He had the good sense to leave her to her thoughts as they made their way toward the small sitting room. Just outside the door, she brought them up short so that she could slip an errant lock of hair behind her ear and smooth down the skirt of her gown.

"Will I do?" she asked, turning back to him.

Adrian wasn't sure he'd ever seen Jane nervous before. And he disliked the idea that her own mother had the ability to put that frown of worry on her face. But that was why he was here with her. With a gentle smile, he nodded and leaned in to kiss her cheek.

"You look lovely," he said truthfully. Then taking her arm again, he led her into the room where her mother and the mysterious escort she'd brought with her were waiting.

Chapter Eighteen

The first thing Jane noticed when she stepped into the sitting room was that her mother seemed smaller. It hadn't occurred to her that during their separation her mother would age. She felt a constriction in her chest at the realization.

"Mama," she said softly and at the sound of her voice, Mrs. Halliwell turned away from the window she'd been staring out of. For a moment Jane saw her mother begin to smile, then, as if realizing her sudden arrival might not be welcomed, her expression turned serious.

"Jane," she said, inclining her head regally. "It is good to see you."

Then before Jane could respond, her mother seemed to notice the man beside her daughter. Her expression—if possible—grew chillier. "Lord Adrian," she said with a gaze that seemed to sweep him from head to toe. "I hadn't expected to find you here. Though I suppose I shouldn't be surprised. You have been with the Foreign Office for some time now, haven't you?"

Beside her, Adrian offered her mother a bow. "Mrs. Halliwell, it is good to see you again."

Mrs. Halliwell's response was a brisk nod. Her attention was all on Jane now. "What has happened here? I arrive thinking to surprise my daughter only to find that Gilford House is in mourning and you are dressed in a new gown and on the arm of a duke's son. Has there been a change in your circumstances since last we spoke? Are you no longer governess to Miss Gilford? And who has died, for heaven's sake? I asked the butler but he said it would be best if I learned it from you."

Before Jane could answer, a gentleman of around fifty, whose reddish hair was sprinkled liberally with silver, stepped forward to slip an arm through her mother's. Jane had been so overwhelmed at the sight of her mother after so many years apart, she'd forgotten completely about the man who'd accompanied her: Sir Ross MacIvor.

Who was he? Was he connected in some way with the man who had murdered her father and his colleagues? Could he be the killer himself?

"My dear, your Jane will think you are not happy to see her. Give her a moment to get her breath. Perhaps you can introduce us."

The man's Scottish burr, in combination with the way her mother colored at his words, made Jane suspect that he was at the very least an acquaintance from her mother's time in Edinburgh. At least she hoped so for Mama's sake.

"Of course." Mama reached back to take MacIvor's arm

and bring him forward. "I'm sorry, my dear. I fear I was overcome with nerves. I should have corrected you, Lord Adrian. I am no longer Mrs. Halliwell, but Mrs. MacIvor."

To her daughter she said in a gentler tone, "Jane, I would like for you to meet my husband, Sir Ross MacIvor."

Jane stiffened, and she held on to Adrian's arm as if he were the only thing keeping her upright. She was suddenly grateful Eversham had suggested he accompany her. "Your husband?"

"Why don't we sit down, my dear?" Adrian asked as he led her to a sofa near the fire. "I'll ring for some refreshments."

Jane wordlessly took a seat and watched as her mother and her new husband sat on a settee across from her.

"Thank you, Lord Adrian," MacIvor said once he'd settled her mother on the settee. "I believe our ladies are rather overset."

Nearing the sofa, Adrian paused at the other man's words. "Oh, I fear we have given you the wrong impression."

Jane flushed and she wasn't sure whether it was at the assumption Sir Ross had leapt to, or Adrian's repudiation of it. " Lord Adrian and I are merely dear friends."

If anything, her mother looked even more disapproving of Adrian than she had before. "I thought at the very least—"

"Mama," Jane said in a warning tone. "Why don't I explain to you a bit about what's been going on."

"That would be appreciated, Jane, because I must say things seem very irregular in this household. I thought at the very least I could rely upon Gilford to keep you safe."

"My dear," said Sir Ross in a quelling tone. "I don't think—"

"Indeed *most* irregular," Jane's mother repeated. "If they are not betrothed, then why is Jane on his arm?"

"Mama." It was impossible for Jane to keep the exasperation from her voice. "I hardly think—"

"Mrs. MacIvor," Adrian interrupted, and despite her annoyance, Jane gestured for him to continue. "You asked for whom the household is in mourning, and I'll begin there. Two nights ago, during a gathering here in Gilford House, Lord Gilford was killed. Murdered, in fact."

At the news, Jane's mother gasped. "Dear God, it's happened again."

"What do you mean?" Jane asked, wondering if she'd heard correctly. "Are you referring to what happened to Papa?"

No one had known that her father had been murdered until she'd brought the pressed rose and Machiavelli quotation found among her father's things to Eversham. At least that was what they'd thought.

Mama shook her head as if to clear it and gave an apologetic look to Jane. "No, I don't know what I meant. You must pay no attention to what I say. As you recall, that was a very difficult time for me. I'm sure Lord Gilford's death had nothing to do with your father's death. After all, Lord Gilford was murdered. Isn't that what you said, Lord Adrian?"

Her mother was lying. Jane was sure of it. But why? Had she known Jane's father hadn't taken his own life? Then why had she allowed everyone else to assume it was true?

A glance at Adrian indicated that he, too, had noticed Mama's prevarication.

"As you can imagine," he continued, "things have been in upheaval since Lord Gilford's death, especially since the house is filled with foreign dignitaries who were invited for a symposium."

"Oh dear," Mrs. McIvor said, a hand to her chest. "Poor Mathilda, she must be beside herself."

To her husband, she said, "Mathilda is Lady Gilford. We were somewhat acquainted when our husbands were both with the Foreign Office."

"That's just it," Adrian said with a nod. "Lady Gilford and her daughter left for the country this morning. Especially given the unusual circumstances of Lord Gilford's death, Will, that is, their son, the new Lord Gilford, thought it best that his mother and sister were removed from the trouble here in London."

"But if you'll excuse me, Miss Halliwell," said Sir Ross with a frown, "if your charge is not at home, then what is your role here? If you wish to come back to Edinburgh with us, then I can assure you, we would be more than happy to have you come live in our home. Indeed, it was our main reason for—"

"Ross," Mrs. MacIvor said in a low voice. "I thought perhaps we could work up to the invitation. Poor Jane has only just learned of our marriage."

Sir Ross made a sound that Jane knew was somehow inherently Scottish. "Your Jane is not some milk and water miss to be gently introduced to her future. She is a sensible young lady. You can see for yourself from the way she and young Lord Adrian look at one another which way the wind blows, no matter what they say, but if she's no longer got a position here, then..."

Jane and her mother both gaped at Sir Ross, but beside her she felt Adrian laughing softly.

"Ross, my goodness," Mama said with a rueful shake of her head. "Poor Jane will never wish to entertain a call from us again."

"No," Jane said weakly. "I am grateful for your offer, though I must insist again that Lord Adrian and I are not—that is to say—there is no—"

She stopped when Adrian took her hand in his and squeezed it. "What Jane is trying to say is that there is no formal agreement between us. But I must reassure you all that my intentions are honorable."

Jane turned to look at him and his gaze was steady, one brow raised in query.

She felt her face flood with color. Goodness. She hadn't blushed this much since she was in the schoolroom. She was going to have a few choice words for Adrian when they were alone again. The wretch.

"Well, I should certainly hope so," Mrs. MacIvor said sharply. "I know I have no right to interfere in your life after so many years away from you, but I will remind you that you are a lady and entirely suitable to be the bride of any gentleman, no matter how elevated his rank."

"Mama," Jane hissed, feeling mortified at her mother's interference. "It is unnecessary for you to say such things.

Adrian was only—that is, *Lord* Adrian was merely trying to assuage any concern on your part. He's a diplomat. It's what he does."

She turned to where Adrian was seated beside her. "Tell them. You were just smoothing the waters, weren't you?"

He gave Jane an exasperated look before turning back to face her mother and Sir Ross. "Contrary to what Jane might think, Mrs. MacIvor, I am not in the habit of telling falsehoods as part of my profession. When I said my intentions are honorable, I meant just that. I fear, however, your daughter and I have not had a chance to discuss the matter since, as I said earlier, things in the house have been at sixes and sevens since Lord Gilford's murder. And we have both been occupied with other things."

Jane was astonished that Adrian had not only reassured her mother and Mr. MacIvor that he'd been entirely serious about his declaration, but also spoken as if he'd merely been waiting for the murder investigation to wind down in order to make his intentions known. He couldn't possibly mean it.

Could he?

Her traitorous heart beat faster at the very idea, despite the way her good sense warned her not to get her hopes up.

"We are so pleased to hear you've gained the attentions of such a decent gentleman, Miss Halliwell. But I'm most admiring of how you've stepped into the breach while poor, bereaved Lady Gilford is away mourning her husband," said Sir Ross, interrupting Jane's thoughts. "But I would not have expected anything different from the girl your dear mother has described to me time and time again. She has every reason to be proud."

Jane looked at her mother with a surprised look. She wasn't sure what she'd expected her mother to have told her new husband about her, but she somehow hadn't imagined the glowing portrait he seemed to suggest.

"Of course I said good things," she said a little chidingly. "I am proud of you, Jane."

"Thank you, Mama," Jane said, and found herself fighting back tears. "And thank you, too, Sir Ross. You are very kind."

"But you won't be wishing to come back to Edinburgh with us, will you, lass?" Sir Ross asked with a none-too-subtle glance in Adrian's direction.

"You needn't decide today," Mrs. MacIvor said with a smile. "We will be here in London for a few more weeks. I suggest you take all the time you need to make the decision that will make you happiest."

At this last, she gave a speaking glance in Adrian's direction and Jane felt him shift uncomfortably beside her.

Rising, Sir Ross stood and said to Adrian, "I wonder if there is a terrace nearby where you can point me in the correct direction of St. Paul's Cathedral. I've a terrible head for directions. And Mrs. MacIvor and I wish to see all the sights."

"Certainly," Adrian said to the other man. To Jane he said, "We'll be right outside. If you have need of us—"

"We will be fine," Jane assured him with a nod. "I have some questions for Mama about our time in Rome."

At her mention of Rome, Adrian gave Jane a quick nod, then led Sir Ross from the room.

"I think you'd better tell me what's going on here, Lord Adrian," said Sir Ross as soon as they stepped out onto the terrace. "I might only be that young lady's stepfather but I will do whatever it takes to keep Amelia happy and it doesn't look to me as if you and Miss Halliwell share the same opinion about intentions. If you've done anything to force the issue—"

"Good God, no!" Adrian said, raising his hands in denial. "It's nothing like that."

"That's not what it looked like to me." The Scot's earlier affability had been replaced by cool suspicion.

Adrian scowled at the other man. "I could call you out for that, you know."

"Dueling is illegal," MacIvor said tartly. "And you can hardly blame me for wondering. Things in this house are most irregular and I need to make sure you're not making circumstances worse for Jane."

"I'm not," Adrian told him with a scowl. "If you must know, I haven't had a chance to make my case to her yet. I've barely had time to realize I've got a case to make."

The kiss that morning had taken them both by surprise, he suspected, though afterward he'd realized he'd been falling under Jane's spell from the moment she entered the drawing room before dinner that first night. But it had been seeing her injured in the carriage accident that jolted him into noticing his heart might be in danger.

Without going into detail about their reason for calling at Attingly's or what they'd learned there, he explained what had happened on the drive back to Gilford House and how Jane had sustained her injury. He also told MacIvor how his feelings had become engaged at that point. It would hardly do to tell him about the kiss, after all.

The older man's jaw clenched in anger at Adrian's description of the cut traces. "So someone was deliberately trying to hurt, possibly kill you both."

"Possibly," Adrian agreed. "Though I suspect now, it was me they were after. Jane was merely harmed because she happened to be with me at the time."

"Now I definitely think we should take Miss Halliwell back to Edinburgh with us." Sir Ross rubbed his chin in thought. "Once all this is sorted out, then you can come up to fetch her. It might do you a bit of good to think things over without the distraction of a pretty face to muddle your mind."

"My mind is not muddled, MacIvor." Adrian heard the note of steel in his voice and knew he shouldn't allow the man to set his back up, but he'd already let Jane get hurt on his watch once and felt like a fool for it. "Of course, if Jane wishes to go with you back to Scotland, that is her choice. But I somehow doubt she will agree to do so."

The Scotsman sighed. "Aye, I suspect she's as stubborn as her mother, that one. And you did say she's been overseeing the household while Lady Gilford is away, did you not?"

They lapsed into discussion of the MacIvors' trip to London and what they'd seen of London thus far. Adrian was offering to take the Scotsman to Tattersalls when Eversham and Langham appeared on the terrace.

Quickly, Adrian made introductions and at the news Eversham was the Scotland Yard detective investigating Gilford's murder, MacIvor's gaze sharpened. "You'll be looking into the circumstances of James Halliwell's death as well, I presume?"

Eversham frowned. "What do you know about Halliwell's death?"

"Just what my wife told me. The whole business was havey-cavey if you ask me."

Langham reached for his quizzing glass, but Adrian's glare was enough to make him drop it. Still, he couldn't stop himself from saying, "I believe Eversham is aware that there were irregularities."

"I should like to speak to Mrs. MacIvor about what she recalls of those days while she is in London," Eversham said. "We believe Halliwell's death and Gilford's may be connected."

"Of course, I want the murderer caught," MacIvor said, "but it's the miscreant who threatened her with the asylum that I want to find."

Adrian gaped at the Scotsman. "What the devil?"

"I believe what my brother, who seems to have lost every bit of eloquence he possesses," Langham said after a raised brow in Adrian's direction, "is trying to say, is that none of us is aware of threats to the former Mrs. Halliwell."

"Someone sent letters to Amelia after Halliwell's death,"

MacIvor said with a scowl. "They threatened that if she ever told the truth about her husband's death they'd make sure she was locked away."

"So, she knew that Halliwell didn't take his own life?" Eversham asked. "How?"

"She didn't know for sure," MacIvor said. "But she suspected. Halliwell had a favorite uncle who did away with himself when Halliwell was a boy and he never forgot it. So when Halliwell turned up dead and it looked like suicide, Amelia wasn't convinced. Then before she could say anything to the authorities, she got the threats."

"Do you recall any of the specifics of the threats Mrs. Halliwell—excuse me, MacIvor, received?" Eversham asked, his brow furrowed in thought.

"It's difficult to forget," MacIvor said with a scowl. "I can tell you the entirety of it. 'You had better keep your mouth shut about how your husband died, or you will find yourself in Wareham's Hospital just like old Mrs. Lymington-Ford did. She was mad as a hatter, but you are not. What a hell it would be for you to be the only sane one in a crowd of insanity. Do not doubt I can make sure it happens if you defy me.'"

"Isn't Wareham's Hospital that place in the wilds of Yorkshire?" Langham's expression turned grim. "Damn awful place that. But who's this Lymington-Ford woman? And what's she got to do with this whole mess?"

"Mrs. Lymington-Ford's son Gareth was ambassador to Portugal," Eversham explained. "She lived in Lisbon with him and his family. That was until she began having fits and became ungovernable to the point where she tried to stab her nurse. Gareth had to escort her back to England and found a place for her at Wareham's. It's generally considered to be one of the better places. And yet—"

"And yet my poor Amelia could have ended up there," Sir Ross interrupted, his tone filled with disgust. "The sooner you catch this scoundrel, the better, Mr. Eversham."

"I intend to do just that, Sir Ross," Eversham assured him. "And I must offer you my thanks, because this threat has given us a vital clue."

"Has it?" Sir Ross asked, his eyes wide.

"Oh, indeed it has," the detective said with a nod. "Because whoever wrote this knew about what happened to Mrs. Lymington-Ford. Which limits our suspect list considerably."

"I wish you would share your deduction with the rest of us, Eversham," Langham drawled, looking at his friend through his quizzing glass.

"It's one of us," Adrian said, feeling as if he'd been given an uppercut from one of his brother's boxing opponents. "The killer is someone who has close enough ties to the Foreign Office to know the circumstances behind the confinement of Mrs. Lymington-Ford—it was kept quiet for obvious reasons. But what's more, they knew that Amelia Halliwell would be familiar with the story."

"I fear you are correct, Lord Adrian," said Eversham. "And if that's the case, then it's possible the culprit is still here with us at Gilford House."

Chapter Nineteen

Y ou're looking well," Mama said to Jane, and it was hard not to note that she seemed happier than Jane had seen her in years. Jane was grateful to MacIvor for that—even if he had mortified her by making assumptions about the relationship between her and Adrian.

"He is a good man," her mother continued and at first Jane thought she was referring to her new husband, but as she continued she realized her mother meant Adrian and Jane felt a headache coming on. "It's just that I associate him with our time in Rome, and the Foreign Office in general. I suppose I wanted you to have a different life. Far removed from the endless travel and diplomatic intrigue."

"Mama, there is no understanding between us," Jane said firmly. "Lord Adrian has been a friend to me in the aftermath of Lord Gilford's death. That is all. I doubt he'd have said anything about intentions at all if Sir Ross hadn't mistaken us for a betrothed couple."

Her mother didn't look convinced, but she let the subject drop. Relieved, Jane turned the conversation to something just as painful but equally important.

"Detective Inspector Eversham would like to speak to you about Papa's death."

Mrs. MacIvor looked startled. "Whatever for? That was years ago."

"There seems to be a connection between Papa's death and Lord Gilford's," Jane explained.

Closing her eyes, Jane's mother shook her head. But when she opened them she said, "Very well. If the detective suspects as much, then I will, of course, speak to him. It's about time whoever killed your father is brought to justice."

"But I don't understand," Jane said, frustration building inside her chest. "I only just learned that there was ever a suggestion that Papa didn't take his own life. But you knew? Why would you keep that from me?"

"You must understand that I could say nothing," her mother said softly. "I was warned, you see. They would have put me in an asylum, and I would never have seen you again. I remained silent for both our sakes."

The mention of an asylum brought Jane up short. "I don't understand. Who threatened you?"

Her mother's mouth tightened. "Can you not simply allow me to tell this Detective Inspector Eversham and leave it at that? I don't want to burden you now any more than I did then."

Jane stepped closer and took her mother's hands.

"Mama, I can assure you I have been involved with the investigation ever since I found Lord Gilford's body."

Her mother's eyes widened, and she leaned forward to pull Jane into her arms. "You never said that you were the one to find Lord Gilford. How dreadful that must have been for you. My poor Jane."

Despite the long separation between them, Jane couldn't help but lose herself in the familiar feel of her mother's arms around her. It had been a long time since she'd felt the comfort that only a mother could offer and she felt her eyes burn with unshed tears.

At last, pulling away and fighting hard to regain her composure, Jane asked, "Please, Mama. Tell me about the threats you received after Papa died."

"I suppose it is foolish for me to treat you like a child," her mother said ruefully. "Especially when you are well past the age when many girls marry."

Just then, the refreshments that Adrian had rung for earlier arrived.

"Come," Jane said, gesturing her mother to a chair near the tea table. "I will pour while you tell me the tale."

Nodding, her mother took her seat and said, "On the day your father died, someone from the embassy called on him. It was one of the senior officials, I know that. I would have recognized Lord Adrian's voice, and lest you fear it was he, be assured that it was not. I never saw who it was, but both your father and his visitor were quite angry. I disliked leaving them to argue like that, but I had to pay a call and when I returned your father had left to go to the embassy. It was later that night, long after he'd returned from their evening's entertainment, that I was awakened by a gunshot. When I went downstairs to see what had happened, I found him in his office, dead."

"Oh, Mama." Jane's hand was shaking so badly she had to put down the teapot before she dropped it. "I had no idea. I never heard the story of what happened that day. No one would tell me."

"I never wanted you to know," her mother said fiercely. "I knew he hadn't killed himself, but even before I had the chance to alert the authorities, someone had already begun to spread the word that he'd taken his own life because he'd lost everything at the gaming tables. Jane, your father wasn't a gamester. And he would never have risked our future on the turn of a card."

"That is what Adrian said about him as well," Jane said thoughtfully, then she revealed to her mother what her father's letter to Attingly had said about the threatening letters he'd been receiving. "If he didn't do whatever it was this person demanded of him, he'd make sure Papa was ruined. Unfortunately, we don't have a way to know what Papa was meant to do in order to escape being ruined."

Her mother's eyes filled with tears. "Oh, your poor father. He must have been beside himself with worry over those threats."

"But what about the letter you received?" Jane asked, wondering how these pieces of the puzzle fit together. "You said you were threatened with being sent to an asylum?"

Quickly, her mother outlined the note she'd received. As she spoke, Jane felt herself grow angrier and angrier. "I never knew that was what happened to Mrs. Lymington-Ford. But this horrible person must have known you were familiar with her and the circumstances around her disappearance. I've heard whispers of other ladies who have been dispatched to Wareham's Hospital, and the very idea of you being confined to such a place is terrifying."

"I must admit that I was terribly afraid," her mother said with a shake of her head. "And I wanted us to be as far away from London as possible. Especially because both the mention of Mrs. Lymington-Ford and whoever it was I overheard in your father's office the day he died seemed to indicate that the culprit was affiliated somehow with the Foreign Office."

"So you went to Scotland to live with cousin Celeste," Jane said, understanding dawning.

"I would have brought you with me," her mother said, "but you were so stubborn and insisted upon becoming a governess. I tried to dissuade you but there was no stopping you."

"Mama, you know as well as I do that Celeste's invitation was primarily for you," Jane said with exasperation. "She mentioned multiple times how small her house was and that it would not be a comfortable household for a 'lively young lady.' I didn't wish to make things more difficult for you, so I sought work as a governess. And I've been happy."

That last was a gross exaggeration, but she had no wish to admit just how miserable she'd been at times, so she turned the conversation to a more pleasant topic. "How did you meet Sir Ross? He seems like a kind man."

Mama looked as if she'd like to continue the discussion

of Jane's refusal to go to Scotland, but she must have seen the implacability in her daughter's expression because she sighed, then smiled and said, "He is. We met at a dinner party in Edinburgh. I was terrified at first of telling him about my past, but eventually he convinced me to trust him. I so wanted you to be at our wedding, but I know how difficult it is for you to get time off. And I thought it best to arrive in London as Mrs. McIvor given all the gossip we endured in the past."

"Why did you come back to London at all?" Jane asked, surprised that her mother would dare such a thing given the threat hanging over her.

"To see you, of course," her mother said fiercely. "I'd already allowed this cowardly stranger to keep us apart, and Ross by my side gave me the courage to finally make peace with you."

She frowned. "Little did I know I'd arrive to find that Lord Gilford had been murdered. It's happening all over again. Just like your father, though I suppose this time the blackguard couldn't risk making it look like the same circumstances that occurred with your father. Or Lord Attingly for that matter."

"I don't even think we'd have made the connection if I hadn't kept the book page and pressed rose that were among Papa's things. I'd thought they held some special meaning for Papa but when I learned similar items were found on Lord Gilford's body I knew I'd misunderstood them completely." Jane shuddered at the memory of learning what she'd seen as sweet remembrances were actually left as a murderer's calling cards.

"I had no idea," her mother said, looking shocked. "I couldn't bear to look at the things that were removed from his pockets that day, so I put them together in a box in his office, where I suppose you found them."

Jane nodded.

Her mother looked thoughtful. "There's something about Machiavelli that reminds me of our time in Rome, but I cannot place it."

"Something to do with the writer himself or one of his books perhaps?" Jane felt a tickle over her spine.

"I don't know," her mother said with a shake of her head. "I wish I could remember. I have some of your father's things in Edinburgh. When we return I'll see if I can find something that might trigger a memory. You might also look through Lord Gilford's things from his time in Rome, too."

Jane gasped. "Lord Gilford was in Rome at the same time we were?"

"Oh, yes," her mother said with a smile. "Not for terribly long, mind you. I believe the foreign secretary at the time—Lord Bathurst and some of his senior aides, including Lord Gilford, as well as Lords Attingly and Ralston, were there for a brief time meeting with the Italian prime minister. Your father died while they were visiting. I don't know what I would have done if Lady Attingly hadn't been there to help me manage."

She was about to ask her mother what else she remembered about that time, but just then Adrian and Sir Ross returned, accompanied by Eversham.

After Eversham had been introduced to Mrs. MacIvor, the detective said with a note of apology in his voice, "I know you have just reunited with your daughter, but I have some questions I'd like to ask you about the time around your first husband's death if that's all right."

Jane's mother agreed, and she relayed everything she'd told Jane, both about the argument she'd overheard between Halliwell and his unknown colleague, and the threatening letter she'd received.

When she was finished, she looked drained, and Jane was glad her mother had Sir Ross to comfort her. "I hope what I've told you will help you find whoever it was that killed my Charles, Mr. Eversham. All these years of not knowing have weighed heavily upon me. And now that I know Attingly and Gilford were killed by the same person, I fear that my keeping what I knew to myself may have led to their deaths as well."

"The only person responsible for their deaths, Mama," said Jane fiercely, "was the murderer. I do not blame you for being frightened of what would happen if you talked."

"Miss Halliwell is correct," Eversham said with sympathy. "But what you've told me today has certainly clarified some things for me and I believe we are close to discovering who is responsible for these deaths. Thank you for trusting me with the details."

"I think we had best get back to the hotel for now," said Sir Ross as he and Jane's mother rose to take their leave. To Jane he said, "It has been a great pleasure to meet you at last, Miss Halliwell. And no matter what happens with all this business, know that you will always have a place with us in Scotland if that is what you wish. Though I suspect you will have other plans."

He gave a none-too-subtle wink and Jane wished that the floor would swallow her up.

"You must visit us at Claridge's for dinner before we return north, Jane," her mother said, smoothing over Sir Ross's teasing. "And you, too, Lord Adrian. If you are able to find time away from your duties here."

Adrian glanced at her before answering. "We would like that very much."

This seemed to please her mother and Jane was suddenly hit with a wave of relief at knowing that their rift was healed. The hug they exchanged at the door was a long one, and when she pulled away, she and her mother both had tears in their eyes.

"I will see you soon, my dear," her mother said with one last squeeze of Jane's hand. Then she and Sir Ross were gone.

When Jane turned from the entry hall, she saw that Eversham and Adrian were waiting for her. "Was there something else we needed to discuss, Mr. Eversham?"

"I thought it would be helpful to go over what we just learned," the detective told her, then after a glance in Adrian's direction, he added, "and I believe Lord Adrian has some new information as well."

That reminded her that she had her own question for Adrian—aside from what he'd meant by his admission of honorable intentions to Sir Ross, which she'd set aside for the moment. "Very well," she agreed, and they all went to confer in Eversham's office.

Once the door was shut behind them, Jane, unable to hold her tongue any longer, turned to Adrian and demanded, "When were you going to tell me that Gilford, Attingly, and Ralston were all in Rome at the time my father was murdered?"

"What do you mean?" Adrian asked, recognizing that Jane was upset but confused as to why. "You were there. You knew they were in Rome at the same time we all were."

"Adrian, I was a girl in the schoolroom. I didn't spend my days following the goings-on at the British embassy. I saw you frequently, but that was only—because you dined with us so often," she said with exasperation. "But you came to us, we didn't go to the embassy. How was I to know which representatives of the Foreign Office were visiting the embassy from week to week?"

Adrian realized with a start that she had a point. He'd taken it for granted that she'd known as much about what was happening among the British diplomats in Rome that week as he had. Or at the very least had known who was there. But of course she wouldn't have known.

"I am sorry, Jane," he said, thrusting a hand into his hair in agitation. "It never occurred to me that you didn't know."

Eversham indicated that they should both take seats and once they were seated across from his desk, the detective turned his attention to Jane. "I know this may seem odd, but bear with me for a moment. Miss Halliwell, what is it about the presence of those three men in Rome at the time of your father's murder that bothers you? Because it is clear that it isn't just their presence, but something else that is niggling at you. What is that?"

Jane frowned, glancing at Adrian before turning back to Eversham. "I suppose it's the fact that two of them—Attingly and Gilford—were also murdered later. And two of them—Gilford and Ralston—were both present at this symposium. It makes me think that perhaps something happened in Rome that Attingly and Gilford, at least, were involved in. Something that got them killed."

Adrian felt a sinking feeling in his gut. "There's one more man who was both in Rome and at the symposium. Lord Payne."

He heard Jane gasp and turned to see she'd gone pale.

Eversham gave a nod to Adrian. "I'll have my men keep an eye on him in addition to you and Lord Ralston. I'd like to ensure this villain is thwarted in the event he decides to eliminate another of your number."

To Eversham she said, "Did you glean anything from your interviews with either Lord Ralston or Payne that gave you a hint as to who could be behind this?"

"No," the detective said with a sigh. "Though it might be a good idea for me to speak to both men again, given that I, too, was unaware that they were in Rome at the time your father was killed."

"You might also ask if they were in England at the time of Attingly's death," Adrian suggested, looking troubled. "Though I find it difficult to believe that the killer is one of us. The diplomatic community is a close-knit one. It is unimaginable to think that sort of betrayal is possible."

"We don't know yet for certain that it is someone within the Foreign Office committing these vile crimes," Jane said softly, though he suspected she was trying to comfort him.

"Correct," Eversham agreed. "Surely there were others known to all three victims who were in Rome at the time of Halliwell's death. It's also possible that someone ordered the killings and had the hired killer place the quotation and the rose on their person after death."

The ormolu clock on the mantel began to chime the hour, and Jane stood. "I thank you for allowing me to continue as part of the investigation, Mr. Eversham. But I had better go dress for dinner."

Both Adrian and Eversham rose with her and after the detective had bid her good afternoon, Adrian followed her from the small chamber.

"I have been lucky to have Poppy stepping in as hostess for me," Jane said as she and Adrian walked toward the family wing, "but since I am no longer suffering the ill effects of our accident yesterday, I should take up my duties again."

As if she'd only just discovered the floors were covered in flames instead of fine Aubusson carpets, Jane all but raced along the hall.

"Jane," Adrian said in an amused tone, "please slow down. I have some things that need to be said and I do not wish to do so while we are running a footrace."

At his words, she slowed and looked over at him. "I was only trying to—"

"Reach your bedchamber before you were forced to listen to what I have to say?" he asked. "I would use many words to describe you, but I hadn't ever thought 'coward' was one of them."

She sighed as they reached the door leading into her rooms. "Come," she said with a shrug. "We can talk undisturbed in my sitting room. But I really do need to dress for dinner."

Before she could open the door, one of the footmen approached from the other end of the hall. Bowing to them both, he offered what looked to be a sealed letter to Jane. Then he turned and hurried back the way he'd come.

Adrian saw Jane's mouth tighten as she looked down at the missive in her hand. The seal looked familiar, though he couldn't place it. Straightening her spine, Jane opened the door leading into her sitting room and indicated that he should follow.

Though it was most improper for them to be closeted in a room alone—especially one attached to her bedchamber—Adrian came inside with her and shut the door firmly behind him.

"If you'll excuse me for a moment," Jane said as she turned to open the letter. Quickly, she scanned the lines and the tightness around her mouth turned into an out-and-out frown.

"Is it bad news?" he asked.

With a lift of her chin, Jane said, "Lady Gilford is simply informing me that my services as Margaret's governess are no longer needed. And that because of my unbecoming airs—that is, not bowing and scraping to her at every turn—she will not be giving me a letter of reference."

She turned to face him, and he saw that despite her show

of indifference, she was upset by the news. "I suppose it's a good thing that my mother and Sir Ross chose today of all days to call. At least I need not fear having nowhere to go."

"Given how unpleasant Lady Gilford has been to you," Adrian said, a little puzzled by her reaction, "I should think you'd jump at the chance to be released from your duties."

Jane sighed. "I do sound foolish, don't I?" she asked with a laugh. "I suppose it's just the cruelty of it. She doesn't know that Mama and I have reconciled, or that Mama has remarried. She simply has no qualms about dismissing me without a reference."

Adrian stepped forward and took her hand in his. Jane didn't try to pull away, for which he was grateful. "There is another option for you, if you do not wish to move to Scotland."

To his disappointment, she pulled away and crossed to the other side of the room.

"Please," she began in a shaky voice. "I know that I perhaps gave you the wrong impression this morning by kissing you. And I apologize for that. But if you are planning to offer for me, I wish you would not."

Adrian hadn't thought his suit would meet with such a resounding refusal even before he was able to say the words. He also couldn't have imagined just how devastated he would be if she denied him.

It was ludicrous to think that three days ago he was barely aware of her and now he felt as if his life would be miserable if she didn't agree to become his wife.

"Will you at least tell me why?" he asked, grateful that

his voice sounded steady. "Because that kiss this morning suggested that you do not have a disgust of me."

It had been the most intoxicating kiss of his life. And he refused to believe that he'd been the only one of them affected thusly.

At the mention of the kiss, her eyes softened for a moment, then she bit her lip. Was she being intentionally distracting? No, he decided. There was not a false bone in Jane's body.

"I do not," she said haltingly. "That is to say, of course you don't disgust me. That is why I was so desperate to get away from you before you could speak."

He frowned. "I'm afraid I'm not following you?"

She shook her head. Taking a deep breath, she said, "I find you all too attractive. That is the problem. Because I knew that if you said the words I would be tempted beyond reason."

"If you find me attractive, and as I suspect, you might even hold me in some affection," he asked as he began walking toward her, "then why not agree to marry me?"

She watched as he approached, and he saw that her expression was one of wistful longing.

When he reached her, he took her hands in his. "What is it that prevents you from accepting me, Jane?"

His words were soft, and as he looked down at her beloved heart-shaped face, he tried to commit it to memory in case she truly did turn him away.

"Oh, Adrian," she said, looking into his eyes. "I would like nothing better than to marry you. But to do so would be denying the one thing I have wished for since Papa's death."

His confusion must have been written plainly on his face because she continued, "I want to have a place of my own. One that will remain the same year after year. I want to put down roots and get to know what village life is like in England. I want the one thing you cannot give me. A home."

Chapter Twenty

"A home?" Adrian repeated. "But what makes you think that's not what I'm offering?"

"The fact that you work for the Foreign Office?" Jane said with a bit of impatience. "I spent the first eighteen years of my life moving from country to country, continent to continent. I have no wish to spend the next twenty doing the same thing."

Before he could respond, she continued, "I know how much your career means to you, Adrian. On one of the few occasions you confided to me when we were in Rome, you told me that you'd fought too hard to establish yourself at the Foreign Office to let your brother's disapproval make you leave it. I hardly think a wife would be able to succeed where your brother has failed."

He stared at her for a long moment, then started laughing softly.

Jane's back went rigid. "I'm sorry you find my desire for

a home to be so amusing, my lord. Clearly there is more that separates us temperamentally than I thought. If you will please leave so that I may—"

"My dear Jane, there is nothing further from the truth," Adrian said, bringing her hands to his lips. "I find your desire for a home to be entirely understandable. What's more, I, too, would like to have a home. One in England, just so we're clear on the matter."

"You can try to use your powers of persuasion all you like, but—" The entirety of Adrian's words finally sank in, and she broke off. "You—you wish to live in England?"

He pulled her into his arms and smiled down at her. "I do, indeed."

"But you were so adamant," Jane said as she looked at him in wonder. "You said you would remain abroad for as long as you possibly could."

Adrian's sensuous mouth twisted into a rueful smile. "I can't believe I prosed on at you about how hard done I'd been by Langham. I'm astonished that you found anything about that immature fellow attractive in the least."

She couldn't stop the laugh that bubbled up in her throat. "I was hardly the picture of maturity at the time. And what you said made a great deal of sense to me. Why should your brother be able to dictate your career choice?"

He brushed a thumb over her cheek. "I understand Langham's point of view now. But we'll discuss that later. What's more important is that I no longer wish to spend my entire adult life far away from my family and friends."

"You don't?" She wondered how a person could go from misery to joy in the space of only a few minutes. She'd been so convinced that no matter how much she wanted to be with him, they were doomed to remain apart because of their incompatible desires.

Now, she was almost afraid to believe what she was hearing.

"Jane, will you marry me?" Adrian's eyes were smiling as he touched his forehead to hers. "Make a home with me? Here in England, where our children can be spoiled by our families?"

"Yes," she said on a breath as she lifted her mouth to meet his. "I will marry you, you infuriating, maddening, adorable man."

Their kiss was, at first, sweetly tender. Jane could tell he was showing her with his every caress just how much he cared for her. And Jane did the same, until they had to break apart for air.

When they came back together, the touches became firmer, the strokes more passionate. Their tongues tangled in a dance that Jane knew mimicked what their eventual coupling would be like, and the thought sent a shiver through her.

Almost as if he'd read her mind, Adrian's hand came up to caress her breast, startling a gasp from her. When he shifted their bodies so her back was against the wall, she almost cried out with frustration. Until, that is, he put his hand back where it had been, and began kissing a trail down her jaw and over the soft skin of her neck, his tongue darting out between kisses, as if he couldn't resist a taste.

"So lovely," he whispered against her skin, while his clever hands worked to lower the neck of her gown so that her breasts were exposed. Jane would have lifted her hands to cover them, but then Adrian replaced his hand with his mouth. And when he stroked his tongue over the bud of first one nipple, then the other, she cried out at the shock of it.

The sensations that jolted through her at his increasingly erotic caresses made Jane ache for things she'd only ever read about. Without conscious thought, she rocked her hips against Adrian's body, and she heard him swear softly.

"Poor darling," he said against her ear, the warmth of his breath sending a tremor through her. "Will this help?"

As he spoke, he gathered her skirts and petticoats and smoothed a hand up her leg to the split in her pantalettes. She would never have imagined such a thing happening where she wasn't abject with embarrassment, but Jane was far beyond caring about such things. She wanted Adrian's fingers on her, and when he stroked over the wetness that had gathered there, she could only gasp at the feel of him.

"That's it," he said in a rough voice as she lifted her hips to meet his touch, "take your pleasure from me."

His mouth took hers as his fingers worked in and out of her and their kiss this time was raw and sexual. The wanting built within her with his every stroke, and soon, she felt herself nearing some height she couldn't name. Then, unexpectedly, bliss suffused her, and she flew over the edge.

Adrian watched as Jane came back to herself, in awe at how utterly beautiful she'd been in the throes of passion. He made a vow to himself then and there that he would endeavor to put that expression on her face as often as possible.

Slowly, she opened her eyes and when she saw him looking at her, her cheeks flushed but to his relief her luscious mouth soon curved into a smile. Unable to resist, he let her skirts fall and took her lips in a slow, thorough kiss.

So engrossed was he in their embrace that Adrian didn't hear the sound of the insistent knocking on the door behind them until he suspected it had been going on for quite a while.

"Jane! Jane! Are you in there?" Poppy called from the other side of the door.

"Oh no!" Jane hissed as she pushed Adrian away and pulled her bodice up until her bosom was safely covered. "One minute, Poppy."

To Adrian she said in a panicked whisper, "She'll guess what we've been doing. She's very good at guessing games."

"I hardly think it's the same as charades," Adrian muttered as he did what he could to smooth her hair back into place as Jane ministered to setting him to rights. "Besides, we are betrothed now."

At that reminder, Jane smiled in such a beatific manner that he almost pulled her into his arms and mussed her up again. But when she caught the glint in his eye, Jane gave him a stern glare that he suspected put Margaret Gilford on her best behavior.

"Go stand over there by the mantel," Jane told him in a low voice.

Following orders, Adrian did as he was told and watched with barely veiled amusement as Jane opened the door to reveal not only Poppy but Langham as well.

"I apologize," Jane said, waving them into the chamber. "We were discussing the investigation and didn't hear you knock."

Adrian noted his sister-in-law's raised brow and doubted she believed Jane's story.

Langham, who had strolled over to stand beside him, said in a tone only Adrian could hear, "That explanation would hold more water if Miss Halliwell didn't have the beginnings of a love bite on her collarbone."

"Damn it." Adrian's eyes flew wide, and he scanned Jane's neckline, where he saw…nothing. "You ass."

Langham gave a low chuckle. "I thought you diplomatic types were supposed to be good at bluffing."

"Why are you even here?" Adrian asked grumpily. "I know you were meant to be doing the pretty with the foreign wives, but surely that's over by now."

"Some of the diplomatic wives were a bit too taken with the ducal personage," Langham said in an aggrieved tone. "Madame Dulac in particular has wandering hands."

Adrian winced. "Pinched you on the arse, did she? She's rather notorious for it. I take care never to turn my back on her."

"A bit of warning would have been nice." The duke scowled.

"Some things a man has to learn for himself," Adrian said with a shrug.

"So, you and the governess?" Langham asked, turning his gaze to where Poppy and Jane were speaking in hushed tones near the door.

"What's wrong with her being a governess?" Adrian asked, turning a cold look on his elder brother. "It's honest work. And there is nothing wrong with her lineage."

Langham raised his hands in a surrendering gesture. "I never said there was. My apologies. I should instead have called her by her name."

"Yes, you should have," Adrian returned. "Especially since she has agreed to become my wife."

There was a pause while Langham digested the announcement. Then he pulled his brother into a hug. "That's wonderful news! Why didn't you tell me that from the first?"

Adrian felt a bit embarrassed by the unexpected emotion from his brother, but was pleased, nonetheless. Thrusting his hands into his trouser pockets, he said with a grin, "It is good news, isn't it?"

Before the brothers could continue their discussion, they were set upon by Poppy and Jane, who came to hug and be hugged in turn.

"I knew there was something between the two of you," Poppy said with a wide smile at Jane and Adrian, who had moved to stand arm in arm. "Didn't I tell you so, Langham?"

"You did indeed, my dear, in fact—" But Langham was

cut off by the sound of a knock at the sitting room door followed by one of the footmen opening it.

"Your graces, Lord Adrian, Miss Halliwell," the young man said breathlessly. "Mr. Eversham said that you're all to come to the parlor at once."

Adrian felt Jane stiffen beside him at the footman's announcement. "What's happened, James?"

"It's Lord Payne," said James. "He's been attacked."

Chapter Twenty-One

It was a somber group who gathered in the drawing room that evening. Beneath the seriousness, however, Jane could feel both fear and resentment hanging heavy in the air.

As Jane sat beside Adrian, wishing propriety didn't prevent her from slipping her hand into his, she noted that in addition to Lord and Lady Payne, the foreign secretary and his wife were also missing.

"Where the devil is Eversham?" Langham asked from where he and Poppy were seated on a sofa across from Jane and Adrian. "If he was so dashed insistent upon everyone being here—including you lovebirds—then he should have the courtesy to be here—ow!"

From the way the duke scowled at his wife, Jane suspected Poppy had pinched him to stop his little speech.

"I'm sure Mr. Eversham is on his way," said the duchess primly. "And we are all so pleased to hear Lord Adrian and

Miss Halliwell's good news, are we not? I, for one, think it is heartwarming to know that love has blossomed amid such sad goings-on."

"I would have thought it considered rude to speak of such things when we are any moment to hear news about a brutal attack on Lord Adrian's colleague," Madame Dulac sniffed, "but les Anglais."

Jane felt Adrian stiffen beside her. "Madame," he began, but was interrupted by Lady Fitzroger, whose husband had been in the diplomatic corps longer than either of them had been alive.

"I believe what we have learned from this dreadful experience, Madame Dulac, is that our time is far too short to waste one moment of it that could be spent in celebration. I'm sure Lord Payne, who is fond of both Lord Adrian and Miss Halliwell, would be the first to raise a toast to this dear couple if he was not resting from his injuries. I should have thought that you, hailing as you do from Paris, the city of love, would be more understanding."

"I didn't know Lady Fitzroger was such a romantic," Adrian said quietly so only Jane would hear.

"Certainly one wouldn't think it of someone married to Lord Fitzroger," Jane whispered, glancing over to where the gentleman in question was snoring quietly into his neckcloth.

"Perhaps it is *because* she is married to Lord Fitzroger," Adrian whispered back.

It took every bit of Jane's self-control to keep from laughing out loud.

"See, look at how they whisper to one another," Mrs. Lindholm said with a beaming smile. "Young love."

Madame Dulac looked sour at having been outnumbered in her opinion that the betrothal announcement had been inappropriate but didn't argue.

Eversham, followed by Lord Ralston—who Jane was glad to see looked to be in good health—came in at that moment, and apologized for his tardiness. "I know you are all doubtless anxious to learn more about what happened to Lord Payne, and I regret forcing you to wait. But certain authorities had to be contacted and Lord Ralston and I were delayed on our way back from Whitehall."

A low murmur began among those gathered. It was not typical for Scotland Yard to need to contact the government when a crime was committed—even if the victim was a member of the aristocracy or the Foreign Office.

Deciding the devil with propriety, Jane gripped Adrian's hand and was gratified to feel the warmth of his strong fingers tight around hers. She held Lord Payne in the highest esteem and it was dreadfully upsetting to know he'd been attacked. And though she was grateful he'd survived, she knew how easily that might not have been the case.

"As some of you already know," Eversham said, standing with his hands behind his back, "Lord Payne was found earlier this evening in his dressing room. As I understand it, he had finished dressing for dinner and thus sent his valet away. But when he didn't come to collect her, Lady Payne became worried and went to fetch him and found him suffering from a head wound."

"Why was he left alive?" Langham asked baldly. "This person murdered Gilford, but only hit Payne over the head."

At his words, some of the ladies gasped, and Jane felt Adrian sigh at his brother's plain speaking.

"From what we can tell," Eversham said, not batting an eye at the duke's words, "the attacker was spooked by something or someone. Payne isn't able to recall what happened, which is not unusual with head wounds, but the bedchamber window was open, so it looks as if his assailant jumped. It isn't a terribly far drop to the garden below."

"Are we to simply wait here like, how do you say, sitting ducks?" Monsieur Dulac—who was rare to speak when compared to his wife—demanded sharply and was echoed by several others who were now voicing their displeasure at being kept at Gilford House under the circumstances.

"Now, ladies and gentlemen," Lord Ralston said in a tone of authority, "of course we understand the gravity of the situation and Mr. Eversham and I have consulted on the matter. And though it would be Scotland Yard's preference to keep you nearby until this brute is apprehended, we have decided that you must be allowed to make your own decisions with regard to your safety. Thus, if you wish it, you will all be allowed to remove yourselves to whichever accommodation you wish."

"And what of Payne? Will he recover?" asked Mr. Woodward above the din of chatter that rose in the wake of Ralston's announcement. At once the talk quieted. "And Gilford, for that matter? Who is responsible for these assaults?"

Eversham nodded, a grim look on his lean face. "We are, of course, still investigating Gilford's death and as Lord Payne recovers I am hopeful that he will be able to tell us more about his attacker. What I can tell you for certain is we do believe that the two incidents are linked. More than that I cannot say at this time. And while I cannot insist that you remain in the country in case we have further questions we need to ask of you, I would strongly request that you do so for at least the next week."

Now that the announcements had been completed, the gathering broke into groups to chat and make plans to leave the next morning, which was the earliest the servants could have them packed and removed to whichever other accommodations they could arrange at such short notice. No one, it seemed, was willing to remain behind at Gilford House.

Dinner had been held back when news of Payne's attack had come to light, and there was still a short while until it would be served.

"I suppose I should have guessed which way the wind was blowing," said Mr. Woodward, who came to offer his good wishes to the newly betrothed couple. "You always did have the devil's own luck, Lord Adrian. If he gives you any trouble, Miss Halliwell, you've only to send me a telegram in Washington and I'll be on the first ship over."

"I have no wish to start another war between our nations, Mr. Woodward," Jane teased.

"Oh, it wouldn't come to that, darling," Adrian said with a lethal smile. "He'd be unconscious long before any armies got involved."

"I do seem to recall you've got a strong right hook," Mr. Woodward said with a rub of his jaw. "Perhaps I'll just write you a letter, Miss Halliwell."

Several others also came by to offer congratulations, and Jane was relieved that no one had mentioned her scandalous career as a governess. But then, no one would dare question her suitability as a bride when the groom's ducal brother was present.

"My felicitations, Miss Halliwell," Eversham said, once he'd finished conferring with Lord Ralston. His genuine smile transformed his usually stern face and rendered the detective devastatingly handsome. "If my scheme to have you remain here to act as hostess—therefore increasing your proximity to one another—had anything to do with this turn of events, then I am glad of it. Something happy should come out of such dismal events, I think."

"I believe it was my scheme, Eversham," Adrian said dryly. "Though your point is well taken."

"Will you be going to stay with your mother and stepfather now that there is no need to remain in Gilford House?" Eversham inquired of Jane. "I only ask because I'll be calling on them tomorrow to ask your mother a few more questions, so I would be happy to escort you, though I suspect your fiancé would like to do the honors."

His question brought her up short, however. Jane hadn't considered that she would need to leave Gilford House so soon. But given that she'd been dismissed as governess, and she was no longer needed as a temporary hostess, she would indeed need somewhere else to stay.

Before she could answer, Poppy and Langham stepped

forward. "We would be delighted if you would stay with us for as long as you wish, Jane," Poppy said with a smile. "We certainly have more than enough room and it would be convenient to have you so nearby when we start planning the wedding."

Jane blinked. Wedding planning. She hadn't thought that far ahead. That morning at breakfast she hadn't even kissed Adrian yet.

Perhaps seeing the alarm on her face, Adrian slipped her arm into his and said, "I believe my fiancée needs a breath of air. If you'll excuse us."

She didn't even have the awareness to realize they'd left without her responding to Poppy's invitation. She only knew that one moment they were in the drawing room, and the next they were out on the terrace.

"Just one more minute," Adrian said in a soothing voice, "and here we are."

And before she knew what was happening, he was sitting down on a bench and pulling her onto his lap and into his arms.

"There," he breathed out into her hair. "You'd gone white as a debutante's gown in there."

Her face buried in his collar, she giggled at his description. "I don't know what came over me. I suppose I simply realized how much had happened and how much there is to do. And there are still three murders to solve and Lord Payne's attack and—"

"Shhh," Adrian said. "No wonder you went pale. That's far too much to think about all at once. For now, Eversham has things under control. It's his job. Let him do it."

Something about the way he said that last part made her pull up short. "Of course it's his job," she said with a frown. "But we've both been looking into what happened to my father and the others, too. And I feel as if we've been making progress. With poor Lord Payne's attack, we have more certainty than ever that the culprit is likely a member of the diplomatic community. And now that we are free to leave Gilford House there are more people we can question. Perhaps there are those who no longer work in the Foreign Office who might know who could have held a grudge against my father and the others."

"All of that is true," Adrian agreed, his brows drawn, "but now that Payne has been attacked, I'm beginning to think it might be safer for you to be out of proximity to me. Haven't you been the one to remind me that I'm the one who's more likely to be a target of the killer? Well, once you are safely tucked away in Langham House, I can assist Eversham as needed without fear of your being in danger as well."

Jane pulled away and glared at him. "And why aren't you, as the one who is more likely to be in danger, going to be safely tucked away in your family's townhouse?"

"I know what you're trying to make me say," Adrian said, his jaw tightening, "and I won't do it."

"What am I trying to make you say?" Jane asked sweetly. "Perhaps that you will continue to investigate because you're a man who gets to do as he pleases?"

"That's not what I would have said," Adrian argued, though she could see that he was getting a bit flustered. "But if I were to say that I prefer for you to not risk being harmed, what about that is unreasonable? It is entirely rational for me to wish you to remain safe."

"And it is entirely rational for me, as the daughter of one of the victims of this killer, to wish to take an active role in the investigation into the man's identity," Jane said, rising from where she'd been sitting in his lap. "I should think that having watched Poppy's courageous efforts to exonerate her sister, you would understand that ladies are well able to do such work."

"Poppy almost died for her efforts," Adrian said in an exasperated tone. Moving to stand before her, he took her in his arms. "I know you are a smart, capable woman. But I can't stand the idea of your being hurt by this villain. And the fact remains that the closer you are to me, the greater the risk."

"And I can't stand the idea of you being harmed by this villain either," Jane said, slipping her arms around his neck. "That is why I refuse to back down. We are a team. Whither thou goest and all that." She felt him sigh against her.

"You aren't going to be talked out of this, are you?"

"On that score at least, you are entirely correct, my darling." And with that she went up on her toes and kissed him.

The next morning, while the guests of Gilford House set about directing servants in their removal to hotels across London, Adrian was meeting with a few key leaders of the Foreign Office in a discreet corner office in Whitehall.

The murder of three British diplomats, along with the

attack on another, had set everyone with even the most tenuous connections with the Foreign Office on edge. And while there was slim likelihood that most of those who had contacted the department had anything to worry about, Foreign Secretary Ralston couldn't be seen to appear as if he didn't care what those who had given years of service to the office thought.

"We should never have agreed to Gilford's plan for a symposium," Lord Payne—who was recovered enough from his injury to have come in for the meeting—said from where he, Adrian, and Eversham sat across from Ralston.

"With respect, my lord," Adrian said aloud, "I do not believe that the symposium is to blame for Gilford's death or your attack. That must be blamed on the culprit."

"But you must agree, Lord Adrian, that had we not been gathered together as we were, Gilford would still be alive and I would not have this blasted headache." Payne's prematurely graying brows formed an upside-down W of disapproval in the middle of his forehead. "No, it was a mistake and I fear Lord Ralston might be the one to pay the ultimate price by losing his position."

"Now see here, Payne," the foreign secretary said with a scowl, "there's no need to—"

But Eversham, who Adrian knew loathed politics, broke in. "Your pardon, my lord, but are you really suggesting that if there were fewer gatherings there would be fewer murders?"

Silence fell over the room as it became clear to everyone both that it was precisely what Payne had been suggesting and that it was a remarkably silly notion. Perhaps the attack had left the man more rattled than he'd let on.

Payne made a sound somewhere between a *humph* and a *tcha* that finally ended in, "Never meant to imply, that is to say, *hmph*."

"Just so, Eversham," said Lord Ralston, with a nod that could have meant anything. "There will, of course, be questions about why Gilford is dead, and you were wounded, Payne, but I believe we can leave the ferreting out of the perpetrator to Detective Inspector Eversham. In the meantime, there will be the matter of assuring those who have honorably served the Foreign Office over the years that we are mindful of their safety."

"But what of Gilford and Attingly, sir?" Payne, having recovered his sangfroid, asked his superior. "I believe it is even believed that the circumstances behind Halliwell's death have now been called into question."

Adrian's head snapped up to look at Payne. *How the devil did he know about Attingly and Halliwell*, he wondered. It was difficult to tell at the best of times what the man was thinking but right now his expression was inscrutable.

Ralston turned to Eversham—his manner much less intense than Payne's, but still, it was evident that the foreign secretary was rattled. "Is this true, Eversham? I thought Attingly was murdered by a cutpurse. And we all know what happened to Halliwell, though for his family's sake we kept it as quiet as we could."

And that had worked out remarkably well, Adrian thought bitterly. Jane and her mother had been ostracized thanks to the rumors that had leaked about Halliwell's supposed suicide. He glanced at both Ralston and Payne and for the first time wondered if either of them had had something to do with leaking the information. It had never occurred to him before to suspect someone from the Foreign Office was responsible for the gossip, but in light of recent events it was worth considering now.

"My lord," Eversham said calmly, "it does appear that both Lord Attingly and Mr. Halliwell were murdered by the same man who killed Lord Gilford and attacked Lord Payne."

Twin flags of color appeared on Ralston's face. It was rare for the man to get angry—strong emotions were a liability in this line of work—but even Ralston, it appeared, was human. "Why wasn't I informed of this at once?" he demanded.

The real subtext of what he was saying was Why did Payne know of this before I did?

"We thought it best that the fewer who knew about this, the better," Adrian said, deciding that Eversham had done enough of the hard work in this meeting. "If you must blame someone, blame me."

Ralston's fingers drummed on the surface of his desk. When he stopped, he turned to glare at Payne. "How did you know about it?"

"I didn't tell him," Adrian said with a look in the other man's direction.

"Nor I," said Eversham, scowling at the fourth man, who was beginning to look uncomfortable.

"I wasn't listening at keyholes, if that's what you're

thinking," Payne said crossly. "I spoke with Miss Halliwell before you both went to visit Attingly that morning. She confided in me where you were going. It was entirely innocent, but I put the pieces together and guessed that it must have something to do with Gilford's murder."

Adrian glanced over at Eversham at Payne's words, but the detective's expression was impossible to read. It was hardly surprising to Adrian, at least, that Payne had taken advantage of Jane's fondness for him in order to winkle out information from her. The man had built his career on his superior intelligence-gathering skills. Still, he was angry at his colleague on Jane's behalf.

"And Halliwell's murder?" Ralston prodded, clearly not willing to let the matter drop.

"The very fact that Miss Halliwell was involved in your investigation was suggestion enough," Payne said with a shrug.

"From now on," Ralston said, not looking particularly mollified by Payne's explanation, "I demand to be kept apprised of any new developments."

Eversham looked as if he were going to object but Ralston raised a hand. "I will not back down from this, Mr. Eversham. I will clear this with the commissioner of Scotland Yard if necessary."

The detective nodded at Ralston's words, but his clenched jaw told Adrian he was not best pleased at the man's intention of going above his head. They discussed a few other matters relating to the various foreign delegates, and soon Adrian and Eversham were stepping outside into the weak sunlight.

"I wonder if Payne deliberately preyed upon Jane's affection in order to gain information," Adrian said as the two men walked toward Trafalgar Square.

"It's possible, I suppose," Eversham said thoughtfully. "I should imagine that a man who has been in his position for so many years is adept at ferreting out information when he wishes it."

Adrian nodded. "Whatever the case, she won't like hearing that she was the source of his intelligence."

"Nor would she appreciate you keeping it from her," Eversham said with a raised brow. "Trust me, as a man who has been married for some years now. Wives do not appreciate being kept in the dark about these things."

Reminded of his argument with Jane last evening about her involvement in the investigation, Adrian asked, "Speaking of marriage and wives, how do you manage to keep Kate from putting herself in danger?"

Eversham blew out a breath and clapped Adrian on the shoulder. "That is a discussion that will require at least a pint of bitters. And maybe two if we're to tackle the subject of 'obey,' in the marriage ceremony. Unfortunately, I have a murder inquiry to conduct."

Adrian groaned. Why hadn't his brother warned him about "obey" for pity's sake?

"What I will say," Eversham continued, "is that you cannot make demands or order her about. Some men will tell you that you're the man of the house and must act it, but that way, I can tell you, lies madness. Instead of working against her, work *with* her. A wife can be as rational a being as any man—in the case of my own wife, more rational than most men I know. Go from there."

Adrian nodded. "Work with her," he repeated. "And that really serves? It does sound much like what Langham has said, but he's not always the one I would go to for advice."

Eversham laughed. "In this case, he is right on the money."

Chapter Twenty-Two

A cross London, in the townhouse of the Duke and Duchess of Langham, Jane was tucked into a fantastically comfortable chair in a private sitting room celebrating her betrothal with Poppy, Caro, and Kate.

It had not taken very long at all to see to the unpacking of her single trunk, and Jane had been feeling a bit down over the realization that her entire life's belongings didn't add up to much more than a shelf full of books and some assorted mementos from her travels with her parents.

It wasn't that she had expected to have a houseful of things at this point in her life, but it brought into focus just how much her father's killer had taken from her. Not only her beloved father, but also the life she'd been meant to live. She'd been ripped from her comfortable existence and forced to fend for herself.

Jane knew, of course, that she'd been luckier than most. She hadn't had to live on the streets, or worse. But there had been moments—like when Lady Carlyle had turned her out without a reference—that Jane had feared it would come to that.

That her mother was now safely married to Sir Ross MacIvor, and she was betrothed to Adrian, meant that for the first time since her father's death both she and her mother would be settled.

But it was more than just physical and financial safety that made her so grateful for Adrian. Feeling a wash of heat at the memory of his hands bringing her such pleasure earlier, she knew that she'd never have allowed him such intimacies if she didn't trust him. If she didn't love him. And though she knew men didn't require love or even affection to engage in such behaviors, she believed in her heart that her feelings for Adrian were reciprocated. At least she hoped they were. Perhaps she'd need to initiate another such encounter so she could make some scientific observations.

"You are very quiet, Jane," said Caro over her teacup. The diminutive brunette was a lively conversationalist and had had them all laughing over the tale of how her Siamese cat, Ludwig, had attacked one of her husband's neckties thinking it was a snake of some sort. (The amusing—or horrifying, depending on one's perspective—part was that Valentine had been wearing the necktie at the time.) "I suppose you've had a difficult few days, given the loss of Lord Gilford."

Pulled out of her improper thoughts and back to the conversation at hand, Jane exchanged a look with Poppy, trying to decide whether it would be prudent to tell the other ladies what she'd learned about her father and Lord Attingly as well. She'd told Poppy, of course, because Poppy had been there when she'd returned from Attingly's. But Kate was married to Mr. Eversham. And Caro was well versed in police matters from her time writing a crime column with Kate.

"I believe they can be trusted, dearest," Poppy said gently. "And if, as I hope, you are to become one of our circle, you may as well leap in with both feet."

At this, Caro's eyes widened comically. "Oh, do you mean to tell me there is more to the story?" She clapped her hands and Kate rolled her eyes.

"Please forgive Caro, Jane," said Kate with a shake of her head. "She means well, but it's sometimes difficult to remind her that not everyone is as fascinated by murder as she is."

"Oh, tush," said Caro crossly. "You say that as if you aren't equally rapt whenever a new case crosses the transom. You even went so far as to marry a detective from Scotland Yard to get closer to the information."

"That's not why I married Eversham and you know it," Kate said with a scowl. "I married him because of his enormous—"

"Lady *Katherine*!" Poppy said with exasperation. "Please."

"I was going to say 'blue eyes,'" Kate said with a sly smile. "I do apologize, Jane, dear. Caro brings out the worst in me sometimes."

"I suppose I should apologize as well," said Caro with a shrug. "Though I see nothing wrong with an enormous—"

"Caroline!" hissed Kate and Poppy in unison, though Jane could tell they weren't as scandalized as they pretended.

"I suppose I can't say 'pair of blue eyes' and get away with it?" Caro asked while trying and failing to appear innocent.

Jane wiped at her streaming eyes. "No need to apologize on my behalf. I'm hardly a girl in the schoolroom and given what's been going on, I must admit I appreciate the chance for a bit of levity."

"So what *has* been happening, Jane?" Kate asked, turning sober. "Please know that whatever you tell us, we will keep it confidential. Unless we tell you we're on the record, there is no danger we'll put what you say in the newspaper."

Jane blanched. It hadn't even occurred to her to fear such a thing. She was grateful for the assurance. Quickly, she outlined what they'd learned about the murders of her father, Lord Attingly, and Lord Gilford being linked, as well as telling them about Lord Payne's attack only the night before.

"Oh, my poor dear girl," Caro said, reaching for Jane's hand. "So you learned after all this time that your father didn't take his own life but was murdered? How horrid that he died at all, but to be shamed by the people who were once your friends is simply not to be borne."

"It was awful," Jane agreed, grateful to be discussing it openly. "But in a way it was a relief. I was so ashamed, but also just very sad on Papa's behalf—the idea that he was so desperate as to take that step, you see—to learn that hadn't been it at all. It was a relief. And it gives me someone to direct my anger toward. At least, I will have once we learn who killed him and the others."

"Oh dear," said Kate wryly, exchanging a look with Caro and Poppy. "You've got the bug."

Jane frowned. "What do you mean? What bug?"

"Perhaps we'd better have a little claret in honor of the occasion," said Caro, moving to a sideboard where she seemed to know there was a decanter of wine and glasses inside.

"What occasion?" Jane whispered to Kate and Poppy. "And do ladies drink wine in the middle of the afternoon?"

"Ladies drink wine whenever they feel the need to, my dear Jane," Caro said over her shoulder. "And the occasion is that you have had a very difficult week. Have no fear. I don't mean for us to get foxed. I leave that to the gentlemen in their clubs. But sometimes life is difficult, and we have been blessed with the gift of wine to help us through."

"You needn't drink it if you don't wish to," said Poppy in a whisper. "But it's quite nice on occasion."

Once Jane had had a couple of sips, she decided it was nice. Quite nice.

"So you see," Kate said a few minutes later, "while the gentlemen would like to keep us from getting involved in matters like murder and the like, they cannot really do anything to stop us."

"We are our own beings and make up our own minds," Caro said, her eyes suspiciously bright. "Kate and I once solved the disappearance of our dear friend all on our own! Valentine and Eversham thought they were rescuing us, but we had already rescued ourselves. And isn't that what marriage is all about?"

Jane blinked. "Is marriage about…rescuing yourself? I thought it was about love and kissing and whatever that was that Adrian did with his fingers last even—" She broke off as the other ladies broke into giggles. "I said that out loud, didn't I?"

"You most certainly did," Caro crooned in a singsong. "Now you must tell us all what it was he did. Perhaps we can have some sort of competition. Whichever of the gentlemen gives the most—"

"Caro!" Kate's hiss finally succeeded in gaining her friend's attention. "Perhaps we can save the, ahem, *pleasure* competition until after Jane and Adrian are actually wed."

Caro blinked owlishly. Then, as if it had taken her a few moments for her friend's words to sink in, she gave a drawn out, "Ohhhhhhhh. That's a good point." She took another sip of wine. "We will save that for after you are wed, Jane," she said, as if Jane hadn't been there listening to the exchange herself. "But it is a very good thing that Adrian is *attentive*." She winked broadly at that last word.

"I am torn," Poppy said to no one in particular. "On the one hand I am pleased to hear that my brother-in-law is good with his hands. On the other hand, he is my brother-in-law…"

"We have much to teach you, Jane. First and foremost is that men are fools," said Kate, pouring more wine into Jane's glass. "I can say that because I am married to one. And he's one of the good ones. But even the good ones are at times lacking in the brain box."

"It's true," Caro said glumly. "Do you know how many times I had to explain to Valentine that just because I have a fondness for a beautifully crafted hat, that doesn't mean that I don't also want to travel to France to see the house where Marie Lafarge poisoned her husband."

"We contain multitudes," Kate said, clinking glasses with Caro.

"In the case of your particular foolish man," Poppy said, bringing the conversation back to the topic at hand, "I cannot tell you how glad I am that he finally admitted to himself that he cares for you. From the time you were at Langham Abbey with the Carlyles he has been desperate to find you. And that was what, almost two years ago?"

Jane nodded. She had no idea he'd been thinking of her that entire time. Though she highly doubted it had been because he was in love with her. It was more likely he'd simply been perplexed by her refusal to speak to him.

A knock sounded on the door just then and the man in question, followed by his brother the duke, stepped inside.

"We thought we'd come upon a sedate afternoon tea party," Langham said, surveying the ladies through his quizzing glass, "and what do we find but a veritable debauch of wine and women."

"We are hardly so depraved as that," said Poppy, looking affronted. "And it's just a bit of wine. Hardly the sort of carousing you men get up to at your clubs."

"If you don't mind, ladies," Adrian said dryly, "I'll be removing my betrothed from this den of iniquity for a bit."

At the groans of disappointment from all the ladies, he

shook his head in amusement. "I will bring her back later. Have no fear."

To her embarrassment, when Jane rose, she swayed a little. "Yes, definitely a little too much wine."

"I've got you," Adrian said, slipping an arm around her back and supporting her as they walked out of the room.

"I *am* allowed to drink wine if I want," Jane said defensively, though she couldn't recall if he'd said she wasn't or if she'd imagined it.

"Of course you are, darling," Adrian said, in a way that annoyed her but she couldn't say why. "But we have an appointment and I fear you cannot arrive in your present condition."

To her surprise, they were in the entrance hall then and Jane's maid was pinning on her hat and Adrian was helping her on with her coat.

"Where are we going?" she asked him as they stepped out into the bracing autumn air. "If I am too inebriated for the appointment, I mean."

"For now," he told her as he handed her into a hansom cab, "we are going for a little drive."

When the cab stopped sometime later, Jane seemed to be much more clear-headed, to Adrian's relief. Because he had a feeling she would have been annoyed if she weren't sober for this particular outing.

He handed her out of the vehicle onto the sidewalk

outside Stafford's Global Bookshop on Charing Cross Road, which was the unofficial street of bookshops in London.

Jane blinked up at the sign above the door. "Stafford's?" she asked. "I don't believe I've ever heard of it."

"That's because it hasn't been open for terribly long," Adrian said as he tucked her arm into his. "But I have a feeling you will enjoy it."

They stepped into the wide space, which boasted a long counter across the back wall and sported a half dozen bookshelves perpendicular to the walls on either side. Behind the counter, dozens of framed maps of cities from all over the world covered every open inch of space.

"Good afternoon, sir, madam," said a sharp-eyed young man as they stepped inside. "What brings you to Stafford's this fine day?"

"I wonder if we might meet with the proprietor," Adrian said as Jane looked around with interest. He handed the young man his card and the man nodded.

"One moment, Lord Adrian," he said with a nod. "I'll just see if Stafford is available."

When they were alone again, Adrian allowed Jane to lead him to one of the shelves.

"These are all books about travel and geography," she said with interest. "I suppose it's no surprise you'd know about this place."

"The owner is an old friend," Adrian told her as he watched her take down a travel memoir by the famous explorer Isabella Bird. "I thought since you're a writer you might enjoy the selection here."

Slipping his arm through hers, he led her to a shelf of

mystery and detective novels. "Perhaps one day soon, your book will be here just between Charles Dickens and Monk Lewis."

Jane's head turned with a snap to face him. "Do you think so?"

There was something in her expression that made his heart ache. Was she so doubtful that she'd find a publisher to put out her novel? He'd simply have to have enough faith for the both of them.

Thrusting his hands into his pockets, Adrian shrugged. "You've always had a way of putting words together. Even when you were a girl, your father often spoke about how eloquent your descriptions of the local sights were. I haven't had the honor of reading your novel yet, but I expect it will be riveting."

Most young ladies indulged in watercolors or other forms of visual arts, but writing—aside from letter writing, of course—was not generally considered a craft for ladies to indulge in.

Jane nodded and smiled, but the idea of Adrian reading her novel put scores of butterflies in her stomach. Though she supposed she'd have to get used to the idea if she wished to have it published, in which case perfect strangers with no feelings at all for her would read and judge her work.

"I hadn't realized Papa ever told anyone about those jottings," she said with a sad smile. "They are one of the many things I regret having left behind in our exodus from Rome."

He recalled that Jane and her mother had been packed

up on a ship bound for London rather quickly after Halliwell's death. He was ashamed that he hadn't wondered before now what had happened to all their belongings.

He was trying to come up with a delicate way of asking, when a tall woman with jet-black hair and almond-shaped eyes wearing an elegant green afternoon gown stepped forward with a broad smile. "Lord Adrian, what a pleasure to see you again."

"Mrs. Stafford," Adrian said, taking her hands and kissing her on the cheek, "may I introduce you to my fiancée, Miss Jane Halliwell?"

Jane's eyes widened at the introduction. "Jane, my dear," he said to her, taking her hand in his, "this is Veronica, Mrs. Stafford. She is the widow of Sir John Stafford, who spent decades in the employ of the Foreign Office."

Some of the surprise in Jane's eyes cleared at that explanation. "Of course, I remember Sir John well," she said with a genuine smile. "But I must not have met you when you called at our home, Mrs. Stafford."

The woman laughed ruefully. "I'm afraid I wasn't received in the homes of most of my husband's colleagues," Mrs. Stafford said. "We met and married in India, and though my father was as blue-blooded as the queen, my mother's caste was such that many of the high-and-mighty chose not to receive me."

"How dreadful," Jane said with a downturned expression. "I fear that though there are many ways in which the English can be said to be on the forefront of progress, in so many others we lag far behind."

"At the time," Mrs. Stafford said, "it was quite painful to

me, but I was younger and more of an idealist then. Now I see it for what it was. Ignorant people behaving in ignorant ways."

Adrian winced inwardly at the thought that Jane's parents might have been among the ignorant acquaintances Veronica was describing. But Jane didn't seem to take the slight personally.

"I am sorry that my own family was among those who snubbed you," Jane said with genuine remorse. "I fear society can be narrow-minded regarding a great many issues, especially where race and class are concerned."

"I don't recall the Halliwells in particular being rude to me," Mrs. Stafford said, "but I appreciate the apology all the same. Now, let us talk about something more pleasant. You are here to find a book, yes?"

"We are here to browse, Mrs. Stafford," Adrian said, grateful for the change of subject. "We have an appointment later this afternoon and I thought Jane, who is a detective novelist, would be interested in seeing some of your selection."

At the mention of Jane's writing, Veronica's eyes lit up. "Oh, a writer. How delightful. Have you written anything I may have read? I am always searching for new works by women to add to the collection."

Jane had turned red at Adrian's declaration that she was a writer, but she answered Veronica's question readily enough. "I don't have anything published yet," she said with a shake of her head. "But I do have a completed detective novel I mean to send off to John Murray soon."

"Impressive," Veronica said with an approving nod.

"But what keeps you from putting it in the post at this very moment? I don't detect any false modesty about you, if you'll forgive my saying so, Miss Halliwell."

Jane shook her head. " Oh, no, nothing like that. It's just that we've suffered the loss of a dear friend this week. But perhaps you know him. Lord Gilford?"

At the mention of Gilford, Mrs. Stafford's eyes widened. "Gilford is dead?"

It hadn't occurred to Adrian that he should tell Veronica about Gilford's death, but now he realized that had been shortsighted of him. "Yes," he told her in a kind tone. "He was murdered at an international symposium that was being held at his home earlier in the week."

Mrs. Stafford moved to a large chair and lowered herself into it. "I apologize," she said, placing a hand over her chest. "It's just that Gilford was one of Stafford's dearest friends in the Foreign Office and to realize they are now both gone is a shock. And he was *murdered*, you say?"

Jane looked at Adrian with a worried expression. "He was," she said, moving to crouch beside the other woman's chair. "And we believe that my father and Lord Attingly might also have been murdered."

"Oh, my dear," said Mrs. Stafford, "I remember when your father died. And it is now thought he was murdered and didn't take his own life? And Attingly was murdered as well? What is this world coming to? So many good men gone before their time. I've always suspected my poor John was murdered, too, though I was never able to prove it."

Adrian had been about to go in search of some water for the woman, but her words brought him up short.

"Murdered? I thought John died of an illness. What's this about murder?"

"I think we'd better go upstairs to my apartments," Mrs. Stafford said, rising to lock the shop door and turn the sign to read *Closed*. "Because it seems as if there is a contagion passing through the ranks of the Foreign Office. And I mean for us to discuss it without fear of interruption."

Chapter Twenty-Three

Mrs. Stafford's apartments were at the top of a narrow staircase in the back room of the shop. It was a large space that ran the entire length and width of the store below, and had been divided into a large parlor, two bedrooms, and a small kitchen with a dining room attached. While the arrangement of the rooms was ordinary, the decor was colorful and comfortable, reflecting the prints and hues of Mrs. Stafford's home country, as well as the elegance of her adopted one.

"Please have a seat in the parlor and I will heat water for tea," the older woman said with a wave toward the chintz-covered sofa in the parlor. "I hope you will not mind that it will be tea as we know it in the East. I do not hold with the insipid drink you call tea here in England."

"We will be pleased with whatever you choose to serve us, Mrs. Stafford," Adrian said from where he and Jane stood near the door leading into the kitchen. "But I first must know what you meant when you said Sir John was murdered. Given that we now believe three men who were in Rome that year have also been murdered, it's important."

Mrs. Stafford led them into the parlor and gestured for them to sit. "At the time, I did indeed believe it had been an illness that took John from me. The physician thought it was typhus, and I believed so, too. It can be quick like that. But a few weeks after he died, I found a packet of the lemon sweets he was so fond of in his things."

She smiled at the mention of the candy. "He could not control himself when he had them. He would eat three or four in a row without stopping. But since he was gone, I thought to give them to a friend who was fond of them as well. But she had only to eat one before she became dreadfully ill. The physician tested them and determined that they'd been poisoned with arsenic."

Jane gasped. "And you believe Sir John ingested these candies before he died."

All the murders they knew of thus far had allowed the killer to inflict a direct wound—and Jane suspected he'd liked it that way—but it wouldn't do to dismiss Lady Stafford's suspicions out of hand.

"I know he did," Mrs. Stafford said with a bitter smile. "I chided him for eating so many of the sweets. Now I wish I'd thrown the whole packet into the fire."

Jane couldn't stop herself from giving the older woman a hug. "I am so sorry. What a dreadful thing for you to go through."

"You are a dear girl," Mrs. Stafford said, pulling away and wiping her eyes with a handkerchief. "Now, the two of you must let me prepare the tea. Perhaps you can look at these photographs John took while we were abroad."

Jane exchanged a look with Adrian as they turned away from the small kitchen.

"It might not be connected," Adrian said in a low voice. "But it does seem suspicious."

Jane began looking at the photographs, while Adrian scanned the bookshelves on the other side of the room.

She picked up a photograph that she assumed based on the setting was of Mrs. Stafford and her husband, standing with her family on her wedding day. Another of Mrs. Stafford holding a long-eared dog with soulful eyes. And still another that showed Mrs. Stafford with, to Jane's surprise, her own mother. She moved closer to the frame to get a better look at the photo.

"My husband was a keen photographer and liked to document his trips and special days, as you can see," said Mrs. Stafford from behind her. "He took that photo when we were in Rome."

Jane looked up quickly and met Adrian's wide eyes across the room. "Were you a part of the special delegation that was sent in the spring of 1865?" she asked Mrs. Stafford. "Around the time that my father died?"

The other woman nodded sadly. "I'm afraid so. I apologize if the photograph brought up sad memories for you, my dear. I will remove it." She moved to take it down from the wall, but Jane shook her head.

"Please don't," she said. "I was simply surprised to learn that you were there that year as well. It seems as if everyone of importance from the Foreign Office attended the gathering."

"If you will sit," Mrs. Stafford said, "I will go retrieve the book of my husband's photographs from that year. Perhaps there will be one of your father you would wish to keep."

Before Jane could protest, the woman had slipped out of the room and could soon be heard shifting items in a room on the other side of the flat.

"It cannot be a coincidence that Sir John was in Rome at the same time as my father and the others," Jane whispered to Adrian.

"It most certainly is not," Adrian agreed. "I wish I'd been more than a minor aide then or I'd have a better idea of what went on. As it was, I'd been relegated to acting as courier between higher-ranking men than I and taking notes at the occasional meeting between Italian officials and the British embassy."

"The only outlier," Jane said thoughtfully, "is Lord Payne. Though I suppose it's possible he was there, too, and I simply hadn't heard about it."

Before Adrian could reply, Mrs. Stafford returned with a large box in her arms.

"Here we are," said Mrs. Stafford as Adrian rose to take the box from her before handing it to Jane. "These are the bulk of John's photographs from our time during his years in the service."

Mrs. Stafford sat down on one side of Jane while Adrian

settled himself on the other. Jane placed the box on her lap, and when she removed the lid, she saw that the photographs were neatly organized by years and countries.

At the pleased sound she made, Mrs. Stafford laughed. "I have always liked to keep things in easy-to-manage arrangements. Rather like the bookshop."

She pointed to the upper right corner of the box. "Here are the pictures from our time in Rome."

Jane lifted out a sheaf of photos, careful not to touch her fingers to the surface of the images. One by one, she stared down at the likenesses in differing shades of gray. There was one of Lord Ralston and a taller man with a clean-shaven face but impressive side-whiskers.

"That's Attingly," Adrian said with a nod. "He and Ralston were close."

"Indeed," Mrs. Stafford said, "they and my John were often to be found of an evening with a glass of whisky and a cigar in hand."

"Are there any photographs of your husband from these years, Mrs. Stafford?" Jane asked, thinking that so far she'd only seen him in the more personal pictures on the walls.

"Alas, he was rarely willing to let anyone else touch his precious camera—Bessie, he called her." She smiled fondly at the memory. "When I think of how jealous I was of that contraption at times. He treated that camera with more care than some mothers give their newborn infants. But I am grateful now to have these reminders of him all these years later."

Jane placed her hand over her hostess's. "I thank you for sharing them with us."

She turned to look through more of the pictures in the box. There were a number of photos that included groups of people, including one that looked to be an assembly of representatives of the Foreign Office with their wives. Upon closer inspection Jane saw her parents among the gathering.

It had been a long time since Jane had seen her father's face—photographs were far from commonplace and Papa hadn't been particularly keen at having his likeness taken.

Jane must have made some sound of distress, because Adrian slipped an arm around her shoulders to offer her comfort.

"They were a handsome couple," Mrs. Stafford said softly. "I was not well acquainted with your parents, but John admired your father very much. He was most distressed when we learned of his death—and the why of it, well, he never believed it."

Jane turned to look at her. "He didn't?"

"No," Mrs. Stafford said firmly. "He was convinced that there had been some 'funny business,' he said. Though he had no way to prove it, that didn't stop him from raising the question with his colleagues. It had angered him so when others in the Foreign Office made clear they believed your father's death was suicide."

"He was far more perceptive about the matter than I was," Adrian said with a sigh. "I simply believed the story I was told."

"You weren't the only one," Jane reassured him. Turning to Mrs. Stafford, she asked, "Do you believe your husband's death had anything to do with his questioning how my father died?"

Mrs. Stafford's lovely face creased with thought. "It had never occurred to me before now. Anyone who knew John would be aware of how fond he was of lemon drops. It would be easy enough to send him some as an anonymous gift."

She stared unseeing into the distance. "I always wondered why anyone would wish to harm him. He was such a gentle man. He was dedicated to his work, of course, but so are many men and they are not murdered for it."

"This might sound like an odd question," Adrian asked, "but was anything unusual found in his clothing or perhaps in his desk after his death?"

Mrs. Stafford started to shake her head, but then a look of realization crossed her face. "Yes," she said, rising to hurry from the room.

She was back only a few seconds later carrying a now familiar page from a book and something else, which Jane knew would be a pressed rose.

"Here," Mrs. Stafford said, handing the items to Adrian and taking a seat in the chair across from them. "I found them in his coat pocket along with the half-eaten tin of lemon drops."

"I am so sorry," Jane said, thinking of how many had been robbed of their loved ones by this unknown killer.

"Thank you, my dear. I know you understand what it is to lose someone you love," Mrs. Stafford said, brushing away a tear. Then seeming to steel herself, she said, "Now, tell me what these things mean? I know the flower was not a love token or anything like that. I never for a moment doubted my John's faithfulness. And if that weren't enough, then the underlined passage would have convinced me of his loyalty. No lover would send such a message."

Jane glanced down at the page in Adrian's hand and read the marked line aloud:

" 'The vulgar crowd always is taken by appearances, and the world consists chiefly of the vulgar.' "

"You are most certainly right," Adrian said wryly.

"It almost seems to be boasting," Jane said thoughtfully. "As if he means to score a point for having succeeded in deceiving Sir John."

"That is how I read it," Mrs. Stafford said with a nod. "But you asked about this for a reason, Lord Adrian. Does that mean that these vile messages have been left on the bodies of other victims?"

"Yes," Adrian agreed. "And the pressed roses as well. We believe it has some meaning for the killer but so far we've been unable to decipher what."

"I cannot guess either," the widow said sadly. "Perhaps we can continue looking through the photographs for pictures of your father and the answer will come to us while we are not coming at the question head-on."

Jane nodded and turned to continue shuffling through the photographs from Rome.

She had just set aside a few more images of her father alongside what she assumed were Italian officials, when she came upon a group photograph of all the senior Foreign Office officials who had been called to the meeting in Rome the week before her father's death. Only this time, none of the wives were in the picture.

From left to right stood Lord Ralston, Jane's father, Sir John, Lord Attingly, and Lord Payne.

"All but Lord Ralston and Lord Payne are now dead," Jane said, showing the image to Adrian.

"I must admit, when your father was found dead, Miss Halliwell," said Mrs. Stafford, "my first thought was that he'd been killed by Lord Payne. But when I suggested the notion to my husband, he thought it absurd."

"Lord Payne?" Jane looked up in astonishment at Mrs. Stafford. She had difficulty believing it of her father's friend. Besides, he had been attacked by the killer. "Why would you think that?"

Jane looked at Adrian, expecting him to be as shocked as she was, but was surprised when instead he looked pensive.

"I was dear friends with his wife, Lady Elizabeth Payne," Mrs. Stafford was saying, "and he could be a terribly cruel man."

"I have never heard anything about him mistreating Lady Payne," Jane said frowning. Turning to Adrian, she asked, "Have you?"

"No," he said thoughtfully, "but that doesn't mean much. Such intimacies within a marriage are often kept quiet."

"The idea that he would treat his wife so poorly is beyond troubling," Jane said, "but just because a man is cruel to his wife doesn't mean he is a murderer. Does it?"

"No, of course not," Mrs. Stafford said. "But Elizabeth had told me that he'd been hoping to receive a prestigious posting to St. Petersburg, but instead he was passed over in favor of Halliwell. Lord Payne was furious about it."

"Papa was meant to go to Russia after Rome?" Jane asked in wonder. "Mama never said a thing."

"It's possible she didn't know," Adrian said gently. "The postings were generally announced at a private dinner held for the diplomats. I'm sure your father would have shared the news with her…but his body was found later that night."

Jane looked down at the group in the picture. "So this is a photo taken the night of that dinner?"

Mrs. Stafford nodded. "The men were all in high spirits because of their new postings. The senior members continued on to a gaming hell that night to celebrate. That was supposedly how your father lost his fortune, though John told me he hadn't seen Halliwell wager above a few pounds."

Adrian nodded at Jane's questioning look. "I had been invited but had to stay behind and finish a report."

"John told me that everyone had left by the end of the evening except for your father and Lord Payne. He hadn't wanted to leave them—John had never been particularly fond of Payne—but he'd promised me to be home at a reasonable hour," Mrs. Stafford said, raising a hand to her lips in alarm. "Perhaps if I hadn't pressed him to return early."

"If anyone is to blame it's the person who killed my father," Jane assured her.

Glancing down at the photographs on the table, she looked more closely at the one of the assembled diplomats and for the first time noticed that they were standing before a blooming plant.

"Do you recognize this particular flower from your time

in Rome, Mrs. Stafford?" Jane asked. "It looks as if it's some variety of rose."

"Yes, it was lovely," Mrs. Stafford said to Jane, looking at the photo with them. "John used that particular trellis alongside the embassy villa as a backdrop for many of his photos. The rose had the most wonderful small blooms, which the gentlemen used for boutonnieres until the housekeeper scolded them for depleting the poor plant."

"What color were the flowers?" Jane asked, not bothering to keep the excitement from her voice.

"Why, they were a deep crimson," Mrs. Stafford began, "just like—"

"This," Adrian said, holding up the pressed flower the widow had found among her husband's things. "Could it be that the pressed rose has been a reminder to the victims of this day in Rome? Of the last time they were all together?"

"And the first time that he was willing to kill to get what he wanted," Jane said softly. It was terrible to believe Lord Payne could be behind the murders, but the evidence was certainly pointing them in that direction. "Could his motives really be so simple as that?"

"I don't know," Adrian said with a shake of his head. "We're getting close but we're still missing the final clue that will prove Payne is the culprit."

"Payne has managed to gain a better role in the Foreign Office after every death," Mrs. Stafford said thoughtfully. "Was there a role that both Gilford and Payne were vying for?"

Adrian swore, and Jane knew whatever he said next would be bad, indeed.

"What is it?" the widow asked Adrian. "What's wrong?"

"It's just that the symposium Lord Gilford and I planned at his home this week was meant to end with an announcement by Lord Ralston. He was planning to resign as foreign secretary and suggest Lord Gilford as his replacement."

"So Lord Payne will expect to be suggested in Lord Gilford's place?" said Mrs. Stafford. "That seems a lofty ambition even for one with such an inflated sense of his importance as Payne."

"But that's just it," Adrian said urgently, rising from his seat. "Ralston confided to a small group today—including Payne—that in light of Gilford's murder, he plans to remain in his position for the foreseeable future."

"Oh no!" Jane leapt to her feet beside him. "We have to warn the foreign secretary. He could be Lord Payne's next target."

Chapter Twenty-Four

"Where are we going? To Ralston's townhouse?" Jane demanded as Adrian handed her into a hansom cab outside Mrs. Stafford's shop. From the tight set of his jaw, it was clear that he was trying to contain his emotions.

"You are going to Langham House where you will be safe," Adrian bit out. "I am going to find Ralston so that I can warn him about Payne."

Jane hissed in frustration. "I am not a child, Adrian. You cannot keep trying to hide me away."

Adrian turned to her and the fierceness in his eyes took her by surprise. "I will not put you in danger again, Jane. It's clear now, thanks to what we learned from Mrs. Stafford, that Payne had the motive and the opportunity to commit all four of the murders. He's already made an attempt on your life once and I won't let it happen again. You mean too much to me to put you at risk like that."

He brought her palm to his mouth and kissed it. "I know

you want to be there when the man who killed your father is caught, but the peril is just too—"

"Perilous?" she asked wryly.

He sighed. "I swear to you that I was once able to speak with eloquence. Something about you robs me of my faculties."

She gripped his hand and said, "I love you whether you're a silver-tongued devil or not. But Adrian, I refuse to be wrapped in gossamer like some precious bit of glass. I do want to be there when we catch Lord Payne and I believe I can be of help."

His brows drew together. "How?"

"He seems to have a soft spot for me. I neglected to inform you I'd even spoken to him before we set out for the Attingly's—I suppose because of my injury. But you should have seen how he behaved the morning after our carriage accident. At the time I thought he was acting far more solicitous than was warranted. Now I know it was because he was remorseful. He was trying to kill you, Adrian. Not me."

Before he could argue, she continued, "I believe he regrets that I was injured, and I think I can use that against him. If the need arises, that is."

He shook his head. "We don't even know that we will find him. I intend to warn Ralston, then inform Eversham of what we've learned from Mrs. Stafford. I doubt I shall even be gone for much more than an hour."

She tilted her head, not bothering to hide her skepticism.

Adrian had the good grace to look sheepish. "Fine, I fully intend to warn Ralston, then seek out Payne myself. But I definitely don't want you there when I confront him. He's already killed four men, for pity's sake."

"Which means if he's cornered, he will very likely try to kill again." Her voice rose with emotion. "I am coming with you and that's final."

To her surprise, he bit back a curse, but then nodded. "Fine, you can come with me. But only because Eversham assures me we won't have 'obey' in the marriage vows."

Jane very much agreed about eliminating "obey" from their vows, and wondered what Eversham had to do with it but decided now was not the time to ask after that particular conversation.

Adrian rapped on the roof of the cab and when the jarvey opened the sliding door between the carriage and the driver's seat, he instructed the man to take them to Belgrave Square.

At her questioning look, he said, "Ralston makes a point of taking tea with his wife on Thursday afternoons when he's able. My hope is that we'll find him there and can warn him before Payne decides to make any attempt."

Jane nodded, then on impulse, kissed him sweetly on the lips.

At least, it was meant to be a sweet kiss. But when she made to pull away, Adrian slid his arms around her and turned it into something far more carnal. When she finally came up for air, he leaned his forehead against hers and said, "That is just to make sure you know how desperate I am for you, Jane. I may lose my ability to speak pretty words around you, but I love you, and when this is all over, I mean to show you every chance I get."

For once, Jane felt it was her wits that had gone

wandering. Nodding fiercely, she clung to his hand and the hansom was soon drawing to a stop.

Not waiting for the driver, Adrian opened the door and jumped down, then helped Jane descend. When they were shown into a sitting room near the entry hall, Jane felt her heart beating like the drum of one of her former charges' toy soldiers.

Unable to remain still, she wandered the room looking at the various decorative items that appeared to have been brought back from Ralston's travels. But it was the series of framed photographs that hung on the far wall that caught her eye.

"Adrian, look," she said as she moved to stand before the trio of images. "These are some of the same photographs we saw at Mrs. Stafford's."

There was one of Lord and Lady Ralston on the terrace of a villa, then another of the house itself from farther away. But it was the group picture in the center that drew Jane's attention, since it was the same one that showed Ralston, Halliwell, Sir John, Attingly, and Payne together before the blooming rose trellis.

"I hope you are not distressed at seeing images of your father, Miss Halliwell," Lady Ralston said from the doorway behind her, startling Jane. "I treasure the few images of my own family I possess. But I can understand why you would find my display upsetting."

"Lady Ralston," said Adrian as he came to stand beside Jane. "Is the foreign secretary in? There is a matter of some urgency I must speak to him about."

Looking a little self-conscious, Lady Ralston gave a small laugh. "I apologize for not greeting you properly, Lord Adrian, Miss Halliwell. Lord Ralston is indeed here. He's in the attic with Lord Payne, searching after photos from our time in Rome. Silly man, I told him they were right here in the parlor. Why they were in such a state to find them, I have no idea. But they were adamant."

"I'll just go join them and let them know that the photographs are here," Adrian told Lady Ralston with a smile. To Jane in a voice only she could hear, he said, "Send for Eversham."

Then without another word, he ran from the room and Jane could hear him outside the door asking the butler if there were any firearms in the house.

"That is very kind of you both, Miss Halliwell," Lady Ralston said. "But the matter is not so serious as all that."

The butler entered the room just then, asking after refreshments, and Jane took the opportunity to ask him to send for Eversham immediately, explaining that his master was in danger.

Lady Ralston looked astonished at Jane's temerity in ordering someone else's butler to do her bidding. "I'm afraid Lord Payne intends to harm your husband, ma'am," Jane said baldly, by way of explanation.

"Why on earth would Payne wish to harm my husband?" Lady Ralston demanded with a scowl. "I know he can be dreadful to his wife, but he and Ralston have been friends for thirty years."

"It is a terribly long story, my lady," Jane said quickly, "but we believe Lord Payne killed not only my own father but also Lord Attingly and Lord Gilford. Not to mention we suspect he may have killed Sir John Stafford as well. There's no telling what he might do next. I think it prudent that you remove yourself from this house until the matter is resolved."

Gasping, Lady Ralston raised a hand to her chest. "Goodness." Then, straightening her spine, she said, "I will not retreat, Miss Halliwell. I have followed that man from one corner of the earth to the other and we have faced down tigers, invading armies, and various sorts of ruffians together. I will not flee my own house for the likes of Payne."

Jane couldn't help but be impressed by the older lady's strength of character. "Very well, my lady. I suppose I can't force you to leave your own home."

"Miss Halliwell, you seem like a young woman of some backbone," Lady Ralston said, looking Jane up and down as if assessing her mettle. "Are you willing to go with me to assist my husband and Lord Adrian?"

Before Jane could answer, a loud crash sounded from the upper floors of the townhouse followed by a shout.

Exchanging a wide-eyed look with her hostess, Jane gave her a nod and they set off toward the staircase.

Adrian crept as quietly as he could up the narrow staircase leading to the door of the attic floor. From above, he heard a loud crash, then a shout that sounded like Ralston. He'd asked the butler who directed him to the attic for a pistol, and while he was glad the man was able to retrieve one so quickly, he worried that the delay might have cost Ralston precious minutes.

The houses in Belgrave Square had been built relatively recently and as such there was an absence of the creaks and groans more frequently found in the older houses of the *ton*. For that, Adrian was grateful. All he needed was for Payne to be alerted to his approach before he actually reached the doorway.

Even so, he was not without trepidation as he made his way to the attic.

The door at the top of the stairs was slightly ajar, and Adrian could hear male voices on the other side. At least, he thought with relief, Payne hadn't managed to kill Ralston yet. Now he only had to make sure Ralston remained alive until Eversham could get here and apprehend Payne.

"Nevil, this isn't like you," Ralston was saying in a calming voice, as Adrian pushed the door open wider—grateful again for the silence of the hinges. "We've been friends for thirty years, for God's sake."

The attic was tidy and organized, Adrian noted, yet it still took him a few moments to find where Ralston and Payne were standing across from each other on the far side of the room. The wide casement window they stood in front of was open, letting in the afternoon breeze—liberally doused with coal smoke and the ripe smells of London.

Peering out from between a pair of tall shelves, Adrian watched as Payne leveled a rifle at the foreign secretary.

"I think you misunderstand what it means to be a friend, Robert." Payne said Ralston's Christian name with a sneer.

"When I got rid of Gilford, you should have appointed me your successor in his place. But it's been nearly five days and you haven't spoken a word to me about it. Which leads me to believe you have someone else in mind. Is that true, Robert? Have you chosen someone else to follow you as foreign secretary?"

Adrian closed his eyes at hearing Payne's angry words. He'd suspected Payne's reason for killing Gilford, but hearing the man announce it so matter-of-factly was chilling nonetheless.

"You're planning to give it to that puppy, Lord Adrian, aren't you?" Payne demanded, seething with fury. "I know you were going to put him in Gilford's old position, but there's been no announcement yet, which leads me to believe you've been moving the chess pieces around. Is it because of his ducal connections?"

Adrian gaped. Payne was well and truly insane if he believed Ralston would back Adrian as foreign secretary. He didn't have nearly the experience or, in truth, inclination for such a position. He hadn't even accepted the promotion to Gilford's newly vacant post yet, for pity's sake.

"Lord Adrian has been working alongside Gilford for years, Payne," said Ralston in a placating tone. "And you know how important it is to maintain continuity in government. You are just as important in your section as Lord Adrian is in his. But surely you can see that you are not as knowledgeable about the politics of the nations along the Mediterranean as you are about the eastern parts of Europe."

"What I can *see*, Ralston," said Payne coldly, "is that you have no understanding of the way our world works. There are certain positions within the Foreign Office that draw the admiration of our peers and I have grown weary of being shunted to the side in favor of your mere underlings. That ends now."

Adrian saw the foreign secretary's face pale in the dim light of the window. "I hope you won't do anything hasty, Payne. I can assure you that if anything were to happen to me there will be consequences."

Payne laughed. "Like there were consequences for all the others? My dear foreign secretary, what makes you think I will be made to pay for your death when I have got away with murder many times before? If the authorities were cleverer, perhaps, but though Eversham has all the pieces, he hasn't managed to put them together. Certainly, he doesn't know I'm the one he's looking for. My little bump on the head took care of that."

"Your own attack was a feint, then." Ralston's words were not a question. "To take suspicion away from you?"

"Yes," Payne said with disgust. "It occurred to me that Miss Halliwell might realize she'd blurted out to me that she and Adrian were going to Attingly's. I couldn't have her telling Eversham I had the opportunity to sabotage the carriage. So I had my valet strike me with a cricket bat. Hurt like the devil but it did turn attention away from looking at me as a suspect, didn't it?"

Adrian had had enough of watching from behind the scenes. If he allowed this to go on for much longer, Ralston would only anger Payne further, which would end in one way: with Ralston dead.

"But why try to harm Adrian and Jane?" Ralston sounded mystified. "I hadn't even appointed Adrian to a new position. And Jane was an innocent in all of this. She certainly didn't have a place in the Foreign Office you coveted."

"I knew that as Gilford's right-hand man Adrian would be destined for a plum position soon," Payne said with a shrug. "It was also apparent that he was working closely with Eversham. Taking Adrian out of the equation would hurt the investigation and slow Eversham down."

"And Jane?" Ralston asked, sounding weary.

"I didn't have any particular enmity to her," Payne said, sounding untroubled by the question. "She just happened to be in the wrong place at the wrong time. Regrettable, but bad things happen sometimes. I quite like the girl, actually. When she's not mooning over that idiot betrothed of hers."

"It seems as if there is no difference between the way you treat those you like," Adrian said, stepping out from his hiding place, "and those you loathe, Payne. Did you 'like' Attingly and Halliwell, too?"

Upon seeing Adrian, Payne's face took on a mask of pure hatred. "I loathed Halliwell," he said through clenched teeth. "Always so jolly and hail-fellow-well-met. Never a bad word to say about anyone. He was disgusting. When he got the position in the Russian embassy, I was almost grateful for the chance to get rid of him. That I was able to do so while ruining his reputation and his family at the same time was like having a birthday and Christmas at once."

"And Attingly?" Ralston asked, scowling. "What did Attingly do? The man was about to walk his daughter down the aisle. Have you no shame?"

"Of course he does not, my dear," called out Lady Ralston from where she approached from the doorway, followed by—to Adrian's alarm—Jane. "I have listened to his rantings for the past while and have come to the conclusion he has neither shame, nor conscience."

Payne snarled and pointed his pistol at Lady Ralston and Jane.

The foreign secretary blanched and held out his hands in supplication. "No, I beg you, Payne. Do not hurt them. I will do whatever you ask."

Adrian tried to catch Jane's eye but she was transfixed by Payne—who'd betrayed her many times over.

"Be careful what promises you make, Robert," Payne said, smiling slyly at Ralston.

"I give you my word as a gentleman," Ralston said, his voice wavering with intensity. "Whatever you wish."

"All right then, Lord Ralston," said Payne with a nod. "But do remember, you've given me your word."

Ralston seemed unable to find his voice again and only nodded.

"Very well, old friend." Payne used his pistol to gesture from Ralston to the window. "I want you to climb up onto the ledge, and then I want you to jump."

Chapter Twenty-Five

J ane gasped and looked over at Adrian, who mouthed the word "run." But there was no way Jane would leave Lady Ralston to face her husband's fate alone. Almost imperceptibly she shook her head and Adrian's expression became grim.

Jane turned to stare at Lord Payne, the man she'd known since she was a schoolgirl, and tried to understand what would make someone turn from an honorable gentleman into a cold-blooded killer. Or perhaps he'd always been this way but was simply adept at hiding his true nature from the rest of the world.

Ralston had begun to step toward the open window, and Jane was trying to think of some way to stop him from reaching it, when Lady Ralston's voice rang out. "No," she said in a firm voice. Jane recognized it as the voice of a woman who has had enough—she herself had used it on Margaret a time or two.

"I will not stand for it, Robert," she told her husband calmly. "From what I understand, Lord Payne has got away with murder after murder. I will not allow him to take you from me."

Ralston turned to Payne, as if he were asking the man's permission for something. With a shrug, Payne gestured toward Lady Ralston and the foreign secretary stepped quickly to his wife's side. He wrapped his arms around her, and Jane had to look away from the emotion between them.

Wiping away a tear, she was surprised when she felt Adrian's arm slip around her waist as he murmured in her ear. "There is a pistol in my coat pocket. When I say so, take it. I will cause a distraction and when I do, I want you to shoot him."

Jane stared at the rifle in Payne's hands. She wanted to argue with Adrian, but there was no time. And if they didn't do something Ralston would die.

In the guise of hugging him, she slipped the pistol from Adrian's pocket and hid it in the folds of her gown. "I love you," she whispered before she pulled away. She saw Adrian mouth the words back.

"Enough of that, you two," Payne said, belatedly noticing Adrian and Jane's embrace. "It's the Ralstons' turn for goodbyes. Yours will be soon, never fear."

"I never knew you to be so heartless, Lord Payne," Jane said evenly. "In fact, I once believed you to be an honorable gentleman. Now you simply disgust me."

Payne rolled his eyes. "Such harsh words, my dear. You will hurt my feelings if you go on in that vein."

He turned to where Lord and Lady Ralston stood

clasping each other's hands. "It's time for you to keep your word as a gentleman, Ralston." He gestured to the open window with his pistol. "Hurry up. We don't have all day."

"Just another moment, Payne, please." Ralston looked as if his feet were rooted to the floor.

Beside her, Jane felt Adrian brush his hand against hers. Realizing that was the signal, she tensed and put her finger on the trigger of the pistol.

Then many things happened at once.

Adrian ran to where a stack of trunks formed a sort of tower to one side of the room and shoved. As they toppled to the floor, Jane saw Eversham enter the room.

But her relief was short-lived. Payne had turned at the commotion and was now aiming his pistol directly at Adrian. Without hesitation, Jane pulled the trigger on her own weapon, and heard Payne's go off a split second later, but the shot went wide and into the wall.

She saw red bloom on Payne's chest, and he looked down in surprised shock at the wound. "You shot me, Jane." And then he collapsed to the floor.

❦

Langham House, London
Late that evening

By the time Adrian returned to his family's Mayfair townhouse, the elegant longcase clock in the entry hall was chiming the midnight hour.

He suspected Jane, along with the rest of the house, had been asleep for hours. But he'd promised to give her a report of Payne's condition when he returned home, no matter how late the hour. And after a quick wash and change of shirt Adrian slipped silently into his betrothed's bedchamber.

Only to find a single gas lamp lit and Jane herself—adorably attired in a gauzy pale pink confection of silk and lace—sitting up in bed, an open book in her lap. When she caught sight of him, she threw off the bedclothes and rushed toward him as if they'd been separated for eight weeks instead of eight hours.

He caught her against him and felt the fatigue that had dogged him for the last hour melt away as his body and senses took note of her scent, her softness, her delicious curves in his arms. On top of all that, though, was something elemental that he'd failed to recognize, but was there all the same the moment they'd been reunited in the Gilford House drawing room. Some unnamed, invisible bond between them that told him they belonged together as sure as the moon belonged in the sky.

"Was it too awful?" Jane asked, her arms clasped round his neck as Adrian held her against him. Answering her own question, she continued, "Of course it was. Hundreds of people who worked with Lord Payne over the years were told he's a murderer. That can't have been comfortable for any of you."

Adrian kissed the top of her head and led her to a chair near the fire, where he unceremoniously pulled her onto his lap. "I suspect many of them were not terribly surprised by Payne's bad actions. He was good at masking his true nature, but as Mrs. Stafford proved, he was not beloved by everyone. And," he added, stroking a hand down Jane's back, "there was a great deal of relief at knowing the man who'd killed your father, Attingly, and Stafford was finally in custody."

Jane nodded and tucked her head against his shoulder. "Has he revealed anything more about his motives, or why he took on the identity of E, or why he felt he had to ruin Papa instead of just murdering him? There's so much about Lord Payne's actions that are still so incomprehensible. I cannot reconcile that vile creature who tried to make Lord Ralston jump with the kindly family friend I knew as a girl."

"Since Payne's gunshot injury was not serious, Eversham and his men were able to question him thoroughly once the wound was dressed." Adrian settled back against the chair, enjoying the simple pleasure of Jane's warm body resting against his. "Though he didn't wish to admit it at first, it does seem that his reasons for killing your father and ruining his reputation were a combination of professional hatred and a dislike of what he called your father's pious attitude. He even gained access to your father's bank accounts and cleared them out in an effort to paint him as a secret gamester."

The information, disclosed to Adrian by Eversham, had made his blood boil. And it had been only Eversham's threat to withhold the rest of Payne's confessions that had kept Adrian from storming into the miscreant's hospital room and shaking the older man until his teeth rattled.

"And he had no qualms about how his actions would

affect Mama and me?" Jane sat up and her voice shook with anger. "Of course he didn't. He had no concern for anyone but himself and his thwarted career ambitions. He didn't care whom he hurt. Even his own wife. At least she's free of him now that he's been caught."

"He didn't care," Adrian agreed. "Indeed, I suspect he thought the pain was well-deserved. Apparently he referred to himself in the letters as 'E' because he considered himself to be Judge, Jury, and most importantly to his own mind, Executioner. Payne thought your father hadn't been deferential enough to him, given that he'd taken his post in the Foreign Office a couple of years before him. Attingly made the mistake of disagreeing with him about a policy in a meeting."

"And Stafford?" she asked, sounding almost as if she didn't wish to know the answer.

"Stafford had begun to suspect Payne of your father's and Attingly's murders," Adrian told her grimly. "Though we'll never know if that was true or simply a conjuring of Payne's guilty mind."

"It's all so senseless." Jane leapt up from his lap to pace the carpet before the fire. "Did Payne truly kill my father over something so trivial—not receiving the deference he thought he deserved?" It was clear from the disbelief in her lapis lazuli eyes that she'd never dreamed of such a thing. "Papa had to die and Mama and I lost everything we'd ever known simply because Lord Payne didn't receive the fawning he thought his due?"

Adrian rose and stepped over to take her fists in his hands. It was clear from the way her chest rose and fell that

Jane was close to tears. And when he pulled her against him, he felt the dam break. "Papa," she sobbed against his chest. "My dear Papa."

Wishing like the devil that he could take her pain from her, Adrian held her as he whispered into her hair. "I'm so sorry, love. So, so sorry. Payne will never hurt anyone again." But he knew that it was too late to stop the man from hurting her and it made him wish he'd been able to see past the killer's mask long before he decided to commit murder. At the very least he'd have to settle for seeing the man tried and convicted in the House of Lords.

After her tears had subsided, and they'd both become aware of the fact that they were in varying degrees of undress, what began as comfort turned into something altogether more incendiary. And by the time they were deliciously naked and skin to skin beneath the cool sheets of Jane's bed, all thoughts of murder and mayhem had been replaced by decidedly more carnal ones.

"Jane." Adrian's voice sounded husky to his own ears as he looked down at her flushed and beloved face. "If we do this, we'll need to marry sooner rather than later. I won't have the gossips speculating should our first child make an early appearance."

"You won't?" Jane asked with a soft laugh as she reached up to brush aside the lock of hair at his forehead. "I thought I was marrying one of the scandalous Fielding brothers. What a disappointment."

She was laughing, and he was desperate to make her his, but Adrian had to say a few more words before he could show her all the ways their bodies could make magic together.

"I love you," he said, taking her mouth in a possessive kiss. "And I won't allow those chattering harpies to make your life a misery ever again. Ever."

He had more to say, but all the control in the world couldn't make him ignore the exquisite torture of Jane's soft breasts and strong thighs pressed against him.

"I love you, too," she said against his mouth, even as she lifted her arms to hold him to her, and he slid his hands beneath her to bring them even closer together. "So much."

It was some time later, when the bedclothes were delightfully rumpled, and Jane's head was pillowed on his chest, with Adrian's leg thrown over hers, that Jane added, "Special license it is."

Adrian gave her a surprised smile. "Yes? Truly?"

"My dear, Lord Adrian," Jane said in her primmest governess voice, "when a gentleman goes to such"—she glanced down the bed a little—"lengths to persuade me, I am always apt to listen."

Epilogue

The Banks of the Serpentine, Hyde Park, London
One Year Later

"This is such exciting news, Miss Halliw—that is, Lady Adrian," Miss Margaret Gilford gushed to her. "When will I be able to read it?"

The young lady and the former Miss Halliwell were gathered, along with several dozen of the *ton*'s most exclusive members, at the Duchess of Langham's picnic, which promised to be the event of the season.

"Sometime next year, I should imagine," Jane told her erstwhile charge with a grin as she pulled the girl toward the elegantly arranged blanket where her husband and friends were already seated and enjoying every manner of delicacy. "I will be sure to tell you when I know the precise date."

"We will undoubtedly read it in the Mischief and

Mayhem book club, Miss Gilford," said Caro from her perch on the blanket beside her husband. "You must join us."

In the year since her marriage, and abandonment of governessing as a profession, Jane had not seen a great deal of Margaret, whose mother had kept the girl in the country during their mourning period. But Jane knew her former pupil had been relieved at having been set free from the schoolroom. At seventeen, she was young to have made her come-out, but not overly so. And Margaret was a lively girl who needed to be in company.

"Where is your brother today, Miss Gilford?" Lord Adrian lounged on the blanket beside Jane, and was looking, in Jane's opinion, even more delectable than the picnic savories.

Somehow, with every passing month, she found some new facet of him to adore. And if the way he loved her in their bed every night was any indication he felt the same.

"Lord Gilford has been scarce at *ton* entertainments since your come-out ball," Caro said, accepting a slice of apple from her husband, Valentine, who sat beside her. "Has he grown tired of us already?"

Margaret toyed with a bit of ham on her plate before she answered. Jane exchanged a look with Adrian. They'd both been worried about Lord Gilford. The man had clearly been devastated by the death of his father. When he'd attended the first several events of Margaret's season, they'd hoped he was emerging from the cloud that had seemed to surround him, but his disappearance again did not bode well.

"He has been tending to estate matters in the country,"

said Margaret with the air of one who is reciting an oft-quoted line. "But he promises to return soon."

"It cannot have been easy for him to step into your father's shoes," Jane said softly to the younger woman, patting her on the hand. "Perhaps he simply needs more time to adjust."

"I hope that's all it is," Margaret said with a scowl, "because I am weary of making excuses for him. And though I know he is grieving for Papa—as am I, and as is Mama—I suspect his difficulty may not be quite so much the new responsibilities as the sea of eligible young ladies and their mamas who swarm him at every *ton* gathering."

"Oh ho," drawled the Duke of Langham from the other side of the blanket. "Young Lord Gilford is dealing with that age-old difficulty that we all have faced in our time— the matchmaking hordes."

"I have never faced such a thing," Eversham said smugly. "In fact, I was never in the sights of the matchmakers, and I am glad for it."

"But I caught you all the same," Kate said sweetly, then popped a bit of scone into her mouth.

"So you did, my dear." The detective took his wife's hand and kissed it.

"There's no need to boast, Eversham," groused Valentine. "You may as well get puffed up that you've never gone to war."

"It's hardly war, darling," Caro said with a roll of her eyes. "Let's not exaggerate."

"This from the woman who once described her cat as

the most intelligent creature on the planet," Valentine said in a stage whisper, then made a yelp as his wife poked him in the ribs.

"Ludwig is cleverer than ninety-eight-point-five percent of the gentlemen at this picnic, at the very least," she told him with a lift of her chin, "and I will not say otherwise."

Adrian gave a shrug. "She's not entirely wrong," he said in a voice that only those on the blanket could hear. His pronouncement was followed by a chorus of agreement.

"If young Gilford is so terrified of being chased about by the matchmakers," Langham said after a minute, "then there is only one solution I've found. And in my case, it worked extremely well."

"What is that, Your Grace?" Margaret asked, her eyes alight with expectation.

"I can answer that for him," Adrian said, slipping his hand into Jane's. "Because it worked for me as well. The best way for Gilford to escape the mamas of the *ton* is to get himself a wife."

"Should we perhaps invite ourselves to Gilford's country house?" Jane asked later, when she and Adrian were gliding over the Serpentine in one of the small boats popular with park visitors. "I know Margaret said that Will is simply avoiding the matchmakers but I fear there may be more afoot. I'd hate to think of him mourning alone."

"I can't say I haven't had the same fears," Adrian said

thoughtfully. "I'll write to him. Say we'll be in the area and would like to stop in."

The estate that Langham had settled on Adrian upon his marriage, Fielding Hall, was located not terribly far from Will's country house, Gilford Cross, and it would not be out of the ordinary for them to break their journey there.

"Oh, thank you," Jane said with a sigh of relief. "His obvious unhappiness has been weighing on my mind. I will feel better once I've spoken to him properly, in a way that simply is not possible at a *ton* party."

Then, as if only now realizing how far from the rest of the party they were, she asked, "Where are we going?"

"Didn't you need to investigate the bridge as a site for the murder in your next book?" He glanced toward the stone structure they were nearing, which divided the lake into the Serpentine on one side and the Long Water on the other.

Jane felt her heart swell with affection for this dear man who had been her first love and would, if heaven were willing, be her last.

"I love you," she told him as he stopped the little boat in the shadow beneath the bridge and carefully moved to kneel at her feet and take her in his arms.

"I love you more," Adrian said, framing her face in his hands.

And with the gentle sound of water lapping at the sides of the boat, he kissed her.

Acknowledgments

It is a truth universally acknowledged—at least by us writer types—that contrary to what one might think, books do not, in fact, become easier to write the more you get under your belt. And since this is my twenty-mumble-mumbleth novel, and it was just as difficult to write as all the other ones, I can, alas, confirm. So, it's super lucky that I've had such an all-star team of folks helping me usher this one into the world. Thanks first and foremost to my always supportive team at Forever Romance. Incisive editor Amy Pierpont for her sharp eye and flawless guidance, and her ability to catch my GenX references because she's old like me (haha, just kidding, Amy, though kinda not?). Rock star status to assistant editor extraordinaire Sam Brody, who is always there to field my 911 emails about things that usually turn out to be more appropriate for the nonemergency line. Sorry, Sam! You're the best! Special thanks to my amazing publicist, Dana Cuadrado, who has skills with the Bookstagram and the TikToks that are beyond this social media dinosaur's understanding. You, my dear, are the best. The production team, especially production editor Luria Rittenberg and copyeditor Shasta Clinch.

Sales, Hachette Audio, and anybody else at Hachette I've forgotten to mention. Y'all are the bomb.

Thanks also to my long-suffering agent, Holly Root, who has been with me since we were both total newbs, and only continues to get better and better. I am so lucky you took a chance on me, lady! Love your guts.

There are more friends than I can possibly remember or mention, but here are a few: Santa, Lindsey, Cindy, Katie, Joan, PJ, Julianne, Limecello, and all my Twitter friends who have been displaced and are now scattered throughout the social media interwebs.

Thanks to my hometown romance-friendly bookstore, The Haunted Book Shop in Mobile, Alabama. Angela and Jodie are a joy to work with and I love having somewhere to direct my readers for signed copies of my books. There's a link on my website, kids. Get your orders in while you can.

My crazy bananas family: Aunt Dee, my first and most enthusiastic reader. Aunt Babe, who wishes I'd just cut out the sexytimes because the books are good without them (lol, no). Aunt Nancy, who can't read them because she hears my voice in every word and it weirds her out (which, valid). And Aunt Sue, who doesn't read them because…I'm not really sure? Also the cousins, and their wives and husbands and babies, cats, dogs, fish, and pets of all sorts.

Jessie, my little sister who is old like me now but will always be younger, so in your face. Love you.

And finally, my little buddy who likes to wake me up by meowing as loudly as she possibly can in my ear and really hates it if I try to write anywhere but on the bed where she can sit beside me while I type, Toast the cat.

Questions for Discussion

1. Why do you think Jane preferred to stay at Gilford House as a governess rather than as a guest like Lord Gilford suggested? Have there been times when you've chosen a more difficult path when an easier one was available to you? Why or why not?

2. Adrian chose to work for the Foreign Office against his brother, the Duke of Langham's, wishes. Why do you think a younger son might want to forge his own path—to make his own decisions? How might this situation be the same as or different from when modern children go against their parents' wishes?

3. When Poppy arrives to bring appropriate gowns for Jane to wear while she's acting as hostess at Gilford

House, she tells Jane, "I know what it is to feel like a fish among fowl." How might clothes and appearance help someone feel more comfortable in a new environment? Can you think of a time when wearing just the right outfit made you feel more powerful? Do you think we as a society place too much importance on clothes and appearances? Why or why not?

4. There are some behaviors that we don't bat an eyelash at in a romance novel that would drive us up a wall in real life. Adrian's declaring his intentions toward Jane when they meet her mother might seem sweet in a book, but in real life it might cause a huge fight. What are some actions that you found attractive or admirable in the book that you would never put up with in real life?

5. When the book begins, Jane is attempting to sell her detective novel to a publisher. How do you think her attitude toward crime and murder might change—if at all—after she experiences the events that take place in the novel?

YOUR
BOOK
CLUB
RESOURCE

VISIT
GCPClubCar.com

to sign up for the **GCP Club Car** newsletter, featuring exclusive promotions, info on other **Club Car** titles, and more.

GRAND
CENTRAL

FOREVER

12
TWELVE

LEGACY
LIT

balance

About the Author

Manda Collins grew up on a combination of Nancy Drew books and Jane Austen novels, and her own brand of historical romantic suspense is the result. A former academic librarian, she holds master's degrees in English and library and information studies. She lives on the Gulf Coast with a squirrel-fighting cat and more books than are strictly necessary.